WIND SPRINTS

Also by Ralph Dennis

The War Heist
A Talent for Killing
The Spy in a Box
Dust in the Heart
The Broken Fixer
Tales of a Sad Fat Word Man
The New Five

The Hardman Series

Atlanta Deathwatch
The Charleston Knife is Back in Town
The Golden Girl and All
Pimp For The Dead
Down Among The Jocks
Murder Is Not an Odd Job
Working For The Man
The Deadly Cotton Heart
The One Dollar Rip-Off
Hump's First Case
The Last of The Armageddon Wars
The Buy Back Blues
All Kinds of Ugly

WIND SPRINTS

RALPH DENNIS

CUTTING EDGE

ISBN-13: 978-1-957868-91-2

Published by
Cutting Edge Books
PO Box 8212
Calabasas, CA 91302
www.cuttingedgebooks.com

INTRODUCTION
BY LEE GOLDBERG

" It's been a good seven weeks or so. I revised completely a novel, *Wind Sprints*, and mailed that poor retarded child up to an agent in New York. To where the flesh-eaters are. Mailed it yesterday and insured it for $15. Which may be more than it is worth. Will wait and see."

— Ralph Dennis, in his *Letter From Atlanta* column for the *North Carolina Anvil*, November 7, 1970

Nearly a decade ago, I fell in love with the twelve, out-of-print, *Hardman* crime novels by the late Ralph Dennis...an obsession that led me to acquire the copyright to his work, published and unpublished, and to co-found a publishing company to get his novels back into print.

His *Hardman* series, with numbered titles like *Hardman #1: Atlanta Deathwatch*, were all released in paperback in the mid-1970s by Popular Library, which packaged them as cheap, sleazy, men's action-adventure novels. Most of the books in the genre were disposable hack work, slim volumes full of violence and sex with titles like *The Butcher* and *The Penetrator,* that were doomed to a short shelf life and oblivion.

But Ralph's *Hardman* novels were something different, terrific crime novels with nuanced characters, strong plots, a remarkable sense of place, and something meaningful to say about race relations in the deep south.

Even so, the novels slipped into obscurity and Ralph never achieved in his lifetime the recognition or success that he deserved, despite publishing three standalone novels outside of the series.

At the time of his death in 1988, Ralph was a destitute alcoholic, sleeping on a cot in the backroom of George's Deli in Atlanta, and working as a clerk at a used bookstore.

However, Ralph wasn't entirely forgotten. His *Hardman* series remained beloved by crime writers, like novelist Joe R. Lansdale (*Hap & Leonard*) and screenwriter Shane Black (*Lethal Weapon*), who credited Ralph for inspiring their work and who passionately recommended the yellowed, hard-to-find paperbacks to their friends.

In fact, that's how I discovered Ralph, because a friend made me read a *Hardman* novel. And I got hooked ... *bad*.

When I set out to republish the *Hardman* novels, I recruited successful authors who were influenced by the series, as well as people who knew Ralph, to write essays for the new, reprint editions. Two of those essays in particular – one by his close friend Ben Jones, the actor and former U.S. Congressman from Georgia, and another by author Cynthia Williams, a former student of Ralph's who declined his marriage proposal — gave me revealing insights into the author I'd been investing my time, money and passion into editing and publishing.

I went on to substantially edit and republish his three standalone novels (*The War Heist* (aka *MacTaggart's War*), *The Broken Fixer* (aka *Atlanta*) and *A Talent for Killing* (aka *Dead Man's Game* combined with the previously unpublished sequel) and to publish his unsold manuscripts *The Spy in a Box* and *Dust in the Heart*.

I'm pleased and proud to say that all of the books, the *Hardman* series and the standalones, received enthusiastic media reviews in the United States and abroad ... the kind of literary respect and acclaim that Ralph Dennis craved, but was sadly denied, in his lifetime.

At that point, I'd read every novel, sold and unsold, that Ralph had written, with the exception of *Wind Sprints,* his long-lost, unpublished first novel. I'd noticed many recurring themes and plot situations in his books, particularly when it came to his portrayals of women, sex, and romantic relationships. After I read the essays by Ben and Cynthia, and traded lengthy emails with them, I was pretty sure that I knew how Ralph's fiction mirrored the experiences and disappointments in his own life.

But I still wanted to learn more.

I knew from Ben and Cynthia, and from articles that I'd read, that Ralph was a student, and later an instructor, at the University of North Carolina at Chapel Hill during the 1960s. So, in the summer of 2019, I went to Chapel Hill on a research trip to read through Ralph's papers at the UNC library, to meet some of his old drinking buddies, and to see the places mentioned in his books.

I spent my days in the library's archives. I read old issues of several Chapel Hill literary magazines that he'd contributed to, first as a writer and later as an editor, in the 1950s through the late 1960s. I read carbon copies of the acceptance and rejection letters that he sent to writers seeking publication in the magazines that he was editing. And I read the letters that Ralph wrote in the 1970s to his colleagues at UNC, after he left Chapel Hill and moved to Atlanta, that chronicled some his early and later life as a novelist.

In the evenings, I spent time with some of Ralph's old friends, who shared with me what they knew about him and their insights into his life.

I learned that Ralph, while a student at UNC in the early 1960s, had an affair with a Chapel Hill woman who was still in a relationship with the man who'd fathered her daughter. She left that man for Ralph and they got married.

Ralph graduated from UNC and moved his family to New Haven so he could pursue a Master's Degree in playwriting at

Yale. Not long after arriving at Yale, he discovered that his wife was having an affair. History repeating. The marriage crumbled. He returned alone to Chapel Hill, where he ultimately received his Masters and stayed as a lecturer in the TV & film department.

I unearthed his marriage license and reached out to his ex-wife (who has since passed away) and to his step-daughter, both of whom kindly and honestly shared their memories of him with me.

I came away from that research, and those interviews, with a much deeper, richer, and nuanced understanding of Ralph Dennis as a man…and the many ways that his life influenced his writing.

But I also wanted others to be able make those same discoveries for themselves. So, in 2020, I collected several of his earliest short stories and poems and published them, along with Ben and Cynthia's essays for my *Hardman* reprints, and some excerpts from articles about Ralph, into a slim collection called *Tales of a Sad, Fat Wordman,* the title borrowed from one of his stories.

The final story in the collection is *Wind Sprints,* which was originally published in the Chapel Hill literary magazine *Lillabulero* in 1967 and is essentially the first few pages, and a short synopsis, of the heavily autobiographical first novel Ralph was writing at the time.

He completed the novel after moving to Atlanta in 1970 and sent it off to his agent. The reaction wasn't good, as Ralph told an *Atlanta Journal-Constitution* reporter in 1974: "As far as I know, the only people who liked it were my agent and me."

He eventually gave up on the book and decided to write a mystery novel instead about Jim Hardman, a disgraced ex-cop turned unlicensed Atlanta private eye, scraping together a living with the help of best friend Hump Evans, a black former NFL player sidelined by a career-ending injury.

Ralph sold *Atlanta Deathwatch* in 1973, two weeks after he finished writing it, finally becoming a published novelist at forty years old.

And *Hardman* was born, a series that he continued writing for eleven more novels.

Actually, it was *twelve* more.

While going through Ralph's papers in Chapel Hill, I discovered some letters he'd written to his friends that revealed that his unpublished manuscript *The Polish Wife,* about a disbarred lawyer-turned-Atlanta lobbyist, was actually a rewrite of an unpublished, final *Hardman* novel. So, I used that evidence as justification to rewrite the book back into a *Hardman* novel, which I published in 2020 as *All Kinds of Ugly* to wide acclaim.

For example, *Mystery Scene Magazine* said that *"All Kinds of Ugly* is a beauty, a pure distillation of grade A, hardboiled pulp that dares to reach for more," while *Publishers Weekly* noted that Ralph's "strong prose and well-paced story-telling place him alongside the likes of George V. Higgins and Ross MacDonald." Best of all, the Private Eye Writers of America chose the book as a Shamus Award finalist for Best Novel of the Year, their highest honor.

That was that, the perfect ending to my Ralph Dennis journey.

Only it wasn't the end.

In late 2022, I got an email out of nowhere from a young woman I didn't know in Atlanta. She was cleaning out her grandparents' basement and stumbled upon a box that contained an undated, yellowed, cob-webbed, typewritten manuscript.

It was *Wind Sprints* by Ralph Dennis.

She google'd Ralph and discovered that I'd been republishing his work. So, she reached out to me and asked if I'd like to have the manuscript.

I told her I couldn't wait to get my hands on it.

I'd never come across the names of her grandparents in my research on Ralph, so I asked her if she knew how they might have known him, or why he might have given them the manuscript of his novel for safe-keeping.

She didn't.

All she knew was that her grandpa used to spend time at the Stein Club, an old Atlanta bar, and perhaps he'd befriended Ralph there.

That made perfect sense. Not only did Ralph hang out at the Stein Club, but the bar figured prominently in many of his books.

She went on to say that her late grandfather was an engineer by trade, but at one point in his life he had taught English at a small college south of Atlanta.

So perhaps, I thought, Ralph saw in him a kindred spirit. Perhaps Ralph gave the manuscript to him for his opinion of it.

What happened next? Who knows.

Maybe they never ran into each other again.

Or, maybe Ralph died before her grandfather could read it, or share his thoughts on the manuscript.

Whatever the reason was, all that mattered was that the manuscript ended up in the basement and wasn't touched again for decades.

She sent me the book.

The cover page didn't have a date, just the title, Ralph's name, and his Atlanta address at the time.

I reached out to Ben Jones and asked if he remembered the address. He did. It was the place Ralph was living when he first moved to Atlanta. I looked at the prologue and I immediately recognized the first few paragraphs from the *Wind Sprints* short story.

If this wasn't the final draft manuscript, it had to be pretty close to it.

⚜ ⚜ ⚜

After the research I'd done, I knew that Ralph had mined his own past for his fiction. But after reading *Wind Sprints*, his auto-biographical first novel, it was clear that he'd been doing that from the very beginning. This was Ralph's own story, tweaked and fictionalized.

It's not surprising that publishers didn't embrace the book. It's not so much a novel as it is a collection of vignettes about a university instructor's miserable love life, beginning with the dissolution of his marriage in 1966, on through his various other relationships with women, and ending with his doomed affair three years later with a younger woman.

The way women in *Wind Sprints* are depicted sexually and otherwise, not only by the first-person narrator, but by every other character, is unpleasant to read today and was probably even more so over fifty years ago. Consider that fair warning.

The narrator desperately wants to be loved by women, but yet he dislikes, distrusts and degrades them. Moreover, the narrator repeatedly abandons any woman who shows real feelings for him. It's a contradiction that makes some sense, once you know about Ralph's past (and you will if you read the two essays that follow this introduction).

The protagonist is obviously, and painfully, Ralph and comes across as a man incapable of loving anybody else because he doesn't like himself much ... but he lacks the courage, or even the interest, to do anything about it. About the only thing he does well, and consistently, is drink. He can down endless pitchers of beer and bottles of cognac while remaining completely sober.

That's not to say there isn't anything positive about *Wind Sprints*. There is much to appreciate — some beautiful, perceptive, and memorable prose and characters who are deftly sketched in just a line or two. It's also a revealing time capsule of New Haven, Chapel Hill and New York in the mid-to-late 1960s ... giving us an early glimpse Ralph's remarkable skill at creating a sense of place.

And, most of all, you can almost hear what would become Ralph's singular, utterly compelling, writing voice, which would find its perfect expression in the *Hardman* series, inspiring a generation of crime writers.

Although Ralph abandoned *Wind Sprints* sometime in the early 1970s, the book did see print before today...in a way. It will be immediately clear to anyone who has read all, or most, of Ralph's books that he repeatedly returned to this manuscript over the years to strip it for parts, using various characters, scenes and even lines of description from it in his other novels.

It's the essential, missing piece in understanding the man himself and his literary work. In that sense, it's remarkably revealing.

It's also haunting.

Because after reading *Wind Sprints*, it's very easy to imagine the narrator's fate matching Ralph's tragic obituary, written eighteen years after this novel was finished.

It almost seems inevitable.

"Ralph Dennis of Atlanta, a writer of paperback mystery novels set in Atlanta, died of kidney failure Monday at Crawford Long Hospital. He was 56. At the time of his death, he was working as an Atlanta bookstore clerk..."

—*The Atlanta Constitution*, July 6, 1988

Lee Goldberg, the co-founder of Brash Books, is the #1 New York Times *bestselling author of over forty novels, including* Malibu Burning, True Fiction, Lost Hills, *fifteen* Monk *mysteries, and five* Fox & O'Hare *adventures (co-written with Janet Evanovich), He's written and/or produced many TV shows, including* Diagnosis Murder, SeaQuest, *and* Monk, *and co-created the Hallmark movie series* Mystery 101.

MY FRIEND HARDMAN
BY BEN JONES

If, on a late summer afternoon in 1973, you had walked into George's Deli on Highland Avenue in Atlanta, you would likely have seen a portly man in his 40's. He would have been on a barstool talking to his friend Sam Najar, the bartender. The customer is balding. It is all gone on top. He has sideburns that are beginning to show grey. His round, mustachioed face is pocked, and his Falstaffian beer gut cannot help but be noticed.

He is wearing a casual white short-sleeved shirt, khaki slacks, and brown loafers. If he knows you and likes you, he will ask you to join him at a booth. If your interests run to literature, writing, pop culture, film history, good wines and liquors, Japanese and Italian food, Southern ribaldry, or the traditionally American sports like baseball, football and basketball, you will soon realize that he knows more about all of these things than you do. And then you will start listening and learning. Because this guy, Ralph Dennis, is a great teacher.

From 1961 until his passing in 1988, Ralph was my friend, my mentor and my sidekick. In a few drunken instances, it fell to me to be his bodyguard. In those 27 years we had only one falling out, over a red-headed woman as it happened, and it was entirely my fault.

We had some things in common. I had grown up in a railroad section house without electricity or indoor plumbing by a railyard on the docks of Portsmouth, Virginia. Our shack was literally on the wrong side of the tracks in segregated Sugar Hill, then a bustling African American community. We were the only "white" folks in Sugar Hill. I know of that now as one of the great blessings of my life.

After a feckless high school career, I worked a series of odd jobs and saved up enough dough to enter East Carolina College in Greenville, North Carolina. While there, I saw a pamphlet about the Radio, Television, and Motion Pictures Department (RTVMP) at the University of North Carolina in Chapel Hill. I sent a handwritten letter to the UNC Admissions Department, and on the basis of that letter I was accepted. The Dean told me that they thought I had some writing talent.

One of the first courses I took was the survey course for RTVMP, a very large class in a vast auditorium. The graduate assistant who taught the writing section of that course was Ralph Dennis. He was very good at what he was doing, a fine and entertaining lecturer, and, though a bit droll and sardonic, he was never, ever boring. I liked his style, and related to his humor.

Most of the Chapel Hill drinking spots were clustered then on East Franklin St., directly across from the North entrance of the campus. But I had noticed a tavern some blocks west of there that piqued my interest, a place called Clarence's. It appeared to be more of a good old fashioned working man's beer joint.

The first time I walked in there, the only guy in there besides Clarence himself was Ralph. He seemed to be totally at home, as if he had lived there for some years.

I introduced myself. He was then 30 years old and I was 20. In that conversation and in thousands of others over the years, I learned a lot about Ralph, and a little bit about myself.

It was at Clarence's that we first bonded over a mutual appreciation of country music, sports, and film. We poured our beer change into the jukebox and as the regulars started coming in, I matched every Budweiser he drank with a Pabst Blue Ribbon, which was a nickel cheaper. He knew that I didn't have much dough, so he would spring for just about every other round. I realized early on that this was a *sympatico* relationship. We were both devoted to that old, but elusive, romantic notion of the artist's drinking life.

Like me, Ralph had come from a bone deep hardscrabble Southern raising. He didn't like to talk about it, but the story emerged over our shared years of lubricated conversation. Ralph was born in 1931, as the Great Depression was sinking ever harder into the American heartland. There were scars from those times that he clearly bore, but they were sealed and protected by a cranky, crusty, and often cynical attitude.

What had gotten him away from a future in the cotton mills was a High School teacher in his hometown of Sumter, South Carolina who recognized and encouraged his gifts of intelligence and writing talent. He spoke of her often as something of a savior.

After high school, Ralph joined the United States Navy, and headed to the Korean War. The highlight for him was a beautiful Geisha girl in Japan he lived with for a year or so. The lowlight was when an angry officer ordered him to drive a jeep across an airfield to his headquarters. Ralph jumped in and drove the jeep into a series of potholes and through a fence into a ditch. The irate officer didn't know that Ralph had never learned to drive. That fact made the officer even more furious.

"Then why in the hell did you do it?!" he yelled.

"Just following orders, sir," Ralph replied. "Just following orders."

And that was the first and last time that Ralph Dennis ever took the wheel of a vehicle.

He came home from Korea and Japan and used the G.I. bill and some scholarship money to pursue his writing ambitions. At Chapel Hill, he got an A.B. and a Masters, which he was working on when we met in the early 60's. There were some wild ass parties around there in those days, when sex, drugs, and rock and roll ruled the roost. Ralph got lucky with women now and then, didn't do any drugs other than alcohol and Pall Malls, and liked his music more nuanced and melodic than most. He was, after all, a bit older. And though it wasn't easy to pick up on, he was also a whole lot cooler than the folks who thought they were cool.

Ralph headed off to the Yale School of Drama for a doctorate somewhere around 1963. I got hitched to a gal from Texas and didn't pick up with Ralph until he got back in 1966. He had gotten another Masters, but he did not leave Yale under good circumstances. My attempts to find out what had transpired would end with a grunted comment about "an enormously stupid asshole." I understood. If nothing else, Ralph Dennis was a proud man, the kind of brilliant Southern country boy who knew what he was trying to do as a writer, and he knew how to do it. Apparently, he felt his Doctoral adviser was condescending and that the guy was trying to jack him around simply because he thought he could. Ralph told him to "put it where the moon don't shine."

There was also a woman up there, a very serious affair which had also ended badly. There was a lot more to it than that, but Ralph was reluctant to discuss it and I was just smart enough not to push it.

The University of North Carolina wanted him back, and he was glad to be back. His daily routine was simple. He would grind himself some good African or Brazilian Coffee, then walk to the campus from his modest apartment to teach at Swain Hall, home of the RTVMP Department. After classes, he would read and critique scripts, and when that was thoroughly finished, he would head to Jeff's Campus Confectionery to hang out with the other regulars who held court there, myself included. We drank a lot of beer in those days. I mean a hell of a lot of beer. We drank staggeringly prodigious, Homeric, Olympian Record amounts of beer.

Jeff's was a little newsstand with a bar in the back. There were no stools, but every day a truly diverse group of beer boozers would stand around for hours, rolling dice to see who was going to buy the next round. There were times when I'd knock off from my job waiting tables at Harry's Deli up the street and head for Jeff's. If I was lucky with the dice, I could drink for hours. There was an ancient bank safe in there, and it became my barstool. There was a bench in the back with a black and white 9 inch television set with extendable "rabbit ears" that someone had to hold and move around when the Tar Heel Basketball team was on.

If Ralph didn't show for a few hours, it was likely because he was working on a short story or some other writing project. He published some in small magazines, and he was at ground zero with the novelist Russell Banks' literary magazine, *Lillabulero*. I wrote a bit, and published a bit, but once I discovered I could make a little dough as an actor, I was hooked on the theatre.

I was in between marriages when I ended up in Atlanta in the fall of 1969. I got a union gig as an actor the day after I got off the bus. My Georgia girlfriend Mary Alice and I got hitched down in Briarpatch, Georgia, and we quickly found that there were a number of former Chapel Hillians in "Hotlanta", celebrating the New South and having a grand old time doing it.

By 1970, Ralph was "getting tired of students" and needed a change. It didn't take much to convince him that Atlanta had fully recovered from General Sherman and was a happening place. We drove up and got him and his belongings and helped him find a bachelor's pad. He got a regular job when his savings started to dwindle a bit, all the while writing every day. He wrote to his friend and agent Elizabeth McKee, pitching the idea for *Hardman*. Ms. McKee secured a contract with Popular Library.

Now, I wasn't there when it happened, but he was so overjoyed with the news that he ran the two and a half miles to our house so that he could tell somebody. Ralph Dennis had given up athletics in High School and was as out of shape as one would expect of a man who had downed 50 beers a week for 25 years, while chain-smoking Pall Malls.

But he made it. I wasn't at home, but Mary Alice was.

"I sold a book!!" he said.

Mary Alice said he was so happy that for years afterwards she found the moment thrilling. And I still can't help but smile when I think of that day.

Jim Hardman and Hump Evans were born that day. The books were excellent. They were the work of a thorough professional, working within a genre he greatly respected. Of course, Ralph had read all of Chandler and Hammett. But he seemed to have also read all of everyone else who ever put ink on paper: Tolstoy, Dostoyevsky, all of the Russians, all of the Classics and all of the Americans, Twain and Faulkner and especially Hemingway, whose style of carving out anything unnecessary was not lost on Ralph.

Ralph would write a first draft in two or three days. "Get the whole thing down as soon as you can," he told me. "The work is in the re-writing."

He loved to polish a sentence until there wasn't a trace of "fat" in it. He did the *Hardman* books with the work ethic of a coal miner, staying at it until there was nothing left to add or subtract.

Those streets and alleys of 1970's Atlanta have greatly disappeared now, paved under and over as a behemoth of a sprawling megalopolis has been birthed from the Georgia red clay; 14 lane super-highways circling through a maze of high-rise glitz and chrome. But if you know where to look…there was the Clermont Lounge…there was Plaza Drugs…there was the Stein Club…there was the "strip at Tight Squeeze".

Ralph and I were both alcoholics, but of a different sort. When I went on a binge, I couldn't stop until the game was over. As the old alkies say, "One drink is too many, a thousand isn't enough." But at a certain time in the evening, Ralph would say, "I need a lift home, I'm really 'schnokered'," and that would be that. I'd drop him off and go back out, looking for more trouble.

I was heading for a bad bottom in 1976. The Georgia lady had enough of my insanity and left. But the drinking got worse. I got married again, and that hardly lasted longer than the first hangover. No one wanted to see me coming down the street.

Ralph and I argued over that red-headed woman and it caused a break in our long friendship. It was entirely my fault.

He got a book deal for *MacTaggart's War* (republished in 2019 as *The War Heist*) and went to England on the advance to do some research. I was making good money doing movie roles and spending it with no regard for anything except to be, as Dylan Thomas said, "the drunkest man in the World!"

I got sober in September of 1977. It was the start of another life for me. Soon afterwards Ralph tired of the Atlanta scene and went back up to Chapel Hill to write and teach. A year later, I was cast in the mega-hit TV series, *The Dukes of Hazzard*. My life changed so dramatically, that it seemed an entirely different life. It was and still is.

I didn't see Ralph for a couple of years, but we kept up through mutual friends. I sent him a letter of amends and he appreciated it. He was proud of how I had changed my ways and found some success.

After five years of sobriety and jumping cars in Hazzard County, I went up to Chapel Hill in 1982 when The Tar Heels were playing for the National Basketball Championship against Georgetown. The game was in New Orleans, but I knew the real action would be in Chapel Hill, especially if the Heels won. I went to where I knew Ralph would be, at Jeff's Campus Confectionery. He greeted me like the long-lost brother I was. He was drinking Michelob; I was drinking Diet Coke.

The Tar Heels won on a last second shot by Michael Jordan, a skinny 19-year-old freshman. The Victory celebration on Franklin Street was beyond wild, as it should have been.

Ralph returned to Atlanta the next year and to his stool at George's Deli. He got a job at the Oxford bookstore and kept writing. When I was in town, I'd pick up Ralph and we'd hit the Atlanta Braves or Hawks games, me drinking green tea, and him downing Budweisers.

When *The Dukes of Hazzard* ended in 1985, I asked Ralph to come up with an idea for an Atlanta detective series. I said that the *Hardman* series would make a terrific television show. He agreed, but he felt I wasn't right to play Jim Hardman. And then he said something that seemed to come from a deeper place.

"Hardman is 'in'." he told me. "But you are 'out'."

I think he was saying that I had escaped from my addictions and my despair, but that Hardman (and Ralph) had not and likely never would.

Instead, he did a half-dozen, two-page outlines of possible stories, and a full treatment for a pilot episode, for a different detective series called *Gunnarson*. Steve Gunnarson was a former jock and Special Forces guy who had inherited the family bookstore, which specialized in rare books and maps. The other side of "Gunnarson, the Hardass" was "Gunnarson, the thoughtful Renaissance Man." Gunnarson "did favors" for friends with problems, a sort of dangerous hobby. I thought the time was right for an Atlanta show. (I played on a softball team there with Isaac Hayes, and we wrote a part for him.)

I pitched *Gunnarson* to CBS in that same endless line with everyone else in Hollywood who could "get a meeting." Nothing happened. It rarely does out there. I think they were just being courteous.

In 1986, I was approached by the Georgia State Democratic Party to see if I was interested in running for Congress. "I've got more bones in my closet than the Smithsonian Institute," I told them. But the Party was desperate. And a lot of folks, including Ralph, told me that I didn't really have anything to lose and that I should jump in just for the hell of it. Ralph wrote my first political speech. He had never written one, and I had never given one. I almost won the race, and ran again in 1988.

George's Deli on Highland Ave. was smack in the middle of that District and I would stop in to see Ralph whenever I had a few minutes. He was having some health problems and job problems and was crankier than ever. While Ralph was looking for a new apartment, George was letting him sleep on a cot in the back of the place. During one night, he had a seizure of some sort and was found in a coma the next morning. He was rushed to Crawford Long Hospital near death, but recovered enough to have several female visitors a couple of days later. Then it went the other way. The day before he died, I spent time at his bedside with his kid sister Irma, who flew in from Michigan. He died on July 4th, 1988, as fireworks exploded everywhere above Atlanta.

When I won that '88 race, I knew that he was as proud as hell of me, as if I was his kid brother. And in a way I surely was.

One day, a few months before he passed, he went into an eloquent chat about the English writer and critic Cyril Connolly. He quoted Connolly as saying, "Inside every fat man there is a thin man wildly signaling to get out." And then, "Whom the Gods wish to destroy, they first call promising."

In one of our last talks, Ralph, deep in his cups, told me of how, at the height of the Great Depression, his mother had taken him and his kid brother and sister and put them out at a state orphanage. He remembered the gates closing. He was about seven years old.

"Sometimes I still get the feeling of watching that car pull away from us," he said. He had never mentioned that before.

Ben Jones is an actor, singer, writer, and recovering politician who lives on a farm in the Blue Ridge Mountains of Virginia. His memoir Redneck Boy in the Promised Land *was published by Random House. He served in the U.S. House of Representatives as a Congressman from Georgia. He has appeared in countless productions and films, but is surely best known as the affable mechanic "Cooter" on the hit television series* The Dukes of Hazzard.

RALPH

BY CYNTHIA WILLIAMS

I knew Ralph Dennis first as a teacher, and later as a friend and mentor. Eventually, he asked me to marry him, but I refused, and our friendship ended.

Obviously, I will remember Ralph differently from the men who knew him, because he was, in some ways, a different person with me.

I met Ralph Dennis in 1966. I was in my junior year at UNC Chapel Hill, majoring in Radio, Television and Motion Picture Production (RTVMP), and as my rather vague intent was to become a screenwriter for motion pictures, I took Mr. Dennis's screenplay writing classes. He was a good teacher, because I still remember the mechanics of writing a film script, yet all I remember of the classes is Ralph sitting on the edge of his desk, coffee cup in one hand and a cigarette in the other, his face expressionless, occasionally flicking cigarette ash at an ashtray. In retrospect, I suspect he may have been bored. Possibly hung over. I liked him. He was cool. I saw him as a Hemingway-esque kind of writer. Undoubtedly, he did, too.

After I graduated in 1968, some circumstance I don't recall brought me back to Chapel Hill while Ralph was still teaching. I remember only that we met in his hangout, a small bar on the downslope of west Franklin Street. Ralph sat across the booth from me and my young husband, clearly uncomfortable.

I intuited that I should not have brought Dewey with me. I came away from the meeting with an inexplicable sense of dissatisfaction, the feeling that I had embarrassed the man—or worse, bored him.

Four or five years later, in 1974, I was divorced, living in east central Tennessee, and working on my first novel. By this time, Ralph had left UNC and was living some 200 miles away from me in Atlanta, trying to make it as a self- supporting writer. I have no idea how I knew where he was, unless we had kept up some kind of occasional correspondence. So many links are missing from my recollections of this time that I can scarcely connect the dots between one event and the next. Not that it matters. All I know is that over the next two years, I drove down to Atlanta a few times to spend a weekend carousing with Ralph and friends of his (including that insanely funny Ben Jones) at George's Deli.

I recall his apartment as being one large room above a garage. As you walked in, his writing desk was to your right. To your left was a small bathroom. Beyond that, to the left, a book case and against the far wall a single- size bed. There must have been some kind of cooking facility and a table because on the one occasion I visited him there, he made shrimp scampi for me—shrimp sautéed in butter with scallions—served with a cold white wine.

I must have brought my unfinished manuscript with me that day, because I remember sitting on the edge of his bed while he sat at his desk reading it. I dared not even look at him while he read.

Finally, he stirred. I put my face in my hands as he got up with the manuscript in his hand and walked across the room to me. He stood over me with his gentle smile. "Lady," he said, "this is a hardback."

We walked in the park across the street one brisk, bright, golden autumn day. Ralph was rather stiffly polite, so I think it was probably during my first visit to him there. In my company, he was always a gentleman. Kind. Gentle. Smiling. Perhaps in deference to my youth and obvious naiveté. I was intelligent and well- educated, but when it came to knowing men, I was dumb as a post.

I was beautiful, you see, with a voluptuous body of which I was oblivious. I was entirely cerebral, impassioned with the life of the intellect. In my eyes, Ralph was still my teacher. He was sending me the books he said were required reading if I seriously wanted to learn how to write. The first book he sent me was Dostoyevsky's *The Idiot*. Told me to read it every year, as he did. He introduced me to Turgenev with *A Sportsman's Sketches*. All of the titles on his reading list were classics, heavy, rich literature. I wallowed in them with such pleasure, with an insatiable appetite for learning.

And I was excited by his interest in me as a writer.

The seduction he practiced upon me was patient. Patiently, over a cheesy French onion soup with a bottle of strong, raw Chianti, he listened, smiling, to my passionate opinions about God-knows-what-all. When he spoke, always quietly and deliberately, I was an eager listener. He must have been encouraged by the warm light in my eyes, unsuspecting that it was the glow of admiration, perhaps affection, but not desire.

Every morning while our friendship lasted, he wrote a letter to me. Called it his ten- finger exercise—a warm- up for the day's writing. I have none of the letters he wrote to me, and of them, I recall only one; he described a recent date involving "one of those sweaty, candlelight suppers" that Southern women insisted upon. Ralph was a disciplined writer and he had to be, because his income from the *Hardman* books depended on the quantity of his output. He was clearly embarrassed to be writing for money, restless and angry at the necessity of it, hoping to make enough from the *Hardman* books to support himself while he wrote some serious hardbacks. He described his life as being a routine of writing by day and drinking beer at George's by night.

Ralph sent me copies of all the *Hardman* books with affectionate inscriptions, but like the Valentine's Day gift of *The Romantic Egoists*, a wonderfully illustrated, coffee table biography of Scott and Zelda Fitzgerald, I let them go with the rest of my library, which I sold in 2011.

The man was a hopeless romantic. He called me one day while I was visiting my brother and his wife in Asheville. Said, "Listen to this," put the phone receiver down by his stereo and left it there all the way through Carmina Burana. Like the literature he shared with me, it was glorious. We were both mind- swerving drunk on it. I was enormously flattered by his attention, by the obvious fact that he had fallen in love with me. I was 28 and writers were my heroes and he was a writer. Again, I lived in my head, and again, for a young woman my age, and a divorcée, no less, I was unbelievably stupid about men. I had no sexual interest in Ralph Dennis, so I ignored his in me. For a long time, he had the good sense, apparently, not to attempt to pressure me into a sexual relationship. As I say, the seduction he practiced upon me was subtle and patient.

Unless his reticence with me was reluctance. He was a balding man with a beer belly in love with a beautiful young thing nearly half his age. He may simply have dreaded my response to any overt demonstration of sexual desire. So, he bided his time.

What he had going for him, and he knew it, was my admiration for his intellect, his self-confidence and skill as a writer.

His Christmas gift to me in 1975 was a solid gold pocket watch with an inscription dated 1906. The watch was slender, as if designed to rest in the palm of a lady's hand. It was exquisite and adored it. But I remember that, as I sat alone by my Christmas tree one night, turning the golden wafer of a timepiece this way and that to reflect the colored lights on the tree, I felt inexpressibly sad. The gift was expensive and fairly radiated Ralph's love for me, and I knew that I did not love him the way he wanted me to and that I should not accept the gift. It was his very declaration of love. I gazed at it ticking softly in the palm of my hand, shimmering.

In hindsight, I realize that, with the gift of the watch, our relationship shifted. Ralph became supplicant. I think it was a couple of months later that Ralph took me to an expensive restaurant in downtown Atlanta and ordered a large plate of oysters oreganata for each of us. I was embarrassed to have to admit that I could not eat oysters (they looked like phlegm on the half shell to me). Ever the compliant gentleman, he ordered me something else and when we left the restaurant, handed the carry- out box of oysters to a homeless man outside the restaurant.

Why in God's name I felt I had to go shopping that afternoon for a lipstick liner I will never know, but we stepped into a department store and while I was at the cosmetic counter, he disappeared. Back outside on the sidewalk in front of the store, he pulled a jewel box from his pocket and opened it. Inside was the largest, most luscious opal (my birthstone) and diamond ring that has ever sparkled before my eyes. He offered it to me as an engagement ring.

I couldn't take it. Although in my selfish desire for his friendship I had ignored all the signs of his having fallen in love with me, I was neither a cruel nor a dishonest young woman.

I was embarrassed, so I hedged at first, saying the ring was much too expensive. He ignored that, urging me to put it on. I must have convinced him that I was not ready to marry again, because he finally went back in the store and returned it. I felt he was trying to force me, as if the extravagance and sheer richness of the gift would prove irresistible, but if he thought so, he did not know me. And although the gesture had discomforted, even irritated me, I have never forgotten the disappointment in his eyes when he closed the box and turned with it back into the store.

He was a sad man. Even in my memories of the fun times, of boozy laughter in smoke-filled bars, I remember him as being quiet, reserved, yet smiling, his eyes amused, and if shaken occasionally with chuckles, I don't remember him participating in our uproarious shouting and laughter. In hindsight, I realize that he was a lonely, middle-aged man watching kids having fun.

Behind the amusement, the sad man waited, watching, defeated. He had been defeated all his life by women who did not want him.

When I was in his apartment, I saw a framed photo of a little boy on a pony. Grinning, I asked if it were a picture of him. He nodded. I think he told me then that he had been orphaned very young. I learned only recently, in reading Ben Jones's, *My Friend Hardman*, that Ralph Dennis had siblings and that their mother had left them in an orphanage when he was six or seven years old. That he remembered watching, through the bars of a closing gate, his mother drive away.

I believe that a child abandoned by his mother will carry within himself always the expectation of rejection, that he will lack the sense of self- worth that is essential to achievement— be his goal winning the love of a woman or winning a Pulitzer. I believe that Ralph Dennis, for all his intellect and education and his skill and confidence as a writer, expected defeat. His very posture was that of a defeated man.

I realize now that as a twenty- something, I intuited his sadness, his hopelessness; I knew that his need for me was emotional; I sensed that he wanted to marry me because he needed to own me. I had the vague idea that, if I married him, I would effectively become the prisoner of a jealous and controlling man.

I lost respect for him. I hotly resisted his attempts to hobble me. To bind me. He'd call me on the phone, arguing his case. He wrote me long letters. Said that if I didn't want to marry him, I could just live with him.

His need was an irritant. Like a fly touching my cheek, my shoulder, the back of my hand. Finally, one day, I sat down at my electric typewriter and furiously typed a letter that stated my feelings in no uncertain terms. I remember the white, hot fury with which I typed that day, the soot- black marks of the ink ribbon upon the white typing paper, and I remember a bit of the phone call I received a few days later. He said that my letter had been "hammering letter," that it was "castrating."

We had a heated exchange. I was shocked and contemptuous of his feeling of having been castrated by my refusal to marry him. Asserted (truthfully) that I had no idea what he was talking about, that if he thought a woman's refusal to marry him was castrating, then he had a real problem, and so on and on, back and forth, until he said goodbye and I knew that he would never speak to me again.

And but for one short and final sentence, he never did. A year or so later, I was in Atlanta again visiting the woman who had been one of the gang in the drunken glory days at George's. I took a notion to go to George's, hoping I'd catch Ralph there and that we could, I don't know, hug like old friends again. Something like that. Who knows what the hell I wanted.

Just to see him, say hey, be friends again. I could have had no idea how deeply my rejection had cut him.

Sure enough, he was at the bar talking with another man when we came in. We took our seats at a booth. He gave no sign that he had seen us. I was fairly bouncing with excitement, so happy to see him again.

Finally, he walked over to the table. I looked up with an eager grin, and he said, "I said goodbye to you a year ago, lady."

The coldness of his eyes stunned me, literally stopped my breath. I don't know whether he turned and went back to the bar or walked out. I don't remember anything after that.

I grew up eventually. Now I understand. Now I know. And I can tell you this much: Ralph Dennis was not Hardman. Hardman was the man he wished to be.

Cynthia Williams is a professional writer whose work includes creative non-fiction, fiction, narrative history, and copy writing for television. She is the author of Hidden History of Fort Myers *and the children's book* Me and the Sky.

WIND SPRINTS

-BEGIN-

All things being equal, and the equality being that of the disturbed and frightened dream, it is time to begin. So much garbage in one life, and that life only thirty-six years spent.

I don't know what has happened. Something has. Maybe as recently as the last year or so. A loss of soul, a death of the spirit. Or, because words mean nothing anyway, a loss of spirit, a death of the soul. High and serious terms for this special malaise.

I have trouble with words now. I am not a professional writer. I am beyond any hope of that now. In fact, the whole effort to keep my bridges intact, to protect myself if nothing came of the writing, has provided me with a good job here at the University of North Carolina, teaching theatre history and dramatic criticism.

The dissertation started and put aside has yet to be done. The Chairman asks me now and then how it is going and I answer at various times, "slow", "hard", and "terribly" and he nods with a kind of smirking understanding.

My students, with their basic understanding of what flattery really is, call me Doctor. I do not correct them because it takes time away from the class when more important matters have to be treated and, I sometimes think, it would be unkind to embarrass them.

The notes on *The Sociological Aspects of Medieval French Drama* fade in my carefully kept and carefully avoided filing cabinet. Until the sap and the energy rise again.

I had not planned to write my autobiography for another twenty-five years. If then. Maybe I'd have waited a full thirty years, for the approaching mellowness, for that one still moment of ripeness before the rot creeps in. No, *thunders* in, whistles in, explodes upon us.

There is a second consideration: by then the gall, the bile, might have thinned down, watered down in the way they say the blood of old men is. Waiting, patient for the full thirty years, my autobiography might have been charming and whimsical. The reviewers would say, "It brings back an America that doesn't exist anymore ... warm, human, bittersweet ... the *yes* to life that has vanished in our time but is still alive in the memory of this man." In time, looking back from a distance and blinded by the shapes and shadows of memory, I might have come to believe that my life had its share of charm and beauty.

My life until now has been a man's version of what a southern lady's life was once supposed to be. Limited, confined in definition to what could be reported properly in the newspapers of the day. Born, married, had children and died.

Born? Check, 1933, In the sandy flat land of South Carolina, in a town called Turbenhorse. Moved to Georgia as a baby. Not sure where my home is now. Millhouse, Chapel Hill, New Haven or New York. Can speak with certainty only about my birthplace.

Married? Check, 1962. After the sullen drive down from Chapel Hill, across the state line into South Carolina where we were in wedlock locked by a J.P. named Miss Angela Slaughter. Who, in a voice that would have frightened God, asked if we were some of those Chapel Hill Red University Reds who believed in integration and that niggers had souls.

Before she would sign the marriage certificate, we had to assure her that we weren't and that we didn't. Because whatever else we were, finally we were more frightened by the accidental meeting of sperm and egg than we were virtuous about equality.

Had children? Check, one daughter, Evadne, born some seven months after the marriage. My child in spirit but never in flesh. The last time I saw Evadne, an ugly, skinny child with arms and legs knotted like the boles on walking sticks, we were on a beach in Connecticut. A polluted beach. Dead black fish washed up by an oil slick sea. Patterns and swarms of flies. Both walking barefoot on the sand, stepping over the fish. My pale chalk feet with the sock fuzz caught under the toenails. Hers bony and tanned, thin and flat as plaster slats. Loving her eye-full face, the pale milk blue of marbles. But there was no way of touching her so that she would know and there were no words that could, with a running start, leap the gap. So that, together, as if on a signal that neither of us had given or seen, we turned and walked back up the beach to where the taxi was parked, waiting. Disgust and shame, I like to think, in both of us. But perhaps not in her. Maybe relief instead. Squinting into the overcast sky, still and patient while I brushed the sand from her feet with my handkerchief.

Evadne was a polite child to the last. "Come and see me again, Daddy." And I, polite also, said that I would ... soon. A lie between us that calmed the fear that we might meet again. That was a year or so ago, more or less, and I have not seen her since. Nor, unless I'm mistaken, does she lean on her window sill and wait for me. If she leans there at all it is to blow her liquid breath against the window panes and cloud out any possibility that she will see me, car parked at the curb behind me, standing on the walk looking up at her.

Divorced? Check, 1967. Not a part of a southern lady's life as defined but a part of mine. Hard to say who was right and who was wrong when there is only a middle, a killing ground where everybody is right and everybody is wrong.

Died? Left blank. Not yet. But sometimes I think my whole shabby and discolored life is a series of wind sprints toward the grave.

BOOK ONE

CHAPTER ONE

NEW HAVEN, 1966

THE TATTOOED LADY'S END OF SUMMER

I remember that it was a spring evening. The hot and dirt-laden air closing about the apartment.

New Haven in the dead of winter has a crisp scent, the bland ice odor of snow piled along the streets. One can smell the ice above the stench of garlic and tomatoes. Or perhaps, if one is honest, it was that the windows were closed and the garlic and tomatoes were bottled up inside.

In the spring in New Haven, all the windows were open and the Italians all across town seemed to eat, drink and bathe in garlic and tomato sauce. In the south, the smell of poverty was something else and for me it was always connected with collards and the raw rank smell of boiled pork neckbones, Grandmama Johnson, almost toothless, picking the slivers of meat from the bones with her fingers and sucking on them a few moments before swallowing them. And the collards, deep green and stalky, mashed by her fork until there was little chewing left to be done.

From the open window, I could look down into the enclosed gravel-covered yard where Evadne played alone. Only minutes earlier, the other children had been called in to their suppers and now with a studied economy, a massive grace, Evadne played alone beside the high wooden fence that separated the Yale student apartments from the Yale Hope Mission. It was an odd game and I am sure there were some assumed rules that were not clear to me. There was an open knot hole at one place in the fence and Evadne would run up to the hole, cover it with a small dirty hand, pull the hand away and look, then scream and run away. Another time she looked first, then covered the hole with her hand and laughed. At other times, she stopped before she reached the knot hole and screamed. The scream hanging in the late afternoon, early evening stillness like a feather.

Starting with the morning, all the clues were there, it was going to be a bad, bad, rotten day. My first class was still over two hours away when I awoke and found her standing naked in front of the full-length mirror. Elaine was fresh from the shower, powdered heavily like a doughnut. The chubby legs and thighs and the magnificent ass enveloped in a fog of body powder.

Because of the dining room clatter of Evadne eating break-fast I whispered, "Bad-ass, come here."

A little surprised she turned, her hands cupping the heavy, blue-veined breasts. "What?"

"Come here. I want a half pound of each."

Elaine sat on the edge of the bed. "What do you want?"

I threw the covers back, and put my arms around her, tilting her easily against me. The smell of the powder was too strong that close, choking me.

"Ball," I said, "let's ball."

"There's no time." Elaine said, pulling away from me easily because I was holding her lightly, gently. "I've already been late once this week." Back at the mirror, she brushed the long brittle hair, the ends cracking like electricity. "I can't be late again."

I tucked the sheet back around me, hiding. "Then who's all this beauty and sweet smell for, if not for me?"

"We're back to that again, are we?" She moved to the chair where the day's clothing was laid out. "I knew we'd get back to that sooner or later."

My head back in the pillow case that needed changing. "Maybe you'll schedule me?"

"Yes," she said, "whatever that means."

"Like this afternoon or later this evening?"

"Yes."

"By then you'll smell like an armpit."

Evadne appeared in the doorway. "Mama, I finished."

"Everything? All the egg?"

The tiny face bobbed. "Yes." Then her face canted toward me, holding the withdrawn, distant look she gave strangers. "Hello, Daddy."

"Hello, baby."

"I'm not a baby." Evadne turned to her mother. "Am I?"

"No, you're almost grown up."

Lies. Lies. I rolled over and buried my face in the pillow and didn't lift it out again until I heard the apartment door slam and the footsteps going down the stairwell. Then, kicking back the covers and standing up, I found that the body powder had transferred, that I was caked with it across my chest and stomach. Me a doughnut, too.

The last afternoon class was over around three. Jim and Dave and I left the annex and walked down Park Street to MacTriff's. It was cool and dark in the bar, empty except for the three of us and a couple of the usual afternoon drunks. Patti opened beers for us and waddled down to the other end of the bar where the longtime customers were.

Jim looked at me over the rim of his beer glass, then put it down and licked at his upper lip. He had a suggestion of a hair-lip so it was hard to tell whether he was licking the beer away or worrying the hair-lip. "How's the paper coming?"

I shrugged. "P.M.L.A. won't take it."

"Just so it keeps you in school, boy. That's what counts."

As if he gave a shit. Jim and I were competing for one of the better fellowships and our conversations hadn't always been this polite.

"It'll be borderline," I said. "I can only hope the Herr Doctor reads it after he's got mind-rot."

"Not him. He reads one a day for ninety days. That's his summer vacation..."

I was watching Dave out of the corner of my eye. Dave was big and solid and bearlike. There was also a kind of childlike quality about the way he looked at people. But I wasn't deceived, it was all deeper than that. He did Navy time like I did and I've never believed that anyone had much of a cherry left after that. There was one odd thing about him and I was probably the only one who knew about it except for his wife. Most of the time, like was then, he kept his left hand closed, as if he was holding something, like a roll of pennies. Once, after we'd been studying all day over a theatre history exam, we'd gone out to a bar. A few drinks and he must have forgotten what he was holding because the hand had opened up. There, looking like pale scar tissue, flattened out palm up on the booth table with the lamp above and slightly behind him striking it full, I'd read the single word, SHIT.

It looked like he'd tried to get it blotted out. There was one method I'd heard about where a skin tone ink was injected over the tattoo and that was supposed to cover it over. Most of the time it didn't work.

Dave had seen me looking and the hand had clenched into a fist, then opened slowly as if he had to force the muscles to react.

"I was drunk in Sasebo at the time and it seemed a valid comment on something or other."

I'd nodded and said that maybe it still was.

After a second beer, Jim left for the library. If I knew him, it was to pick up a book that I'd need in the next day or two.

Dave and I sat at the bar and enjoyed each other's silence until it was time for me to pick up Evadne.

The kindergarten was four blocks from MacTriff's, in one of the old neighborhoods where, on three side, urban renewal was chipping away at it. It was only a matter of time.

I have a way of closing myself off when I walk any distance at all. On that day, I was thinking about one element in the paper I was researching, a description of one of the flying machines in *Mystere de la Passion.*

At the kindergarten, as I expected, Evadne was waiting in the play yard and her face, just for a split second, showed the disappointment that I was there instead of her mother. Then she smoothed it away and said, "Hello, Daddy," and took my hand and we walked the three blocks to the apartment.

There were breakfast and lunch dishes in the sink and a can of spaghetti on the dining table anchored a scrawled note.

Don't wait supper for me. The girls at the office and I have supper plans. Should be back by ten.

Around seven I cleared my books from the table and set a place for Evadne. The canned spaghetti was warm and I'd fixed her a small salad that I knew she wouldn't eat and a couple of warm rolls with butter.

While Evadne ate, I ran the water for her bath and added Soaky. When she'd eaten all that she'd wanted, I undressed her and put her in the tub.

It was getting dark as I stood at the living room window, listening to the splashing in the bathroom, and watched the Yale gothic spires and rooftops in the distance. Gothic is godawful anyway if you've grown up on southern Greek colonial like I had and the dingy, dirty night falling across the city seemed to be exactly what it deserved.

After I tucked-in Evadne, I told her a bedtime story about Pete Gray, the one-armed outfielder who made it to the major leagues during World War Two when a lot of the two-armed ballplayers were in the service. It was not one of my better stories, though I tried to spice it up a bit by adding a little one-legged match girl who sold Pete matches outside the stadium every day. I think the only part of the story that interested Evadne was when I, with one arm held behind my back, gripping my belt, demonstrated how Pete, cheered on by the little match girl, would catch a fly ball, toss the ball into the air, place the glove under the stump of his other "arm", catch the ball as it came down and then throw it toward home plate. I had to act this out for her several times. The last time, when I was reaching up for the ball, I looked over at her and saw that she was asleep.

Around nine o'clock I gave up on the books. The account of the flying machine used by Bruneleschi in Vasari's *Lives of the Artists* had been helpful but it didn't answer all the question and in a strict scholarly sense I didn't know if I could use Italian flying machine to explain how French flying machines had worked.

Fuck it anyway.

I opened a quart of beer and, after looking in at Evadne to be sure she was all right, I grunted my way through the window and out onto the porch. There was a camp stool I left out there and I put it against the wall near the window and watched the lights in the distance and drank my beer.

I'd met Elaine when I was living on the Alley, the ten rooms that overlooked the main street of Chapel Hill, just above the center of the business district. It had been a good, few years up there, listening to the last gasps of the Beat Generation. And I'd been writing then, poetry and short stories, and the last thing I wanted to do was go back to school. There were a couple of painters living up there then and a friend, Miles, who was writing a novel. The other rooms were taken by what we called the Steinbeck people, the ones we didn't mix with. There were girls too, a lot of girls passing through at all hours, though the Dean of Women had listed the Alley as one of the places that was off limits to her girls.

I met Elaine at a swimming party out at Hogan's Lake. We were in the water. There had been some casual talk, my best line of bullshit, and then it was like somebody had sucked our breath away and left her gasping. We were hanging onto the ladder that led up to the pier and I reached out and caught the strap of her one-piece bathing suit and pulled down the top.

If she said anything, I didn't hear her because I ducked under the water and caught one of the water-wrinkled nipples in my mouth and after that we almost drowned. She let go of the ladder too and for the longest time, we didn't seem to need air. We were sinking into the dark water, with the black night sky above us, and somehow she'd gotten a hand down the front of my bathing trunks and she was pulling at it, so hard it felt that it might come off in her hand. I had to let the nipple go because she was writhing, and the only way I could have held it was to bite into it.

9

And I said, "no, no, in case I don't drown I have plans for that nipple and the other one too."

But I wouldn't let go of her either and she was holding me and the only thing that saved us was that Miles chose that moment to dive off the end of the pier. The shock of him striking the water near us exploded us toward the surface where we leaned against the ladder again, gasping and sputtering water.

Starting that night, she was a regular up on the Alley. Her friends didn't understand what she saw in me and the Alley people had some questions about what I saw in her ... though they didn't ask them.

A year later, she began to get morning sickness. A couple of times she threw up in the sink in the back corner of my room. It was then we drove down to South Carolina and got married. The next fall, because I felt that I ought to accept my new responsibility, I started work on a Masters in English. Evadne was born during final exams three and a half months later.

By midnight, having listened to the distant campus clock strike the hours of ten and eleven and then twelve, I began to worry. Apart from the campus, New Haven can be a pretty tough town. It wasn't like Chapel Hill at all. One time, I got as far as dialing the first three digits of the police number before I talked myself out of it. I knew I'd feel silly if I reported Elaine missing and then had her walk in a few minutes later. So, I waited.

A few minutes before one, I heard Evadne cry out in her sleep and I went into the bedroom and sat on the edge of her bed and waited until the nightmare passed. I was wiping the perspiration from her forehead with a towel when I heard the apartment door open and close. Then no sound at all.

At first, when I entered the living room, I thought she was winded from a fast climb up the three flights of stairs. She was leaning back against the closed door, her pocketbook dropped and on its side at her feet, her hands held low and pressing back against the door as if to hold it closed.

"You're late."

"Huh?" Her chin pressed down upon her breast bone, eyes closed, and breath bubbling through her slack lips. "What?" Her eyes opened, fluttered.

"Where have you been?"

"Around."

"Where's around?" I stopped by the coffee table to get a cigarette.

I was lighting it when she took a faltering step away from the door and fell flat on her face. It was a smell I remembered from the days on the Alley but I couldn't place it right away. I caught it first when my nose got buried in her hair as I was lifting her onto the sofa. I considered the possibility that it might be a sense memory, so I went over to the window and took a deep breath to clear my head.

When I came back and leaned over her, it was there — the smoky acrid scent. My sweet little wife's been smoking grass and she's stoned. I recalled the few times we'd had grass up on the Alley and how afraid she'd acted when Miles had passed the foil lined pipe around.

Some girls at the office you've got there, I thought, and you've got some tall explaining to do in the morning.

I went into the bedroom and pulled back the covers on the bed.

You're going to give me a goddam hernia, I thought as I carried her from the living room down the narrow hallway to the bed room.

It was like undressing a rag doll, only the rag doll weighed around a hundred and twenty pounds. I got the dress off by a lot of twisting and turning and rolling her this way and that. I think I heard the seam give in a place or two but I said to shit with it and balled it up and threw it across the room. I was leaning over pulling the covers over her feet when I stopped. The thin slice of light from the hallway had been there the whole time but I hadn't really been looking at Elaine. Now, narrowing my eyes, I could see that there was something dark right over her navel. I couldn't make it out so I turned on the overhead light.

Over her navel there were the initials "R.T.T" in black, probably written with a felt tipped pen. I pulled the bra up and away from her and found that there was an "R" in red ink on one breast and "H" in green ink on the other.

When I turned her over on her stomach, through the sheer white underpants, I could see the blur of other lettering on her buttocks. I didn't remove the underpants to read these initials. It didn't seem to matter. I covered her and turned off the overhead light. I stood over the bed for a long time, thinking that was some party you went to, badass, and how would you like to get good and dead?

But I talked myself out of it and closed the bedroom door behind me. There was one quart of beer left in the refrigerator and I got it out and opened it and went through the window again. I stood against the wooden railing of the porch and looked down into the courtyard.

Sometime later, there was blue spears of lightning in the distance, beyond the black gothic spires. A light, misty rain followed the lightning and I didn't move back against the wall until the rain thickened. I leaned back against the wall and drank my beer and watched the wind walk the rain across the porch boards toward me. The rain across my face was fresh and cool but it tasted like sea water.

CHAPTER TWO

MILLHOUSE, GEORGIA, 1966

UNCLE BOB'S NIGHT OUT

There wasn't much night life in Millhouse, but Uncle Bob wasn't about to let that change his mind once he'd made it up. Here I was, his favorite nephew, down from the North for the summer and all I did was sit out on the front porch and read or, in the evening, sit on the same dark and leaf-shaded porch and drink bottle after bottle of beer.

"Sure," he said, "I know you've got marriage problems back up North, but that's no reason for you to vegetate here at home." He leaned toward me and out his eyes toward the living room where Mama was watching television. "Hell, you can't let any woman think she's got you de-balled."

I nodded and pried the top off another bottle of beer.

"You might have something there," I said, but I was wondering how Elaine would know what I was doing or if she'd care even if she knew. She was back in New Haven, having a ball and probably balling half the male population.

But I didn't tell Uncle Bob that. It would give him another argument and I knew he'd say something about the goose and the gander and it would sound very southern and very wise. Arguments were his thing. He was a lawyer. So, I just nodded a couple of times, jerky little nods that meant to him that I agreed.

When it was settled to his satisfaction, he accepted a beer from me and moved his chair forward a few feet so that he could brace his heels against the banister. He sighed and finished off the bottle of beer in two swallows.

Later, before he left, he went in to say goodnight to Mama and I heard the sound of the TV turned down and I could hear Uncle Bob telling Mama that he and I were going out Saturday night and do the town.

Mama, who has a kind of dry wit when she tries, said that doing Millhouse ought to take all of five minutes. And then the sound went back up to full volume on the TV set.

There were a few girls I still knew in town. One who had been mousey and frightened behind thick glasses all through high school was now librarian at the Carnegie Public Library just off Main Street.

She still looked frightened, but she'd replaced the glasses with contact lenses and she was trying to do something with the thin, wispy blonde hair. She'd been friendly enough when I'd gone by to check out some books, but I'd held myself back, still somewhat unsure of myself and knowing that I'd have to explain too much. Ass wasn't worth that much. Maybe it would be in time, or maybe I'd meet somebody who didn't know me and I wouldn't have to explain at all.

And back in New Haven, the wife-beast was shacking with some of those Italians whose dreams of pie-in-the-sky was real, home-made, hand churned, garlic ice cream.

I got through the rest of the week all right. When I wasn't on the porch reading, I amused myself by imagining Uncle Bob's campaign to convince Aunt Ethel that the Saturday night out was his personal sacrifice to my mental health.

It would go something like this:

Aunt Ethel, her skin the color and texture of dried seed corn, with what had been a cute, pert turned up nose now sagging a little at the edges, would be seated after supper in her reading chair. Floating around her, warring with the smell of boiled supper cabbage, the medicinal stench of Airwick.

"Ethel, I'm worried about that boy."

One finger holding her place in McCall's, she'd close the magazine and drop it into her lap. "He seems fine to me. Just needs to go to church more often." That she'd added "more often" showed the real extent of her affection for me.

Uncle Bob would sigh sadly. "Oh, I admit, on the surface, he seems to be holding his own. But inside, inside where it really counts, he's really torn up."

"All the more reason he should pray more," Ethel said. "That's certain."

"And I told his Mama at the time, warned her when the phone call came, that marrying that girl from the North would be nothing but trouble. Of course, by then it was too late for his poor Mama to do anything about it."

"Well, he's paying for his mistakes now."

"Coming home to roost," Ethel said.

"It bothers me, him just sitting on the porch hour after hour, ruining his eyes reading in bad light. Why, I told his Mama just the other night that I thought that boy needed a change of environment."

"It might help." This said tentatively.

"Help?" Uncle Bob would almost shout. "Help? It would be just the tonic that boy needs." Having made this point, he'd settle back into the rump sprung contour he'd created on his end of the sofa. He'd let that hang in the air for another minute or two. "Yes, sir, just the tonic he needs."

And by Saturday, dropping a few words here and a few words there, he'd create a patchwork quilt of his good intentions. Oh, he had better things to do with his own time. That suit against the Newbold Lumber Yard going to court in a week or so. Hell, he wasn't the one needed the change of environment. If he didn't think so much of me, hadn't looked up to me all these years, I'd let him stew in his own juices. And on and on until Aunt Ethel must have, in a moment of weakness, agreed that it certainly couldn't hurt to try it.

After an early supper on Saturday Uncle Bob and I drove out to the VFW Club for a few beers and a few hands of penny-nickel-dime, dealer's choice.

"It's not that I don't lie to Ethel," Uncle Bob said. We were in the slot machine room at the VFW Club. He was drinking a double bourbon and branch water and I was drinking a beer. "It's just that if there's some truth in what I tell her, even ten words worth, then I believe those ten words and usually she does too." He fed another dollar into the machine, sliding the quarters one after another from the roll in his hand.

"You ever win in here?"

"Hardly ever." He turned to the table I was leaning on and picked up his bourbon. He took a long sip without missing a stroke with the slot machine handle. He finished off his drink and handed me the glass. "You know, branch water doesn't taste the same since the town council and the mayor decided to put fluoride in the water."

"Progress," I said.

"It sure plays hell with good ten-year-old bourbon." He shook the quarters in his hand, as if weighing them. "Here," he said, "you lose a few while I get us another drink."

When he came back, he brought me another beer and stood just past my shoulder watching while I lost the rest of the roll of quarters. We went back into the bar and drank some more and ate two bowls of popcorn.

He seemed to be waiting for something but I wasn't sure what it was. Then, exactly at ten o'clock, he pushed away from the bar.

"Come on, son, let's go see if it's too wet to plow."

Fat's Place was a poolhall and beer joint just a fraction of a mile outside the city limits. Poolhalls weren't legal within the city limits of Millhouse. The law went back to a knifing that took place back around the turn of the century. Nobody remembers who got cut or if the wounds were serious.

As far as I know, nobody had ever tried to have the law changed. Fat Jack Burtram would have probably mustered the support to keep the law on the books. He believed in a little vice and larceny and I'd heard him say, more than once, that it's less troublesome out in the county. He was probably right: his B girls worked some long hours on the army cot back in the beer storage room and he'd been known to supply white whiskey if the price is right.

Some people thought he even booked a bet now and then.

Fat Jack saw me before he saw Uncle Bob. He let out a yell you could hear over the juke box

"Professor!"

He'd been calling me that since high school when his kid brother, Ernie, and I had played football together and we used to sneak out to the pool hall now and then for a game. We don't mention Ernie anymore. It was something understood between us, a link, but it was better not to talk about it.

I'd been on Guam in the Navy when Mama had sent me the clipping from the newspaper. Ernie had gone down to Florida after high school and he'd got involved in his first love affair ... with an older woman. He'd needed money and he wasn't making it fast enough to satisfy her so he'd held up a grocery store with a rusty old .32 he took from the gas station where he worked. The old grocer had been slow about handing over the money and Ernie had been scared and the gun had gone off, the bullet hitting the old grocer at the bridge of his nose and splattering his brains all over the canned goods behind him.

Florida executed Ernie although the town of Millhouse had sent the governor a petition with five thousand names on it, asking that the sentence be changed to life in prison.

After I got the clipping, I wrote Fat Jack a letter telling him how sorry I was about it, and how I thought Ernie had been a good guy and had just had the bad luck to get mixed up with a pig-assed woman like that.

I had trouble reading the letter I got back from Fat Jack. The part I could make out thanked me and said that it meant a lot coming from me, more than it did from a "lot of those shits who don't mean it when they say it." But all the time since then we'd never mention Ernie again.

"The first one's on me, Professor." Fat Jack opened a beer and put it in front of me. He added a spotted, yellowish glass that I tried to ignore. "You can even have a chaser if you want," he said. I shook my head. Uncle Bob edged around me to shake hands with

Fat Jack. "I'll have a beer and a double chaser."

"Done." Fat Jack gave him the beer first and then leaned under the counter for a moment. When he straightened up, he placed a beer glass about half full of an almost clear but slightly brownish liquid on the bar.

He leaned on the counter and waited while Uncle Bob poured a little trickle on his tongue and kept it there for about a count of thirty before he swallowed.

"Smooth."

Nodding, satisfied, Fat Jack pushed away from the counter. "It's Art Baker's runoff, but I cured it for a couple of weeks myself. My girls must have bought up all the dried apricots in town."

Uncle Bob tried to pay but Fat Jack wouldn't touch the money. "It ain't every day the Professor's in town."

"Speaking of your girls....." Uncle Bob let that trail off and turned on his stool to look toward the back dark area of the room.

"Slow for a Saturday, so far anyway." Fat Jack shrugged like it didn't matter. "Nadine's back in the store room stacking empties and Billie's in the back booth resting before the rush starts."

Uncle Bob eased himself off the bar stool. "Billie by herself?"

Fat Jack scratched at his crotch, fondly, slowly, as if he was doing a braille reading. "Some construction worker's keeping her company while she's resting."

Uncle Bob went into an elaborate stretch as if that had been why he'd left the stool in the first place. He managed a yawn too before he sat down again. "That Billie's some girl."

"So, they tell me. A man my age has to depend on what his friends tell him."

"Shit, Jack."

"The Lord's truth." Fat Jack smiled sadly. "A man my age has got to be satisfied with scratching and trying to find it."

"I'm your age," Uncle Bob said, "and I don't have any trouble finding it."

"The Lord treated some people kinder than others."

They talked on and I shut them off like I might turn off a radio or a light. I was thinking about New Haven, the beast with two backs being made, maybe even on my bed, the bed I'd bought new right after we got married. Elaine was damned good at making one half of the beast and the memory of some of the times when it had really been good flashed past my mind like a film. I could feel the blood flowing, almost hear it seeping in, until my groin was tight and swollen and aching. I was sweating too and I tried to think about something else but that didn't work. The film was still running in my mind and I couldn't stop it. She was riding me, leaning back and supported by my raised knees, her hair whipping around her head as she moved, teeth clenched and groaning, deep in the frenzy before it would all fall apart, calling my name over and over.

I got up and ordered another beer and paid for it before I went down the aisle, past the dark booth where a girl was giggling, and into the bathroom. I tried for a long time to piss but couldn't, not looking at it but looking at the crudely lettered sign over the trough. Short horns stand close to the trough. Long horns can stand where you want to. After a while, I gave up and splashed cold water on my face and washed my hands.

When I passed the booth again, I heard a man's voice: "The shit you say. It must be made out of gold."

I could hear the faint rumble of her answer before I was out of earshot and away. I stood at the bar and drank my second beer and watched the dark booth. I wasn't surprised when the construction worker said in a loud voice, "That'll be the day," just like John Wayne used to in the movies and stalked down the aisle outside.

Fat Jack said, "'Night, George," but George didn't answer or show that he'd heard.

Billie cleared off the table before she came over to the bar. She was a little on the short side, blonde hair in a kind of feather cut with the dark roots just beginning to show. She wore a mini skirt and a white t-shirt. When she moved, breasts the size and shape of winesap apples moved freely under the t-shirt.

Uncle Bob spun around on his stool and watched her. "Somebody steal your underwear off the clothes line, Billie?"

Billie put the bottles and glasses on the bar before she threw back her shoulders and did a little dance step, "You complaining, Bob?"

"Not me. I hear it's the fashion in London, Paris, New York and Atlanta."

"Millhouse, Georgia too," Fat Jack added, "courtesy of Fat's Place."

"That fashion continues, I might move in here full time." Uncle Bob pushed the empty beer glass toward Fat Jack. "I need a bit more chaser."

from the time, she'd come up to the bar. I'd been trying to lock eyes with her. Her eyes, when she did notice me, were dull and dis interested. "Who's the ugly fellow on the other side of you, Bob?"

"Him?" Uncle Bob turned slowly and looked at me. "Probably some hitchhiker who came in for the air conditioning."

After Fat Jack put the glass in front of Uncle Bob he waved Billie down to the end of the bar. "If his own uncle won't own him I will." He introduced us and added, "But I call him The Professor."

Closer I could see that she was very young, maybe no more than eighteen. "Professor of what?" The eyes relaxed, gaining depth.

"Muff diving," Uncle Bob said and went into a spasm of laughter.

⚜ ⚜ ⚜

A few minutes later, a crowd started arriving. It seemed from the talk that an American Legion baseball game had just ended out at John J. Moss Memorial Park. Looking at the gathering crowd, Uncle Bob ordered two more beers and told Fat Jack we were going to take a booth. "Take three or four," Fat Jack said. "Hell, you're friends, so take five."

When the rush was over, Billie came to the booth and sat next to Uncle Bob. For an instant she'd hesitated and I thought she was going to sit next to me but something had shifted in her and pushed her away from me. "Are you really a professor?"

Before I could answer, Uncle Bob's hand dropped under the table and she jerked slightly, then settled down once more. "Are you?"

"Not yet. Maybe in another two years or so."

"He's working on his P.H.D. at Yale," Uncle Bob added. The hand was back on the table top, turning his beer glass around and around in wet circles.

"Does that pay much, being a professor?"

"Twenty-five thousand a year," Uncle Bob said. Either he didn't know any better or he was building me up.

"Not that much," I said, "Not to begin."

"But later, if you do good, it could be that much?"

I nodded, deciding to let it go, and I could see her eyes close with the strain of dividing that by twelve and then by fifty-two. I could have given her another problem by telling her to use nine instead of twelve but that seemed an unnecessary complication. Before she got very far with it, she had to leave to take orders at a booth near the front door.

Uncle Bob leaned across the booth toward me. "That girl seems taken with you."

"Could be," I said, smiling though I hadn't intended to. "It just could be."

The other bar girl, Nadine, came from the back a few minutes later followed by a sheepish looking sailor. The sailor stopped at the back end of the bar and had one beer before he left. Nadine waited a couple of tables before she saw Uncle Bob and came over and dropped into the seat next to him. "Been sleeping," she said after we were introduced, "and it was a good nap."

"You sleep on your back or your front?" Uncle Bob asked.

"Whatever seems handy at the time."

Billie finished clearing a couple of tables and joined us, sliding into the seat next to me, her bare leg and thigh pressed against me for just long enough for me to feel the warmth, then easing away as she moved toward the outer end of the booth.

"I thought we might drop by for a visit after closing, if you girls don't have other plans." Uncle Bob was canted toward Nadine but I could see that he was trying to watch Billie out of the corner of his eye. I was watching Billie too and I saw the faint dip of her head when Nadine looked at her.

"Maybe just for a little while," Nadine said. "I got to get my sleep."

We stayed until closing time. We were going to make a stop at his office to pick up a bottle he had there.

At the door, I turned and looked back at Billie where she was standing under the strong bar lights. She seemed waif-like, a little lost and that was such a change, a change I'd noticed all evening from the way she'd been when I first saw her.

I said, "Wait a minute," and went over to her.

Billie met me halfway, in the shadow away from the strong lights. I fumbled for a few second, trying to find the right way to say it. But the words were tumbling end-over-end and they wouldn't straighten out. "If you'd rather we didn't come by, we won't."

"I don't care."

"What I mean is, that you don't have to feel that you have to put up with me if you don't want to." But that wasn't right either and I said, "I don't want you to feel forced."

"I don't feel forced. All right?"

"All right."

"I never dated a professor before."

On the way over to Uncle Bob's office, I thought about what "date" meant in whore talk. I had the feeling, just from the way she'd said it, that that wasn't what she meant at all.

It was around an hour after we'd left Fat's Place when we drove up to the house where Billie and Nadine lived. There was a light on in the upstairs rooms but the screened-in front porch was dark.

We'd spent the hour in Uncle Bob's law office overlooking the main square of Millhouse. from his window, you looked down on an authentic slave auction block and the monument to the Confederate dead. It was still and quiet on the square as only a small southern town can be after midnight. While I was looking out of the window, a police cruiser stopped on the square and a policeman got out and inspected the slave block and the monument. In the black protests of 1964, an attempt had been made to blow up the auction block but the bomb hadn't gone off.

While we waited in the office, he had a short drink of Wild Turkey and I had a cup of instant coffee I made on the secretary's hot plate in the outer office.

The policeman, satisfied that the historical artifacts weren't in any danger, drove out of sight past the far corner of the court house.

I left the window and sat in the client's chair across the desk from Uncle Bob. The just seal-broken bottle of Wild Turkey jutted partly out of the crushed brown paper bag.

"Since it might all hang out before the night's over," I said, "how about telling me how you met the girls?"

"Official capacity, of course."

"Huh?"

He smiled. "I represented Nadine on a disorderly conduct charge about six months ago. I didn't want to, but Fat Jack talked me into it. Said if she was convicted, it would give his place a bad name." His voice shifted from matter of fact to a kind of wry twist ... Of course, if I was going to take the case I had to go to the scene of the supposed crime and find out exactly what the nature of the conduct had been."

"Of course."

"It happens that I had a full schedule of appointments that week and I couldn't fit her in until around one a.m. It seemed to me at the time that while her conduct might seem interesting, even exciting, it wasn't what I'd call disorderly."

"What was the verdict?"

"It never went to trial. Saved the county some money that way. Had a little talk with Bud Bliss. He was in school about the time that Jerry was." He hesitated and I knew that the mention of Jerry was a mistake.

Nobody mentioned him anymore. It hadn't been long since Jerry had died, and for all the talking we'd done about him since, you'd think I'd never had an older brother, or Mama another son, or Uncle Bob another nephew. "It turned out that Bud had some progressive ideas about the law. It was dropped for insufficient evidence..."

The house was a mile or so from Fat's Place. It had been a farm house once but the land had been farmed out and the newest owner had put it in the soil bank.

"Think anybody's home?" I held the bottle while Uncle Bob carefully folded his coat and draped it over the back of the seat.

"Not sure," he said.

He tried the screen door and found it latched. He rapped on the door frame a couple of times. "Hey, anybody home?"

When there was no answer, he grabbed the door handle and jerked at it. The latch held. After the third or fourth pull, the handle came off in his hand.

He staggered back a step or two and I caught him with my free hand and steadied him. from the dazed way he stared down at the handle in his hand, I realized that all the whiskey he'd been drinking all evening was finally getting to him. I made a note that I'd do the driving on the way home.

"Shit." Then, with his eyes on the lighted window above him, as if unaware of what he was doing, he dropped the door handle into his shirt pocket and scooped up a handful of gravel from the walk. On the second spray of gravel the window creaked up and Nadine leaned out. "Is that you, Bob?"

Billie let us into the house. As soon as I saw her, I knew that I'd been right before about our date. She was wearing a blue linen dress and stockings and heels. It was obviously her Sunday best.

Being right tightened me up a bit but I covered it over and said,"Hey, you look great, Billie," with what seemed to be the proper amount of enthusiasm.

Uncle Bob tried to undercut her by saying, "I see you found your underwear." That didn't spoil it for her. The way she was acting reminded me of a girl I'd taken out when I was a senior in high school. She'd been a freshman and it had been her first date.

While Billie was in the kitchen mixing us a drink, Uncle Bob shook his head. "Dolled up for you, boy. You don't watch out, about the time the sun comes up she's going to make you brush your teeth and take her to church."

There wasn't anything I could say to that. I was still trying to think of an answering remark when Billie returned with a drink for Uncle Bob and a bottle of beer for me. She blushed when she handed me the beer.

"You didn't drink hard stuff so I brought a six-pack home from the Place." When she turned away from me, I saw that there was a damp spot in the back of her hair. That probably meant that she'd just had a shower. With that in mind, I made another guess that she probably had on brand new, never worn before underwear. But there was, I thought wryly, a damn good chance the way the evening was going, that I'd never find out for sure.

"Where's Nadine?" Uncle Bob was swirling the ice cubes around in his glass and looking up the stairwell that faced the sofa.

"She's taking a shower."

"Really?" Uncle Bob swayed a little as he got to his feet. "It's Sunday morning and I could use one myself."

He mixed another drink in the kitchen for Nadine and, with the bottle under one arm, crossed to the base of the stairwell. "We'll chaperon you two young people from a good vantage point upstairs."

He went up the stairs and out of sight. We'd agreed on the drive over that we'd only stay an hour. Aunt Ethel was going to raise hell anyway. Maybe an hour wasn't enough. I could feel the time ticking away inside me like I had a clock for a heart.

I got to my feet and stretched. Then asking," Aren't you drinking?" I moved to the sofa and sat down beside her.

"I don't like the taste yet. I guess I'll have to develop a liking for it."

I shook my head. "It might be better for you if you don't."

"Sometimes I take a shot in a coke." She was looking at me with all the barriers down, as if she'd grown her innocence back in the last two or three hours. "It's not that I'm against drinking at all." That hung in the air for a long while, static and flat. Then she said, "It must take a lot of work to become a professor."

I said that I guessed it did. I'd been in school so long that I was getting tired of it. "A couple of years more in New Haven and I can come south again."

While I was talking, I put down my beer and eased an arm around her shoulders. I think she'd been waiting for that because there wasn't any hesitation as she turned and faced me.

It started out like a high school first date kiss but, as it lengthened, I could feel myself becoming more and more demanding, so much so that she pulled away from me.

"I wish you wouldn't kiss me that hard. It makes my lips swell up." It was said softly, as if she were afraid of offending me and I said that I was sorry, that I'd be more careful.

I kissed her gently, slowly, my tongue in her mouth against the almost imagined sting of the Listerine she'd used, nibbling at the corners of her mouth, sucking the breath out of her lungs into my lungs. She was panting for breath and as we fell back against the sofa I pushed my hand under her dress, past the stocking tops, to the change of texture when I touched the inner thigh. It was so incredibly smooth and soft that I opened my eyes and looked at her.

Billie's eyes were open too. Surprise had frozen on her face. "I thought.." but she broke off. Her mouth moved without sound, as if she were chewing up the rest of what she'd started to say. She sat up straight, away from me, and took a long shuddering breath. Then softly, almost inaudible, "No, I guess I wished..." She stood up and looked at the wrinkles on the front of her dress. "There's another room down here."

I followed her to the small room that was off the hallway near the kitchen. I stopped in the doorway while she stripped back the covers and clicked on the small lamp beside the bed. Then, with her back to me, she began the practiced and fluid process of undressing. I didn't start undressing until she was rolling down her stockings. She was naked first and sat on the edge of the bed watching me, eyes dulling and glazing over as if she wasn't seeing me at all but some kind of shadow movement.

When I was naked too, she stood up and met me at the side of the bed. She put out her hand and caught me, peeling back the foreskin with the palm of her hand as she pushed against me. "I didn't ask you before. You want it French or straight?"

I could feel her pain and it was like my pain and we made love in the lighted room. She moved very little under me and I began to wish what she'd wished but it was all ruined and impossible anyway and that was all there was to it. And then, in the short rows, feeling it slipping away from me, raw with anger and frustration, I lunged against her as harshly, as brutally as possible and she opened up to me, becoming limitless, and I felt the defeat at the moment I exploded inside her.

I heard Uncle Bob moving around in the living room. I got up and dressed. Billie was curled up on the far side of the bed, back to me and unmoving. I couldn't even hear her breathing.

Uncle Bob met me out in the hallway and said that ten dollars was the usual for a short time. I said I'd meet him out at the car and went back into Billie's room. I stood there for a long time wanting to say something. I guess I realized there wasn't anything to say so I left twenty dollars on the table beside the bed and went out to the car.

As expected, Aunt Ethel was mad. She was trying not to show it in front of me and I suppose that was why Uncle Bob had insisted that I have a cup of coffee with him before I headed home. I knew that all hell was going to break loose as soon as I left so I accepted the second cup of coffee that Aunt Ethel offered me out of politeness. She'd offered it but she hadn't intended that I drink it. Her hand was shaking as she tilted the pot over my cup. Then she moved past me and topped off Uncle Bob's cup.

"What's that?" she asked.

"What?" Uncle Bob's mouth dropped open and he looked down at the front of shirt as if he half-expected to find Nadine's name written there in lipstick.

"What's that in your shirt pocket?"

"Huh? This?" Uncle Bob lifted a hand and dug out the screen door handle. He shrugged and tossed it into the center of the kitchen table.

"It looks to me like the handle off a whore house door," he said.

CHAPTER THREE
MILLHOUSE, GEORGIA, 1966
WAR BUDDY

It was late August. I'd gone back to reading and drinking beer on the front porch. The girl at the Carnegie Library had given up on the possibility of an affair. She'd go into a fury of stamping BOOKS DUE on post cards when I'd enter the library and when I'd leave. Once, looking past the other librarian who was checking out the books for me, I watched her run out of post cards and stamp the whole front page of the Millhouse Daily Southerner.

Twice, seeing the weekend stretch out in front of me like a length of curved rope, I borrowed Mama's 1959 Ford and set out for the beach. Each time I got a hundred miles away from Millhouse and each time I stopped for supper at the Red Dot Bar-B-Que Pit and Dance Hall. I'd have a plate of barbeque and some ribs and I'd drink a couple of slow beers and listen to the J piece country band in the other room shit kick for a while. The band must have doing requests because they'd play *Cold, Cold Heart* about every fifth number. They played it kind of fast and jerky and if it hadn't been for the nasal female singer

I wouldn't have known what it was. After eating and resting, I'd go out and turn the car around and head back for Millhouse. Maybe I didn't really want the beach that much. Not in the summer anyway, with all the fun and excitement around me while I was as still and heavy as a stone inside.

After the second abortive trip, I didn't have the heart to try again. Mama had been waiting in the living room for me that second time, though it was past her usual bed time, and all she said was, "I'm beginning to wonder about you, son."

So, I sat on the porch while the late August temperature stuck around the hundred mark and stayed there. One of the Junior Chamber of Commerce wags repeated again what he did every year: he had his picture taken frying bacon and eggs on the bare sidewalk outside his insurance office. It didn't say in the newspaper caption whether he ate the bacon and eggs or not.

Uncle Bob passed by on the average of once or twice a week. He'd drink one of my beers if he was on his way to the office or the VFW or somewhere else, iced tea if he was on the way home. Each visit he'd work up to telling me that Billie was asking about me, that she wasn't mad anymore, and that she liked me better than anybody else in town. "That little girl feels bad about that misunderstanding and, she wants to make it up to you."

"There's nothing to make up."

"She thinks there is."

"There isn't," I'd say and the silence would blow around us, chilling us both until he'd finish his beer or iced tea and get up to leave.

Around 8:30 one Friday night, Mama came out on the porch and broke the stillness of my exercise in not-think and said, "There's a phone call for you."

"Who is it?"

"I think it's Bert Campbell ... "

On the way to the phone table, I tried to remember his face but I couldn't. It had been a long time and the face blurred in the center, though the outline was firm enough: round like a slightly misshapen cookie. I got my high school annual from the book shelf and opened it on the phone table before I picked up the phone.

"Hey, Bert."

"Man, I heard you were in town," he said.

The annual cracked with an old dry rot when I opened it in the center and flipped this way and that, trying to find the senior pictures.

"I'm out at the VFW having a few drinks." He said.

I hesitated at the football picture section and found myself in one of the group pictures. The caption noted that we were interior linemen.

I had a lot more hair then and I looked out at the camera with a kind of shy innocence.

"I heard you were up north studying to be a teacher," he said.

Bert Campbell was on my left in the picture. He was shorter by an inch or two and not as heavy, I'd been right about the shape of his face but I'd forgotten the bent, broken nose.

"Bob told me the other night when he was out here," he said.

Bert and I had been sort of friends during each football season, forced into it by the fact that neither of us was very good at the game,

I'd been a second-string tackle and he'd been a second-string guard and we'd played side by side. When we played, which wasn't often.

"I was thinking about you the other day," he said, "I'd been out to practice watching this year's team begin the fall workouts, I swear a couple of them look like we used to."

I found the senior pictures and skipped through the A's and B's until I found his class photo. He'd written beside his picture in pencil: *Now, go out and get your share, buddy.*

"I even stayed around for the wind sprints. Coach ran them until half the team was down on their faces."

I thought about the wind sprints. It would be after the practice was over and you'd get in a line with the rest of the players, down into a three-point stance and the coach would shout, "Hike" and you'd charge out of the stance, staying low, and run ten yards as fast as you could.

Then you'd get into the stance again and wait for the coach to trot up beside you. Then he'd shout again and you'd go another ten yards and another ten yards until you reached the goal line. Then you'd turn around and get into a line again and start down the field in the other direction. It would continue until the coach saw that he'd pushed you as far as you could go. Sometimes the wind sprints would last an hour or longer, until the sun was down and the coach couldn't see us anymore.

"I thought you might want to come out for a drink."

I felt trapped by an old friendship that didn't exist anymore. I wanted to say that I couldn't, that it wouldn't mean anything, that

I didn't have anything to say to him. Instead, because it had been a long afternoon on the porch, I said that I would come out for one drink.

I found him in the main bar room. I didn't recognize him at first. He called my name and I turned and saw him. I tried to keep the shock and surprise off my face as I walked toward him. Bert was sitting in a wheelchair pushed up tight against one of the tables. He looked like he weighed between three and four hundred pounds. The loose flesh hung down in folds from his face. Under the loud sport shirt his torso seemed a shapeless mass.

"Maybe I should have told you," he said, "but I thought you'd heard." I pulled out a chair and sat down. "The Korean one. Damaged my spine. That's the way the ball bounces."

He made it sound vaguely heroic, understated and sort of stiff upper lip. Later, from Uncle Bob I found out that he'd been refueling a plane during a rain storm and he'd slipped on the wing and fallen on his back on the concrete runway. That had been twelve or thirteen years before. Now all he did was sit around the VFW like someone out of one of those old Republic Studios World War Two movies.

"I was thinking about you the other day even before I saw your uncle." Bert laughed, his mouth opening slowly, as if he had to will it to open. "Those crazy things we used to do in high school."

I nodded and watched while the bartender ducked under the counter and brought over the drinks Bert had ordered. A sour mash for him and a beer for me. I was surprised by the table service. Usually, you had to get your drinks from the bar. Bert signed the check and waved aside my offer to buy the round.

"I settle up once a month when the disability check comes." It took both hands for him to get the glass to his mouth and I tried not to watch as part of the drink dribbled down his chin and onto his shirt.

Instead, I turned my head and watched two couples enter and cross to the bar. One of the women had a swing to her hips that froze everyone in the room into a still watchfulness.

Bert looked at her too.

"That's what I miss most," he said. "Ass." I nodded. There wasn't much to say. "Not like the old days in high school, huh?"

"Not a bit," I said, wanting to agree with him.

"Sore cocks all the time from all that tight, young stuff."

"Great days," I said.

"The greatest." He seemed to be tasting those days again and I sat and let without saying anything. "Those last two years, that senior year when we won eight in a row, I don't think there was a single night I didn't tear me off some." His voice was getting louder and I was beginning to look around to see if they could hear him at the nearby tables. "Shit, some nights I'd tear off three pieces."

"That was before old age hit us," I said.

"Man, I had a cock like a hoe handle in those days."

"All of us did," I said.

"Like a goddam hoe handle."

"Great days," I said.

"To those days." He lifted his glass but the difficulty in his movement combined with the passion in his toast spilled the last of his drink across the table. "I wish they'd come again."

His voice cracked and I said to myself, "Oh, shit.." and got up to go to the bar to buy another round. Before I got away from the table a man left the bar and came over to the table.

"I'm Bert's brother, Sam." He put out his hand and we shook hands.

He was a few years older than Bert, gray hair cut very short and deep wrinkles plowed into his face. "It's time," he said to Bert.

"An hour more," Bert said. "He just got here ... "

Sam shook his head.

"Half an hour then," Bert said. "I'm just beginning to enjoy myself."

"You know what the V.A. doctor said."

I followed them out of the club and into the parking lot. When it came time to transfeRobert from the wheel chair into the car, I fought back the revulsion and helped. Bert's body felt like a sack, not quite full, of some kind of liquid. Before he would leave, Bert insisted that I come out again. I said that I would. There was a lot to talk about. He agreed and leaned away to let me close the car door.

After they turned onto the highway, I went back to Mama's car and drove over to Fat's Place. Billie saw me as soon as I entered. She looked unsure at first. I walked over to her and said, "Hello, Billie" and smiled at her.

It was all right then, and she sat with me in a booth when she wasn't waiting tables. She made a big thing out of drinking a little of my beer now and then.

When they closed for the night, I sat at the bar with Fat Jack and drank an illegal beer or two while she and Nadine cleaned up.

There was a kind of life and lust force running through my body, the kind of tingle I've had after a steam bath and a cold shower. I was aware enough to know that it felt a little unclean but I knew I couldn't stop it if I tried.

Later that night, while Billie was upstairs showering, I stretched out on the bed in the small room. The room dark except for a narrow slash of light from the hallway. I knew it had all been a cripple man's lies.

It hadn't been that way at all. The memories blew over my body like a breeze from the window and I thought about the Junior-Senior dance our senior year. Bert and Russell Hart and I had gone to the dance stag, telling ourselves that was what we really wanted. The truth was that we didn't know any girls to ask, any that we wanted to take who would go with us. We stayed an hour, not dancing, as if waiting for some of the girls to come over and ask us. They didn't and we left and got some beer from a service station outside of town. We drove all over the county in Russell Hart's car until it was almost dawn. That was the way it had been and I closed off my mind and waited in the darkness until I heard Billie's bare feet in the hallway coming toward me.

CHAPTER FOUR
CHAPEL HILL, N.C., 1966
THE OLD MAN

Millhouse was sweltering. A few more days in the 120's and everything and everybody in town would be as dry as old toast. On the plane to Raleigh-Durham I read the *Daily Southerner* and saw that the insurance man was at it again. He'd made the front page once more, this time cooking hamburgers and toasting buns on the pavement outside his office. That man showed a lot of wit. He'd somehow contrived to have the name and address of his agency printed on his apron this time.

The Carolina Inn had a vacancy and I checked in for one night. I hoped it would only be one night. After I'd unpacked and showered, I took the elevator down to the lobby and went outside, cradling a half gallon of white whiskey in a paper bag in my arm like a loaf of bread. The whiskey had been a present from Fat Jack and I knew it was probably some of his private drinking stock, the stuff he aged in an oak barrel for a year. The other farewells hadn't been that easy. Mama, losing some of her usual distance, asked when I was going to decide that I had enough education. "It's going to school as long as you have that got you into that mess up north."

Billie had broken down the night before and had offered me back all the money I'd given her.

"It would make me feel better," she said. "Like I wasn't a whore with you." I said that she'd never been a whore with me except that first time and that had been my fault. I told her I wanted her to keep the money and buy herself something nice. After a long time, she put the money back in the envelope where she'd been keeping it and nodded. "I might buy me a bus ticket to New Haven." she said. "That would be something nice ... "

I turned left where Columbia cut across Franklin Street. I walked down West Franklin without seeing much of it, thinking instead of what might happen if Billie did come up to New Haven. Part of me wanted it and part of me didn't. I'd gone through the problems and I'd started on the benefits when I found myself about to pass Pop's Grill. I went inside and felt the cool darkness close in around me.

The early afternoon crowd was there: a few undergraduates, a pair of med students with the plastic tubing tied through their belt loops, and, bunched together at the far end of the counter, several construction workers. In the time I'd been away, there'd been some changes. Now there was a juke box and coin receivers at each booth and there was a bowling machine against the back wall near the kitchen.

Pop wasn't out front, so I ordered a beer from his helper and sat at the bar, first very careful to place the half gallon jar out of the way of the traffic. When I finished the first beer, he still hadn't appeared. I called the helper to my end of the counter. "Pop here?"

"In the kitchen."

I ordered another beer and with that in one hand and the jar the other, I had to push my way into the kitchen with my shoulder.

Pop was at the range, his back to me, bent over a twenty-quart sauce pot. He was stirring the sauce and whistling low and tunelessly between his teeth. He looked around when the kitchen door slammed behind me, "Yes?" One of the stainless-steel racks was between us, the high shelf blocking me when I took a couple of steps to the right.

"Delivery," I said.

"I don't remember ... " He rounded the rack and saw me, "You? Of all people?" He opened his arms and made a clumsy rush for me.

"I said delivery." I backed away from him and placed the jar and my beer on the dish washer.

When I turned back, he got me in a bear hug and squeezed me until I was out of breath.

"All this time and not one letter. Not even a single line." One last hug and he stepped back.

"You didn't write either." I got my breath and looked around for my beer. "You could have sent me a grocery order or a menu or something."

"Why should I send you a menu? The menu's the same."

I looked at him closely to see if there had been any change in him. He looked the same, the way he'd looked for the last ten years: Huge shining head without a hair on it, heavy hooded eyelids that moved slowly open to reveal pale blue eyes. He had the thick solid body of a wrestler.

He was over seventy and he carried himself like a man half that old.

"I brought you something." I handed him the jar of white whiskey.

He peeled off the paper bag. "What is it?"

"Wild Georgia white honey."

He tipped the jar on its side. "No, it's not thick enough." Righting the jar once more, he unscrewed the top and smelled it. His nose wrinkled and he tilted the jar and took a long swallow. "I think it's something you start charcoal fires with."

"You can kill fleas on a dog with it too," I said.

"Kill the dog too." He locked the jar away in a cabinet with the vanilla extract and the cooking wine. "My glass is out front."

I sat at a booth and sipped at my beer while he worked his way down the bar. It took time because he had a few words for everybody, a joke, a friendly remark. In time he reached the draft tap and filled a large tea glass he kept beside the cash register.

"I haven't got much time now," he said, sitting down across from me. "The supper help will be in soon. You stay for supper. We'll drink some later."

I said that I wanted to look around town some, but that I'd stop by later.

Pop nodded. "I'll call in an extra bar boy so we can sit and talk."

"How's Mama?"

The hooded eyes closed briefly and then opened. "Fine. And she misses you." He shook his head slowly, as if a little embarrassed. "Sometimes she doesn't remember names. You know how it is when a person gets old. But she says that she wishes the nice boy would bring his wife and the baby to see her."

"I'll stop by and see her before I leave."

"It's strange but she always took a special interest in you and Elaine. When you'd bring her here on a date, Mama would whisper to me that you two were like she and I were forty years ago."

Not anymore, Pop. But I smiled.

"Send her a picture of the baby," Pop said. "The baby means something special to her. She thinks of the baby like it was a granddaughter to her."

"As soon as I get back to New Haven," I said.

"She talks about the baby all the time. Mama is a little silly now and then and thinks that she's dying. If we had children and grandchildren she says she could look at them and see where her life had gone."

He shrugged and I thought I saw a dampness under the heavy hoods. "As it is now, she worries too much about that." He drained off the last of his beer in a huge swallow. "Women are silly, don't you think?"

"No," I said as I slid out of the booth, "no, there's nothing silly about Mama."

"I don't think so either," Pop said, "but I was afraid you might not understand."

A few minutes later, as I was leaving, I could hear him roaring away in the kitchen. He wasn't mad. It was just an overflow of life and joy and energy and that was his way of running a kitchen

Around eleven, I could feel the depression settling upon me. During the day I'd been all right. Daylight washed all the shadows out and thoughts and words in the sun were matter of fact, surface, set in concrete. Night was the time for the qualifiers, for *seems, appears, might be, maybe,* and *perhaps.* What was true in the afternoon only *seemed* to be true in the late night. If it only *seemed* to be true, there was also a chance that it wasn't true.

Maybe part of it was that I was moving back toward New Haven. from Millhouse to Chapel Hill was about half way, a stopover on the way to all the hassle that waited up there for me. Back on the porch in Millhouse, those hot afternoons, it had been clear what I needed to do and why I needed to do it. Now it wasn't clear at all.

There was no way to cover it up. Pop must have understood it or at least he knew that something was wrong. At eleven-thirty, he gave the last call for beer and the crowd began thinning out. By midnight, the Grill was empty and Pop locked the front door.

"I think," he said, stopping beside me at the bar, "that we need something special to finish off the day with." He switched off the overhead light and I followed him back to the kitchen. "I have a friend who goes to Washington pretty often and I have a standing order with him. The ABC store doesn't carry it for some reason."

He returned with an unopened bottle of Metaxa from one of the locked cabinets. He peeled the foil away and pulled the cork.

"Sit there," he said, pointing to the stainless-steel counter across from him. When I was seated, legs dangling down but not touching the tile floor, he eased himself onto the counter facing me. Leaning forward, he offered the bottle to me. "Friends don't need glasses. They have the same diseases anyway."

I took a swallow and held the Metaxa in my mouth, rolling it around my mouth. I swallowed and felt the jolt in the bottom of my stomach. I handed the bottle across the aisle to him and watched him tip back his head and pour it down his throat. He passed the bottle back to me. "Without any proof, of course, I've always felt that Metaxa was what Ulysses used to get the Cyclops drunk."

"Am I supposed to be the Cyclops?"

He shook his head. "You have too many eyes." He watched while I drank and waited until I passed the bottle back to him. "I have eyes too. Enough to know that something's wrong."

"The degree program up there, that's the problem."

"No, that's not it." He lowered the bottle and braced it against his thigh. "It's probably a woman ...

"That's a good guess."

"Only a guess? Here ... He passed the Metaxa. "I've known you for how long? Seven, eight, nine years?"

"One of those," I said.

"You worked for me here for two years. I watched you with all those girls. You whored around too much. But I decided that you were just young and that you'd grow up."

"I meant to." I barely wet my tongue and passed the bottle back. "All things don't work out the way you plan them."

"Maybe I'm just an old man. Maybe I don't understand any-more." He put the bottle aside and eased himself off the counter. He walked into the back of the kitchen. When he returned, he carried a steaming coffee pot and two cups. He poured two cups of black coffee and handed one to me.

"I was seven years old when I came to this country," he said. "It was so long ago that I don't count it in years but tens of years. At twelve, I got a job as a busboy in a restaurant. That was in Baltimore, when I was living with my uncle, who was a street cleaner. By the time I was fifteen, I was a cook's helper. I made salads and I was learning to make sauces when the chef had time to show me." He took a pull at the Metaxa and followed it with a sip of coffee. "That was the first time I knew a woman, when I was fifteen. One night, four of us who worked in the restaurant went to Raybal Street. It wasn't really a street. It was a narrow alley where the women lived." He smiled and shook his head. "I was so afraid that it didn't take long. It cost a dollar and that was a lot of money in those days. The woman had a sour smell that perfume couldn't cover up and the foot of the bed had black marks on it. That was because some of the men didn't even take their shoes off. Shoe polish wasn't as good in those days and it came off easy."

I motioned toward the Metaxa and Pop took a quick swallow and passed it to me. I poured some into my coffee and handed it back.

"The next day, except for being afraid that I'd caught a disease, I was over being afraid and I thought that I was a man. I'd known a woman and I wanted to swagger around because of it. But I used to think a lot in those day when I was young and I wasn't satisfied with the way it had been with me and the woman. I'd gone to that woman looking for something and it hadn't been there. So, I thought about it and I thought about it and I discovered something. If you go to a woman without some love for her, then you're going to her not because you want to have some closeness with her, but because you're afraid to be close and you want a distance between you."

When he paused I stepped down from the counter and refilled our coffee cups. While I watched him his face changed, softened.

"I didn't go back to Raybal Street and two years later I met Elena…Mama. A year after that we got married. It was everything I thought that it should be." Pop paused and leaned toward me. "You see, life flows back and forth between people who love each other. It flows out of you and into them and then out of them and back into you. It's never the same, it's always changing." He sipped at his coffee and put the cup aside. "It's like breathing the breath of someone when you kiss them."

He corked the Metaxa and locked it away. "I'm tired. I'm not used to talking this much."

I put the coffee pot back on the range and rinsed out the two cups. "I'm tired too."

He drove me to the Carolina Inn and parked in front. I looked at the long porch with the empty rocking chairs on it and then I turned back to him. I was about to thank him when he stopped me by shaking his head.

"Maybe it's the Metaxa. I'm not too embarrassed to say this. "I've loved you like you're my son, my own son." I nodded. "Mama too. That's why what I've seen today worries me. Life is flowing out of you faster than it's flowing it. There's no balance in your life."

"I know."

"You have to find it."

I said goodnight and closed the car door behind me. When I reached the porch, I turned and saw that the car hadn't moved. A sleepy elevator operator took me up to my floor.

CHAPTER FIVE
CHAPEL HILL, 1966
BEFORE I WAKE

It was a usual Chapel Hill late August day, humid and hot, with the temperature around eighty degrees by nine-thirty in the morning. There had been lightning and winds during the early morning but no rain. *The Weekly* had a headline about the water shortage. The mayor was considering a ban against washing cars and watering lawns.

Pop met me at the door after I'd paid off the cab. He led me through the living room and dining room and into the kitchen. "How's your head this morning?"

"My head feels like solid bone."

"Now you know how the Cyclops felt." He motioned me to a chair at the kitchen table. "I don't usually believe in this. Hair of a dog..it makes me think how a dog smells." He got two beers from the refrigerator and twisted off the caps. He pushed one beer across to me and sat down facing the dining room door. "Mama's awake but the nurse is with her."

Nurse? I wanted to ask why there was a nurse with Mama but I didn't. Pop would tell me what he wanted me to know. I lifted the cold bottle and pressed it against my forehead.

"I told her you were coming. You should have seen her smile."

In the distance, somewhere in the house, a radio was playing hard rock music. My mind was running ahead, knowing even before Pop told me anything else, and the music seemed shocking.

"The nurse," Pop said. "The music helps the time pass for her and Mama doesn't mind." He whirled the bottle around and around on the table top, the large hands surprisingly delicate but the tension was there beneath the surface of the movement. "Sometimes I think Mama's gotten to like the music."

"Mama always was a swinger," I said.

Pop smiled, remembering. "Yes, you'd say that to tease her." His hands fell away from the bottle and remained palm down on the Formica surface. "She wasn't certain that it was a nice thing to be a swinger. It was what you called your girls. She didn't approve of all those girls."

"I'm sorry."

"Don't be. Secretly, she was pleased. It appealed to her vanity." He looked down at the backs of his hands. A thick blue vein began a violent jerking and leaping on the back of his left hand. He balled it into a fist. "She loved you too much to be really insulted."

When I'd finished my beer, he stood up and placed the two bottles on the sink drain. "I think we can see Mama now." He hesitated at the dining room doorway. "I know you'll try to do the right thing. Still, I have to ask you not to seem surprised at how she looks. I spoiled her when we were young by telling her all the time that she was beautiful. Now I won't let her have a mirror and she sees herself only by what our faces show her."

Mama was lost in the large hospital bed. It had been cranked up into a sitting position and the blinds behind the bed were adjusted so that the room was in a kind of twilight.

Pop stopped just inside the room while I crossed to the bed and leaned over to kiss Mama on the cheek. When I straightened up, I could hear the muscles in my face crack as I managed a smile.

"Mama, it's good to see you." That close to her the smell of death was on her and it choked me. The plump and ample body had wasted away so that only the bones and the skin that covered them remained. Her face was a death's head, the roundness gone so that the teeth seemed enlarged and out of proportion. Her lips moved and she said something.

Pop leaned past me, his ear toward her, nodding. "Mama says you look very good."

I turned toward him. "I can't understand her."

"Sometimes she forgets and speaks Greek," Pop leaned over her. "Speak English, Mama." He patted her arm and moved away, to return a moment later with two chairs. "Doesn't Mama look beautiful today?"

"Like a swinger," I said, "like a beautiful swinger."

"You see? Mama, what did I tell you?"

Mama's lips moved, the sound that came out more like a hissing than anything else. Beside me, Pop whispered,

"She asked about the baby."

"Evadne's fine, Mama." I fumbled in my pocket and brought out the small photograph that I'd found in my suitcase, "She sent this to you," I held it toward her. "She asks about you all the time."

"You see?" Pop said. "I said Evadne hadn't forgotten you."

Mama stared at the picture and then her eyes closed. Pop stood up. "I think she's tired."

I started to push back my chair but before I could move, I saw that her hand was picking its way slowly down the covers toward me and there was nothing I could do but reach out and take it. Her fingers moved inside my hand like claws and then stilled. I sat there holding her hand for a long time, until Pop said, "She's asleep."

While Pop placed the chairs back against the wall, I walked out of the room, not sure where I was going. I passed the nurse in the hall without really seeing her. When I stopped walking, when I knew where I was, I was standing at the back door, the kitchen neat and still around me and the backyard, seen through the small door panes, was bathed in the fierce heat of the morning sun.

I didn't hear Pop come up behind me. "She didn't want to die in the hospital."

That broke it loose inside me. It poured out of me like vomit, racking cough and choking, struggling to breathe against the weight of the anger and the helplessness. It was like having the breath knocked out of me, like it had been done a few times when I'd played football. I don't know whether he turned toward me or I turned toward him, but somehow he was pounding me on the back to force the breath back in me and we were both crying harshly, violently. I was glad the rock music was loud because I wouldn't have wanted Mama to hear us.

Afterwards we dried our faces and could look at each other without embarrassment.

I left the Carolina Inn after lunch and walked across campus. The second summer session had ended a week or so before and a kind of desolation had settled over the University. My progress around the campus was like one of those children's puzzles where the child connects the numbers and discovers that he's drawn a tiger. Moving from air conditioned building to air conditioned building, in each only a minute or so, until I felt cool enough to leave, I think I must have drawn a pattern of confusion and aimlessness.

After an hour or so, I was in Battle Woods. The wooden area seemed to have shrunk, to have pulled away from the buildings pushing in all around them. The undergrowth was stunted and dry brittle, cracking flat and dull in the air like pistol shots in the distance.

I walked deeper into the wood, perhaps as far as I'd ever been.

I saw very few animals. That might have been because of the heat. A mangey-tailed squirrel now and then and once, a house cat gone wild. Sitting and washing itself.

A little out of breath I topped a small rise and looked down into a clearing where a young boy and girl were making love. They were in their teens, perhaps as young as fifteen or sixteen. I saw them only for a moment before I backed away, their pale white skin a glare against the vivid plaid blanket. There was difficulty and anguish in their love-making and looking back on it, the image caught in the back of my eye, held there but fading hour by hour into a dark gray shadow, I decided that it was their first discovery, their first flight. My own first time but quite different, remembering it as I pointed myself toward where the road was. I'd finally won my football letter in my junior year. The day after the banquet, I wore my monogram sweater to school and a girl named Essie Martin asked if she could try it on. Then she wouldn't give it back and a whole semester went by, until just after the Junior-Senior dance. Essie was a mill girl. That is, her mother and father worked in one of the mills, and she seemed to have a knowledge and boldness in her that wasn't in most of the girls.

One afternoon, I asked if I could come by that night and get my sweater back. There was a sly interest in her agreement and that night when I found her house, down a pocked unpaved road, she came to the door in tight shorts and a t-shirt. Almost before I was through the doorway, she told me that her mother and father had gone to the Wednesday night prayer meeting at the Church of God and wouldn't be back until after ten o'clock. Frightened, not sure what to do, I watched the minutes cluster against each other until, with a surprising passion and boldness, I pushed her down on the sofa and fell on top of her.

Essie looked at me with an expression I've never forgotten, a face without passion, composed and unruffled, and said, "I don't mind doing this for you, but would you mind waiting until I get this damned coke bottle out of my back?" And sure enough, while I waited, she reached under her and brought out an empty coke bottle. That put aside, she stretched out on the sofa once more, shifting from side to side as if to be sure there weren't any more bottle under her, and opened her arms to me, saying, "Now … "

I believe I saw her again, years after that. I was driving around town and I made a wrong turn and before I could find my way back to the highway, I realized that I was in the mill district. It was a spring morning and as I drove past one house, I looked into the side yard and saw a woman hanging still slightly soiled diapers on a clothesline.

At the sound of the ear passing, she stopped and turned and I saw the same face grown older, the throat and facial skin tone gone, and then the sun struck the windshield and blinded me. When I could see again, I was passing a different house, another clothesline and another woman shaking out her wash, the wet wash popping like wind in a sail.

Two days later, after another visit to Mama when she held onto my thumb and wouldn't let it go, I caught an afternoon flight for New York.

CHAPTER SIX
NEW YORK, N.Y., 1966
GREENWICH VILLAGE
WON'T GO AWAY

Usually, although I regret it afterwards for one reason or another, I stay at the Hotel Earle when I'm in New York. The hotel is rundown and needs cleaning and painting. The clerks treat you in a suspicious and patronizing manner, as if they'd learned all your secrets from your baggage while you were out having breakfast. Once I stayed there for a few days with Elaine while friends watched Evadne back in New Haven. The way the clerks acted toward us, I began to wonder if we were married. At least, I began to feel that we weren't. That led to some renewed and passionate love-making in a creaking and lumpy bed, with a precautionary look now and then at the transom to be certain that the clerks hadn't come to watch. Still, all that put aside, it was located on one corner of Washington Square and it was an area I'd liked once before it started changing. Also, I'd read somewhere that Ernest Hemingway had stayed at the Earle once, during World War I, when he'd been awaiting shipment to Italy where he was going to drive ambulances. And, finally, I'd received a short letter from my brother, Jerry, placed and dated at the Hotel Earle, just before he started the swing west that was his last trip anywhere. It was curiosity about that last stay in New

York, how Jerry had lived, that prompted me to stay at the Earle that first time. Now, I guess, staying there was habit.

The area had been changing the last few years. For a time, it seemed that the teeny boppers had moved into the Square to live on the spring and summer weekends especially when they flooded in by train, bus and car. In their outlandish clothes, carrying the guitars they could hardly play. Then, with the growth of the East Village, they moved there and only came over to the Square to panhandle the tourists.

I left my bag at the Earle and walked across to Sheridan Square and angled across the brick-covered street to Christopher. Behind and a few doors beyond the United Cigar store I turned into Geo. Herdt's Bar and sat on one of the stools near the front door. It was just a small neighborhood tavern with a short L-shaped bar, a row of booths along the left wall and some tables in the center. A friend had taken me to the bar one of the first times I'd been in New York and I'd liked the simplicity and unassuming quality of it. Somebody'd asked me once what my favorite bar was in the City and I'd said Geo. Herdt's and they'd looked at me like I was crazy.

I took my second glass of porter back to the phone booth. I tried to reach Joe-John but there wasn't any answer and I stood in the booth, saying oh, shit, I should have written him or called him and said I was coming. He and his wife, Rachel, might be back in North Carolina or off on one of those reading tours where he'd read a few sections of the book he was working on and then answer a few questions about the future of the novel. Then cocktails with the English faculty and a few selected students from the creative writing classes, the male students surly and unimpressed, the coeds itchy-crotched and wide eyed. Then a bad night's sleep and off the next day to another college where he'd read the same sections and answer the same questions about the future of the novel. In a few weeks, he could make enough from the tour to keep him going in New York for another five or six months. But, Joe-John had said once, he needed a month to recover from the gin and the coeds. Especially the coeds.

The first tour he'd gone on, he'd left Rachel back in New York and the coeds had screwed about ten pounds and a lot of sleep away from him. Now he took Rachel with him for protection and that was almost as bad. Some cute little piece of trim would introduce herself, portfolio of short stories or poems hugged against her flat hard stomach and the passionate rumbling would begin in the lower part of Joe-John's gut. It really didn't completely vanish when Rachel crossed the room and steered him away to another group.

"Rachel got a lot of leftovers that trip," Joe-John said once. "But being a good wife, she didn't complain ... she tried to think of it as a second honeymoon. Instead of mail that was delivered to the wrong address."

It was seven-twenty by the clock behind the bar. Joe-John might be out at an early dinner before a play or, hell, he might be at Martha's Vineyard with some of the literary establishment. Not with the real establishment but the fringe, the shadow group, the ones that didn't belong but sometimes got asked to mingle as if they did. With the tacit understanding that they wouldn't presume.

Around eight-thirty, it was still light outside and I could turn in my seat and watch people walking down Christopher Street. It was what I did best now ... the watching. I'd look at a couple across the street and I'd study them for the short time they were within the range of the bar's window. I'd try to decide from the way they acted toward each other whether they were happy. Or unhappy. When I'd made my decision about five or six couples, I had to admit to myself that I wasn't sure what all this meant anyway.

I tried Joe-John again at nine and let the phone ring seven or eight times. Then I gave up and left the bar. It was dark outside now and cooling some and I passed through Washington Square and headed into the East Village. I didn't know my way around too well and I must have strayed some. I felt like I was losing time but that didn't seem to matter much. There was just the Hotel Earle to look forward to, the grubby room there in the dark, and the faraway and next door wheezing of other lost people.

I was fairly sure that I was in the East Village when the panhandlers thickened on the street corners and in the open doorways. Some of them looked like high school kids in town for the weekend, trying out this aspect of the hip life while they had money hidden away on them for the trip home. I didn't stop for any of them and I didn't react to the obscenity that they threw after me.

When I felt I'd had enough of it, I turned and headed back in the direction of the Square. I'd gone only a block or so when I ran into the three of them … four 1f you count the little girl perched on the shoulder of one of the men. The man holding the little girl was huge, maybe six feet six, but round shouldered. His face was cleanshaven and his long hair pulled back and tied with a piece of string. The other man was smaller, under six feet, with a soft wilted looking beard. He wore the Ben Franklin half-glasses. The woman with them had red hair and very pale, fair skin, the kind that sunburns so easily.

I would have passed them as I did the others. I'd prepared my shake of the head, distant and only mildly irritated, for the question when it came. But the standard, usual question stopped me anyway. It was in the thin and mildly musical voice of the little girl. "Spare change, mister?"

The huge man dipped his shoulder and the little girl slipped off.

He caught her in the air and whirled her around to face him. "Now Donna, I told you not to beg."

"But, Pete, I wanted to."

"We do the begging. You be quiet. That was our bargain."

"I don't see why I can't … " the little girl began.

The large man pulled her in against his chest and hugged her. "Because I said not to."

"But, Pete … "

"Ssssshhhh." Pete muffled the rest of what Donna said in the= hollow of his shoulder.

The woman had seen me stop. She circled Pete and the child, patting Donna on the head as she went. "She wasn't supposed to do that. But if you've got any spare change..?"

"What do you want it for?"

"For a quarter you want a penny-by-penny breakdown?" This from the smaller man with Ben Franklin glasses. "Shit."

"Shut up, Jimmy." There was an edge in the woman's voice. "Food. We need it for food."

"All right." I took out a dollar bill and handed it to her.

"Hash … Donna squirmed around on Pete's shoulder and faced me. "We need it for hash."

The woman's hand closed over the dollar bill. "Hush, Donna."

Jimmy leaned toward me. "Donna's right. We all got to have supper, right?"

"We had supper," Donna said. "Pizza."

"Well, you can always have a late supper." I smiled at her and she smiled back.

"It's cough medicine," Donna said. "It makes you cough."

I walked around Jimmy until I was close to the little girl. "I've got a little girl about your age. She might be a little older."

"What's her name?" Pete turned her and placed her on his shoulder. "Is her name Donna?"

"Her name's Evadne." I got a quarter from my pocket and turned and showed it to the woman. "If you don't mind … ?" The woman shook her head. I opened Donna's hand and put the quarter in it. "That's for you. That's not for hash. That's for candy or anything else you want."

"Chewing gum?"

"Sure," I said, "all you can chew."

"You." Jimmy said.

I turned and looked at Jimmy who'd spoken behind me. "Yeah?"

"You want to turn on?"

The woman caught Jimmy by the arm and pulled him away from me, until his back whammed against the building front. "Haven't you got any sense at all?"

"He's straight. He's middle class straight." Jimmy turned to Pete. "Pete, can't I smell a narc? Didn't I point out the one who busted Ed and Grace? Didn't I? The first time he showed up but nobody'd believe me?"

Pete nodded. "But that was just one. You missed some others."

"Come on, now," Jimmy said. "We're going to be here all night. All the tourists but him are back in their hotel rooms getting air conditioned." He stepped up closer so that I could smell the garlic on his breath. "You want to turn on with us?"

"Not hard drugs?"

"No, soft," he said, "soft as cream of wheat."

"I don't know."

"You see?" Jimmy said. "He's dying to." Then back to me, "Two ways it can happen. You can stand here until we panhandle another two dollars or you can lay another two on us and save a lot of waiting. It's that simple."

Pete looked over at the woman and back at Jimmy. "Maybe he doesn't want to turn on."

Jimmy grinned. "Everybody wants to turn on."

The woman and Pete and Jimmy looked at me, waiting. from a little above me Donna stared at me, her small mouth moving as if she wanted to ask the question but was afraid to.

"Why not?" I gave Jimmy two ones. He balled them up and stuffed them in his pocket.

"I think we've got enough for a ten-cent slice," Jimmy said as he left to "find a spade I know."

The rest of us — Pete, and Donna and the woman, whose name I learned was Beth — I walked over the five or six blocks to their place to wait for Jimmy. All the way over, passing the panhandlers who didn't bother us, I kept asking myself if I really want to try hash.

I'd smoked grass, of course, everybody had. The first few times I'd been afraid of it, not sure how I'd act, and nothing had happened. Later, when I could relax it had been a pleasant high, if you stopped early enough before you got too stoned. Looking into myself now, I wasn't sure I wanted to smoke it. Maybe it was just that I didn't want to be alone. If I didn't like it, I could just pass it on. I doubt that the others would care one way or the other.

The loft apartment was over an old garage building. It had been one long room at one time. Somebody had raised a few two-by-fours and nailed on some quarter-inch plywood to partition off the back third. Through the door opening, I could see a dresser and a double bed. There was a dining area against the right wall – a two burned hot plate, a table, and chairs, and a noisy old refrigerator with a compressor on top. At the front, in the area that overlooked the street, there was a worn old sofa with an army blanket covering it and a couple of straight backed chairs.

Pete bent over and dropped Donna into the center of the sofa. "Time for your lesson," he said. He turned to Beth. "How about some coffee while we wait?"

"We're out of sugar and cream," Beth said as she passed us with a sauce pan and entered a little room to the right, which I assumed was the bathroom.

"Black all right with you?" Pete asked.

"Sure," I said, moving a shirt off one of the chairs and sitting so that I faced the sofa. "Sounds fine to me."

"What lesson today?" Donna asked.

"Spelling." Pete leaned past Donna and felt around under the sofa until he brought out a thick bundle of large file cards. He slipped the rubber band off the cards and onto his wrist. He decided upon a card and held it out toward her. "Boy," he said.

Looking around him, I could see that the letters were written out on the card in thick, double strokes of a felt tip pen.

Donna stared at the card. "B-O-Y."

"Girl," Pete said, changing the card.

"G-I-R-L."

"Cat."

"C-A-T."

I leaned in close to them. "How about cats?"

"How many cats?" Donna turned from Pete to me.

"Two cats," I said.

Pete shook his head. "She's not that far yet."

Donna squirmed on the sofa. "No, Pete, I can spell two cats."

Beth, returning after putting the sauce pan on the burner, sat on the sofa next to Donna. "What's the problem?"

Pete winked at her. "How to spell two cats."

"I know," Donna said. "C-C-A-A-T-T."

Pete choked back a laugh. Donna heard him and turned an angry little face toward him. "That is how to spell two cats."

I looked at Beth. "There's some logic in that." Then to Donna: "Three cats?"

"Pete will laugh," Donna said.

"No, I won't. I promise." Pete snapped the rubber band back around the cards.

"C-C-C-A-A-A-T-T-T."

I nodded and smiled at Donna. "I know somebody in linguistics who'd be interested in this." I brought out my pack of cigarettes and passed them around. "Donna, that's what I call creative spelling."

"See?" Donna said proudly to Pete.

"If this man says it's so it must be so," Pete said, dropping the file cards under the sofa and hugging her to him. He grinned at me over Donna's head. "But I still think something's wrong with that system ...

The water in the sauce pan began to hum and steam and Beth left us to make the instant coffee.

An hour passed and I could see that Pete and Beth were getting a little nervous. Either that, or it was a fine acting job. I was offered a third cup of coffee and a cheese sandwich.

I said, "Thanks anyway," and offered the cigarettes around once more.

Tamping the cigarette against his thumbnail Pete said, "The spade dealer must not have been where she was supposed to be."

"It's tight in New York right now," Donna said. "Maybe she got busted."

"Maybe if Jimmy found her, she didn't have any stuff." Pete said.

"Maybe the price went up," I said, trying to play their game.

Then, while we sat in silence, Donna yawned and gave up the struggle. Already leaning, she tucked her head into Pete's thigh and sighed. The balled-up hand opened and the quarter I'd given her dropped to the floor and rolled toward me. I leaned down and caught it on the roll. I flipped it into the air and caught it, "I could always cut my losses. Then I'd just be out three dollars."

Pete's face didn't change, remained distant and remote, but he must have thought I was serious. "She'll remember. She'll tear up the place looking for it."

"Yeah, I know." I leaned toward Beth, offering the quarter. "You can put it under her pillow."

"I'll let you do it," Beth said. "It's past her bed time anyway."

She lifted Donna and carried her toward the partitioned off end of the loft. I followed.

"She sleeps there." Beth pointed toward the side of the bed flush against the wall.

I lifted the pillow and put the quarter under it. Then I sat on the end of the bed while Beth undressed her down to her underpants. "She's a lot like my little girl ... though, to tell the truth, there's not a thing about her that's like Evadne."

"You divorced?"

"In the process," I said.

"It's a rotten process," Beth said. "I did it myself a year ago. Had to fly to Mexico for it."

She lifted Donna and placed her on the pillow near the wall. I pulled the sheet up around her and stood up.

Beth looked at me, "It hurts sometimes, huh?"

"Not me," I said, "nerves of steel, ulcers the size of silver dollars."

"It must be the same with everybody."

"It's mainly the child," I said.

"Sure," she said, but her voice and the twist of her mouth said that she didn't believe me. "That's what George, my ex, said. He used to say it by the hour but he hasn't come to see Donna in a year and he's that far behind in behind in support."

"Sorry."

"It's not your fault and maybe you do mean it ... She crossed to the door and stopped. When she turned back to me, she was open and vulnerable. "If you want to stay a little longer, I can send Pete out to find Jimmy,"

I looked down at Donna, mouth slack, a bubble of a snore beginning. "I can't."

I followed her back into the living room area where Pete was standing at the window eating a cheese sandwich. He looked at me and then at Beth closely, as if trying to read something in our faces.

Whatever he was looking for must have been there because he nodded once firmly to himself and stuffed the rest of the sandwich into his mouth.

"It was there if you wanted it," Pete said. "She's a crazy girl when the moon's full."

We were out on the muggy hot street and Pete was showing me the way to the Cooper Union before he looked into a few bars for Jimmy. I knew the way back to the Square from the Union.

"I guess I'm not up for it," I said

"Her marriage fucked her up some," Pete said.

That bounced around in the silence, echoing against the dark building fronts until we reached the Cooper Union and split, going off in opposite directions with only a wave and a nod.

CHAPTER SEVEN
NEW YORK, N.Y., 1966
AND WHO ASKED
FOR IT ANYWAY?

"It sounds like a drug cult version of a murphy game," Joe-John said.

"Maybe but I don't think so."

It was late afternoon and we were standing in front of a fish market just off 6th Avenue. I'd reached Joe-John in the morning but I'd had to wait until he'd finished his writing quota for the day. We'd met at O'Henry's for a few beers out at one of the sidewalk tables. Then we'd gone down to the fish market because Joe-John said he wanted a dozen or so raw oysters. He'd eaten the first dozen in a couple of minutes and now we were waiting for the man to shuck another dozen for him. Joe-John had the tabasco bottle in one hand, shaking it.

"You ought to try some. They'll keep your hammer up."

"Worry about your own hammer," I said.

"That's what I'm doing, good buddy."

The fish man brought out the second dozen oysters on the half shell. Joe-John shook a careful dot of tabasco on the center of each of the oysters. "Like I told you, Rachel's down visiting her mother in Sanford."

"I might have passed her in the Raleigh-Durham airport."

Joe-John sucked an oyster off the shell and chewed at it. "Wouldn't fly. Took the train down to Baleigh. Train service has gone to hell."

"The south's gone to hell."

"That's why I'm up north," he said.

"Is that right?"

"No, that's a lie." He chewed another oyster and swallowed.

"I got tired of all that mush-mouth, grit and redneck shit. Funky smelling Bible belt, All that salt pork and collard greens. That unwashed gentility and.."

"Is that in your new book?"

"Not yet." He smiled, "But it might be in by tomorrow afternoon." He paid for the oysters and we walked back up 6th.

"The only thing is," I said after a long silence, "up here you're the grit."

"Not anymore. I've been taking speech lessons to lose my accent, table manners so I'll know which fork to use," He stopped and grinned at me. "Even got circumcised so people might get to think I was Jewish. So far, very few people have noticed the difference. Rachel doesn't like it. She says the foreskin was the best part of me." We started walking again, "Hell, I've even learned to eat raw oysters and clams. You know what my Daddy would have thought of eating raw shellfish? He'd have puked just from the thought of it."

Joe-John's father would have. I met him once. It'd been in the late 1950's, a Sunday in the spring, and his father had driven to Chapel Hill. I think his father came to ask Joe-John if he was going to spend the summer on the farm, helping out, but I don't think he ever got to ask. Just the way Joe-John acted must have answered the question for him. He wore a shiny black suit that had been brushed off and sponged, that didn't have a crease on it anywhere. The shirt was almost yellow with age and the black tie had a knot in it about the size of a peanut. Above the tie and the skinny adam's apple, his face was as coarse and tanned as leather.

He brought a lunch with him, two shoeboxes of fried chicken and fried pork chops, heavy large biscuits, a jar of homemade pickles and fresh sliced tomatoes in vinegar and sugar. For dessert, there was half a chocolate cake with whole pecans pressed in the hard frosting.

We ate in the kitchen of Joe-John's air conditioned apartment on Rosemary Street. The whole time he was there I don't think Joe-John's father said more than a hundred words. He seemed a little lost and hopeless and when his set time for the visit was over, he got up abruptly and said that he had cows to milk at home. Joe-John got up too and was going to walk down to the car with him but his father said, "No, you stay up here with your friend where it's cool" and went out, closing the door so gently behind him that I could hear the lock click into place.

"Yes, sir," I said, "you've come a long way." We turned onto 8th Street and headed for 5th Avenue. "I can remember when you said you could hear the oysters scream when you bit into them."

"That was a long time ago. Now I don't hear anything scream." He stopped me with his arm and we dodged a cab and cut cross to the other side of the street. "Want to show you something." We reached the 8th Street Bookstore and he leaned against the window and pointed into a book display. "There."

I followed the tapping finger and found a copy of his latest book. The cover was a photograph of a blonde girl sitting on a bar stool, her short skirt hiked so high that you could see her red underpants.

"That's fame for you," I said.

"If you·go by Marlboro, you'll find the others on sale for ninetyeight cents. Remaindered."

"That's fame for you," I said.

"You shit." We started out again, still walking toward 5th Avenue. "You never told me what you thought about *Who Asked for It, Anyway?*"

"You want the truth or literary lies?"

"The truth," Joe-John said, "if it kills you."

"You're not going to like it."

"Tell me anyway."

"Joe-John, you're getting cute and precious. Turning your back on the guts, like you're afraid of being serious, like you could layer … "

"Jesus," he interrupted me, "tell me some literary lies." His face was flushed and I knew I'd hurt him.

"All right, literary lie number one. It is gratifying to find that a young writer of such obvious talent has broadened his horizon, proof that he is no longer a southern writer but an American writer." I looked at him. "How's that?.."

"That's good crap but crap anyway."

"I'm sorry." We reached 5th Avenue and waited for the light to change. "I guess I ought to know enough to know that when somebody says they want the truth, what they really mean is that they want a pleasant truth."

"I think I was trying to see if I conned you too," Joe-John said. "The book's a pile of shit and I know it. I was just hoping nobody else knew it."

We crossed the street and turned up 5th Avenue. We fought the tide of the early evening crowds headed toward the Village. "Where're we headed, Joe-John?"·

"I thought I'd surprise you and introduce you to my first rich mistress." He winked at me and lengthened his stride. "The grit's first social conquest. And she thinks that pile of shit novel is the great American novel … or one of them."

A few more minutes of walking and we turned under a long gray awning and entered an apartment building. The black doorman recognized Joe-John and touched the bill of his cap. "Miss Carling is expecting you, sir."

"Thank you, Mark."

We entered the lobby. Joe-John caught my arm and jerked me to a stop.

"Look at this." We stood in front of a bank of four television monitors. "This gets me."

Three of the four elevators were empty. The fourth, on the far right, carried a woman. It was hard to tell if she was young or old because she was facing the back of the elevator and we could only see the back of her head and her shoulders.

"One time," Joe-John said, "I was in one of the elevators here and I forgot about the camera." We moved down the lobby toward the elevators. "I must have been thinking about something else and I reached up and dug a gigantic booger out of my nose. It must have weighed a pound. They're bigger up here because of all the dirt in the air. And then, while I was inspecting it and comparing it, I realized I was on TV and that Mark or somebody who lived in the building might be watching. I almost peed in my pants."

On the way to the tenth floor, Joe-John pointed out the lens of the camera. As soon as I knew where it was, I felt myself tightening up, not sure whether to smile or look serious. And my nose, dull and forgotten all day, began an itching. It took all my strength to keep my hands down by my side. After what seemed a long time, the elevator opened onto the tenth floor hallway.

Marcia Carling, dressed in a see-through blouse and a miniskirt, poured the martinis and Joe-John passed me one and took one for himself. She looked to be in her mid or late twenties, black hair worn shoulder length, her body starved model thin, flat stomach accented by out thrust hip bones.

"I think you're early, Joe. I hardly had time to mix these after Mark called from the lobby and I'd meant to shower ... "

"Couldn't stay away from your pretty hide," Joe-John said. Marcia looked at him questioningly.

Joe-John laughed. "I have to talk that way in front of all my old friends from the south. Otherwise, they go back and tell everybody that I'm putting on airs."

Marcia nodded.

"I'm supposed to use certain words at least once a day. Chittlins, cowflop, horse apples, cracklin' bread, hopping john, paper poke, poontang, grits, streaked meat, hog jowl, change your luck, coon, KKK George Wallace..." He broke off and looked at me. "Is that enough?"

"I think that puts you ahead for a week."

"Most of this is beyond me," Marcia said. "What's hopping john?"

"Dried black-eyed peas and rice cooked together, usually served on New Year's along with hog jowl, for luck." He looked at me. "Did I leave anything out?"

"Only that it looks like hell and doesn't taste much better."

"I've never seen it," Joe-John said, "or tasted it." He sipped the last of his martini and went over to the bar and poured another. "I think you're the only person I've met lately who says he's eaten it. I thought it might be something that unicorns ate." He brought the pitcher over to me and topped off my glass. He stopped short of refilling her glass. "Look, sugar, why don't you go ahead and take that shower?"

Marcia hesitated, looking at me.

"Don't mind me," I said.

"Hell, country boys like him don't know what's done and what isn't done." He put out a hand to her and pulled her gracefully to her feet. "And put on something pretty. We'll try out a new restaurant."

When the bedroom door closed behind her, Joe-John said, "Nice, huh?" He moved over to the console and shifted the FM from a classical music station to hard rock. We listened to some hard rock and sipped our drinks. He seemed poised on the edge of his chair, waiting for something. When the faint hiss of the shower was heard, he put his glass aside and pushed up from his chair. "No use wasting those oysters." On the way to the bedroom, he turned up the rock a notch or two. "But for the sake of decorum and face-saving, we'll pretend you think I'm going in there to rest on the bed. Right?"

"Right," I said.

The shower ran for a long time. I finished off the last of the pitcher of martinis.

"I balled your wife about a month ago."

It was after midnight and Joe-John and I were in a quiet bar off Sheridan Square. We were both a little drunk. There'd been wine with dinner and some brandy afterwards. We'd dropped Marcia at her apartment and set out to crawl a few bars. We'd been in five or six already and I'd switched to beer. Joe-John continued with scotch on the rocks.

"Go ahead and throw the punch," Joe-John said. "I'll take one punch and call it the going price for ass."

I looked down at my right hand and found that it was balled up, the skin white and tight across the knuckles. Carefully, forcing it, I opened the fist and left the hand palm up on the table top, "I'm confused. Did this follow something we were talking about?"

My throat felt shut down, choking off a word or two, but I got it all out.

He shut his eyes and shook his head. "I couldn't find a place where it fitted into the conversation."

"It works well at the end of a conversation."

"Just thought I'd better tell you."

I felt the edge sliding into the open. "Remorse?"

"No." He made a sign to the waiter. "Before somebody else tells you."

"Who?"

"Make a guess. Look, good buddy, at the moment, the way to Elaine's pants is through being a friend of yours."

I shook my head. It didn't make sense.

"It's some kind of bedroom revenge," Joe-John said. "It took me about the whole month to figure it out."

The waiter brought his drink and my beer. I took a long pull from the bottle and looked across the table at Joe-John.

He said, "It's like this. A wife is a fuck that wears out. A friend, for a man, is somebody who usually lasts a lifetime, right? So here you are, no wife and she's got Evadne and all you've got left are a few friends. If she really wanted to gut you, clean you out, isolate you, what does she do? Ball your friends and then let you know somehow. Right now, the people with *satisfied* written on their foreheads are all friends of yours."

"That's crazy."

"Not to her." He sipped at his scotch. "Look, there's even a fool proof script for it. You want to hear about it?" When I didn't answer he went on. "It starts with a call to one of your friends. She's upset about the way you're acting and she needs to talk to one of your friends and get some advice. With me, she knew that Rachel worked and she suggested lunch. At lunch, she gets upset and cries a little. She asks, fighting back the tears, if there is some private place where we can talk. The apartment, of course, and at the apartment she implies that you were really a closet queen, that you really only balled her as a duty. Then she breaks down and cries again and the first thing you know she's in the friend's arms and he's comforting her and she's sobbing that she's lonely, which gets translated as horny, and the next thing you know the friend is balling her on the rug, on the sofa, against the wall, on the ceiling, on the toilet, or under water in the bath tub. Afterwards, the friend doesn't feel too guilty because he convinces himself that it was all for the good of Elaine's mental health, and that they've been playing knights and fair ladies and he's been protecting her and using his cock like a sword. Right?"

"That's hard to believe."

"Hell," Joe-John said, "if it was turned around, and it was Rachel working the same script on you, you'd put horns on me and feel like you'd done your Boy Scout deed for the day."

"Maybe," I said.

"You'd better believe it."

"And then again I'd try like hell not to." I stood up, heading for the bathroom, the chair rasping on the floor behind me. "I'd try hard. I'd try harder than you did."

When I came back from the bathroom, he was nodding slowly, head down over his scotch. I could feel the sickness passing from me to him, washing over him, eating under his skin. I sat down across from him and we started talking about professional football.

The next morning, I checked out of the Hotel Earle and caught an early train for New Haven.

CHAPTER EIGHT

NEW HAVEN, 1966

LOVE SUCKS AND CHILDREN FLY LIKE JUNE BUGS

Back to grubby town. The Gothic nightmare of Yale University where, at any moment, one expects the Man in the Iron Mask to step out of one of the dark doorways. Or Douglas Fairbanks, Jr. to prance down the stairs, a dagger in his teeth and a dueling sword in one hand.

Grubby Gothic nightmare surrounded by crumbling and garlic-impregnated slums. Winds that taste of rotten garlic and wino's cheap red. Sidewalks banked with snow in the winter and pigeon shit in the summer. Streets full of the harsh sound of people speaking English with difficulty and unfamiliarity, speech rhythms corrupted by the shadows of other languages. Bars where I argue that Arnold Palmer is not the world's greatest athlete. Bars where I drink bitter Hull's Export Beer as if doing Hail Marys for a lifetime of sins. And the room where I live on Park Street, a dark room smelling of mold and aged sperm. A single narrow bed pushed against and under the single window, hunting a breeze from the alley that cuts between my building and the next.

Cockroaches as big as geese waddling across the cigarette burn scarred floor. Broken skylight above the bathroom, where I stand looking up at the sky as if from a sewer. Or when it rains, I stand pissing into the toilet while the sky pisses on me. The phone disconnected because it did not ring. Never rang. Or rang only when I wasn't there.

A letter from my lawyer has been forwarded from Millhouse. "…as soon as you have funds and can deposit with my office a sum of four hundred and fifty dollars ($450.00)…the minimum fee set by the New Haven Law Association for a court action of this type…we can serve your wife with due notice that divorce proceedings have been instituted..hear from you soon since you have delayed this matter for a full summer."

I write him a check and a simple note that tells him to turn the dogs loose. The summer has made no difference in my thinking. The tattoos will not wash out and the blue film that runs in my mind will not run down. Not always the same film but she is always the star. The man wears a children's cardboard black mustache and has a whang that will not wear out. A whang like red stone that will not wear out and never stops moving. Maybe when the divorce is final the projector lamp will burn out and even if the film continues to run, I won't see it. For those other films, the ones where I am the star, where I do not have a whang like red stone, where I wear out, there's no help for it. Only time perhaps. Time and the brain rot that time brings. When passion is only a sad memory.

It is around noon when I stop by the kindergarten for Evadne. It's the same place where Evadne had gone the year before. It is run by a large black woman who is a Catholic and secretly she teaches the children to cross themselves. I found Evadne crossing herself one night during a thunder storm. I had spoken to Mrs. Durant about it but she tried to explain it away. Many of the other children are Catholics and they cross themselves before lunch or before the afternoon nap. "It is obvious," she had said, "that Evadne learned from them." I couldn't call Mrs. Durant a liar, no matter what Evadne told me. I counteracted Mrs. Durant's influence by telling Evadne that if she continued to cross herself, it would make her arm fat and ugly.

I'm about a half hour late. For a time, looking at myself in the mirror while I dressed, I considered not going. I'd call and say that I was sick. There was a certain amount of truth in that. The face that looked back at me from the mirror was sick and frightened. Three months, the whole summer to bridge. Evadne would hardly know me or if she knew me, it would be shaped by what Elaine had said about me those months. Or, indirectly, from attitudes Elaine had toward me: a sour mouth when I'm mentioned, perhaps the way she read my letters to Evadne, as if they'd been written by an idiot.

Evadne was angry with me. Not only had I kept her waiting on the front porch but inside, with the clatter of dishes and silverware. The other children were eating lunch. "Daddy, you're late and I'm hungry."

"I'm a little late," I agreed, "And I'm hungry too." She accepted my hug and kiss without complaint, as a duty. Taking her hand as we walked across the porch I said, "We're going to have spaghetti, baby, real Italian spaghetti."

Evadne brightened up at that but I knew that she probably wouldn't like it as much as the canned spaghetti her mother warmed up for her. But, what the hell, I didn't feel like buying her another goddamn hamburger or hotdog.

Starting down the steps, Evadne turned slightly toward the dining room noises. "Daddy," she said, "they're having fish cakes and beans."

Her small face contorted with disgust, like I'd seen once when a wino, just in front of us, hawked and spat a pale, quivering oyster on the sidewalk.

DiNocolas was just down the street from where I lived. It was there, in the bar itself, that I used suffered large glasses of Hull's Export Beer. In the evening, my neck sore from looking up at the TV set, watching the Mets play on a field of blue or purple grass. Or, in the late afternoon talking sports with the bartender: Wilt Chamberlain, or Bill Russell, Arnie or Jack, run and shoot or control ball, head full of surfaces so I won't think about the rotting heart, the festering spirit.

We arrived at the restaurant during a slack period between the early and late lunch rushes. The dining room was only about half full and I let Evadne choose our table. She sat in the aisle in the special children's chair and I sat across from her in the cushioned booth seat. I ordered a children's platter of spaghetti with meat sauce for Evadne and baked stuffed shrimp for myself. As an afterthought, I asked the waitress if it was possible to get a meat sauce that wasn't too strong with garlic. The waitress smiled at Evadne and said that she would see.

While we waited, Evadne sipped a Coke and I drank a goblet of beer. Other people drift in, filling the tables around us. Except for the children's chair, Evadne felt grown up, sitting up straight and looking around calmly at the people at the tables near us. One elderly gentleman with a gray bushy mustache smiled at her and winked. Evadne blushed and looked down at the tablecloth.

"Daddy," she said, "this is a nice place." I said that I thought so too. "Mama never takes me out to eat. Sometimes she brings home a pizza."

"Your mama works hard. She's tired." I said this carefully, trying to get conviction into it. She was only a child but I had the feeling that she played her mother and me off against each other. I didn't want any part of that kind of domestic politics.

The waitress, when she brought the lazy susan of relishes to our table, said, "The cook is fixing a special sauce for the lady."

"Does she mean me?" Evadne asked after the waitress hurried away.

"Sure, she does." I spooned out a small portion of corn relish and pickled beans onto a plate and put it in front of her. "You're the only lady here, aren't you?"

"I guess so." Amazement and wonder colored her voice. Very ladylike, she speared a couple of kidney beans and put them in her mouth. The vinegar and spices must have stung her but she forced herself to chew and swallow. "Daddy," she said after a swallow of Coke, "those are funny tasting beans."

The spaghetti, when it arrived, had been made especially for her.

It was mainly tomato sauce, lightly spiced, with large chunks of meat in it. After a few bites, Evadne pronounced it the best spaghetti she'd even eaten. The baked stuffed shrimp were, as usual, excellent. I sat in the warm glow of her pleasure and hoped that it would last all afternoon.

It is a distance of some five or six blocks to the Green and we stopped several times to let Evadne rest. She was already tired from the walk to the restaurant. When we reached the Green, we sat on the church steps and watched the people passing by. The bus stop in front of the church was crowded with the afternoon shoppers clutching their brightly lettered bags. People came and went, sat beside us on the steps, arose when they sighted their bus. Evadne watched them all with her clear innocent eyes.

On impulse, after we'd been there for a time, noticing the mass of teenagers with their bathing suits and towels lining up as the beach bus angled in toward curb, I said: "Let's go to the beach," and took her hand and hurried to join the crowd.

Seated, Evadne said, "I don't have a bathing suit."

"We'll just look or go wading."

The bus started and stopped, started and stopped. We passed the Urban Renewal area where the ugly old buildings had been torn down and ugly new buildings erected. Then out past the industrial slums. Ten minutes later, the bus turned onto a long tree lined street. In the far distance, the street butted against the ocean. The blue green ocean was like a lowered sky.

"See the ocean?"

"Mama brings me here," Evadne said, "but we come in a car." There was a snobbish distaste for the bus. "Why don't you have a car, Daddy?"

"I do, but your mama has it."

"Oh," The small oval of her mouth showed her realization that she'd touched upon dangerous ground. "I thought you had another car."

"Not yet."

At the last stop we left the bus with the rest of the crowd. I took her hand and we walked the last block down to the ocean. It was the same beautiful ocean running against an ugly, uncared-for beach. It didn't have the pure white sand of the beaches farther down the southeast coast. It seemed to be partly black dirt.

We crossed the highway and trudged over the squat dunes to the beach. The tide was low and the reach of the ocean was a hundred yards or so away.

"Here." I bent over and removed her canvas shoes and white cotton socks. "Is that better?"

I stuffed the socks into the shoes and folded the shoes together so that I could hold them in one hand. I took her hand and we moved down the slight decline of the shelf to the edge of the water.

"Get your feet wet, baby,"

Evadne hesitated, looking out at the froth, her toes curling under into the wet sand. "It looks cold."

"No, it isn't."

"Yes, it is."

"How do you know?" I asked.

"I went in and it was too cold."

"When was that?"

"Sunday..." Evadne looked down at her feet. "It was cold when Mommy and Uncle Mark brought me and it was cold when Uncle Bob brought me."

I tried to keep the heavy weight out of my voice. "How many Uncles do you have?"

Her mouth shut tight, the lips clamped together in a straight line. She had said too much and she knew it. She shook her head and pulled her hand out of mine.

"Baby?"

Then, without warning, she ran down the beach away from me, her thin arms swinging, her feet slapping in the wasted froth of the tail end of the waves.

"Evadne." I ran after her, trying to dodge the water but splashing into it, feeling it soak into my shoes, wet my pants to the calf. At the last moment, instead of grabbing her from behind, I sprinted past her, turned, and I caught her. I lifted her, pulling her tightly against my chest. Her legs kicked against me, wetting me, her face closed to me, twisted and frozen into a harsh set.

"I'm not going to hurt you, baby. Have I ever hurt you?" She relaxed and went limp against me.

"I don't want any more Uncles."

"Quiet, baby. It's all right."

"There's Uncle Mark and Uncle Bob and Uncle Fred and..."

"Sssssshhhh." I pulled her closer to me, shaking her, rocking her gently. "I don't want to know."

"I have too many Uncles. I don't want any more. I don't want any Daddies either." Her voice dropped. "Not even you."

Still holding her, I walked back down the beach to where I'd dropped her shoes. It was awkward, but somehow I bent down and got her shoes without releasing her. She was a dead weight, slack against my shoulder. I walked up the beach toward the flattened-out dunes. Everything was still except for the angry striking of her heart and the thin hiss of her breath.

It was a long wait for the bus back to New Haven.

CHAPTER NINE

NEW HAVEN, 1966

HELLO, BIRTHDAY BOY

On the almost silent ride back to New Haven, she'd complained that I hadn't brushed all the sand away before I'd replaced her socks and shoes. "It hurts, Daddy."

"I thought you didn't want a Daddy."

But I couldn't hold out against her and I took off her socks and shoes. I used the socks to wipe away the sand away, put the socks in my pocket and put the sneakers back on.

Near the bus stop, I flagged down a cab and gave the driver Elaine's new address. I hadn't been there yet. It was, I thought, a new apartment building near the hospital. The driver shook his head and said that he didn't think there was such a building in that area. He said he'd find the address. We almost missed it altogether but Evadne sat up in the back seat and pointed out the back window.

"That's it, Daddy."

The driver bounced the cab off the curb and backed up. I told the driver to wait and helped Evadne out of the cab and turned and looked at the house. It was an old wooden frame house with a long narrow porch. It had been painted a kind of battleship gray with blue trim around the windows and doors. As we started up the walk, the front door opened.

"Mommy." Evadne jerked her hand free of mine and ran toward her mother. "Mommy."

I watched the thin, sad little legs running away from me. Elaine caught her in her arms and lifted her. The face I knew, saw often in the dark places of my mind, looking past Evadne toward me. Then, without a word or even a nod of recognition, she carried Evadne into the house and closed the door behind her.

An hour later, sitting in the Castaways, I found Evadne's dirty socks in my pocket.

That was a month ago and I hadn't seen Evadne since that day. School was in session. I would be the final year of my course work and then I could go away. I'd thought about leaving before but that would seem like running away, like sprinting ahead of her shadow, knowing if the sun was behind her, the shadow would catch me no matter where she was and no matter where I was.

My friends knew by then. I'd tried to hide the breakup during the spring, as the year closed out. I'd stayed in the apartment in the married student housing until exams were over, sleeping on the ragged old sofa in the living room. The bedroom was empty except for my clothes, an old trunk, and some boxes of books that I'd never unpacked. When the exams were over, I went by the Yale Housing Office and told them I was living in the apartment alone. I was told that that broke the lease and I'd have to move out. That afternoon, I rented a truck and loaded my things in it. I found the room and bath on Park Street and moved in. I'd kept the room during the summer I'd spent in Millhouse and left most of my things there.

Now, back from Millhouse, there wasn't any reason to hide the break-up any longer. I told a few friends, certain that the word would get around in time. It did.

In a few days, the first invitations started coming in for suppers with married friends, aware even as I accepted, that while kindness was a factor there was also the hope that I'd fill in the gaps about the breakup.

from the single friends, it was much more casual, a few beers in the evening, a play or a movie, or some information about a party. They didn't push the parties. After all, I was still married and it wasn't quite the same.

I felt much more comfortable with the single friends. It was "let's have another drink" and "look at the ass on that" and "screw class tomorrow, let's play some penny-nickel-dime stud." And we would, drinking until the bars closed and then playing cards all night and then going out to the Toddle House for breakfast.

Two of the best of these drinkers and card players were Rick and Buzz, both from the north, both bright, young and Jewish and both from well-to-do families.

Rick was short and squat, beginning to bald at twenty-three, with a five o'clock shadow like steel wool. He was shy and timid with people at first.

Buzz was the exact opposite. He was tall, slim and athletic, handsome except for a broken, bent-looking nose. The nose didn't hold him back. When he walked down the street or into a room where a party was going on, it was like he was saying, "here it is girls, so come and get it." Many of the girls did come and did get it and yet there was something oddly effeminate about him. There was so much vanity about the way he fussed over his appearance. Sometimes he'd take fifteen minutes to get his hair combed and shaped just right and I'd been at his apartment when he was getting ready to go out for a few beers and I'd squirmed for half an hour while he tried to decide which shirt and which jacket to wear.

Rick was from Philadelphia. His father ran a couple of fashionable restaurants and did catering.

Buzz was from Long Island and his father was in the fur business.

Both Rick and Buzz, though their fathers, don't know each other, seemed to live on under the table money. At the first of the month, they each received a book of ten and twenty dollar American Express traveler's checks. They used these instead of a checking account.

Buzz explained it to me once by saying that a checking account could be audited in terms of how much money his father spent. Traveler's checks couldn't. Paid for in cash they existed only in a kind of financial limbo.

Rick and Buzz and I did a lot of helling around that first month that all the students were back in town.

One night, in a solemn ceremony up in Rick's apartment, while we were finishing off a kosher care package from Rick's mother, they made me an honorary Jew. I was a little drunk at the time and I was moved by it. They thought I was acting, putting them on, and they said if I was going to act that way, they weren't going to waive the circumcision rite after all. It would have to be done by a chicken killer in the old way and I'd have to go through a bar mitzvah. If I was lucky, maybe I'd be a real Jew by the time I was fifty-five.

Then it was Buzz's birthday. His father came to New Haven for the day. We had dinner at a steak house, the four of us. It looked like the usual wealthy father takes his son and his son's friends out to dinner. Mr. Hartman was having a good time spending his money and after a time

I got over being embarrassed, got over feeling like a sponge. It all went smoothly except for one tense moment when Mr. Hartman complained about the wine. The waiter, knowing money when he saw it, replaced the bottle with another, saying that the first had been a little "off."

This bottle Mr. Hartman pronounced excellent. When the waiter had left, Buzz leaned toward his father. "When did you become an expert on wine?"

"It's all crap," Mr. Hartman said. "I thought I'd tell him."

The steaks were beautiful and the waiter, after the wine episode, hovered over us, doing everything but wipe our mouths with his coat sleeve.

After we'd ordered brandy and coffee, I got up and headed for the men's room. I was a little surprised when Mr. Hartman appeared in the men's room a minute or so after me. He stood at the mirror while I pissed.

When I came out, he was combing his hair. He was shorter than Buzz, perhaps five-six or five-seven. There was a weight and squareness in his shoulders, a sense of power and strength. His hair was graying around the edges. High across his cheekbones there were the dark pits and craters of an old case of acne he must have had thirty years ago. "I want to ask a favor of you."

I washed my hands and looked at him. "Sure."

He put his comb away in his inside jacket pocket. "You and Rick have to keep Buzz busy for an hour or so and then bring him over to his apartment at ten o'clock." His rinsed off his hands and dried them. "A minute or two after ten but not before."

"All right."

We left the men's room and made our way through the tables. "Rick knows already. I'll beg off for an hour to see an old friend. You two suggest a drink or two at the bar." He stopped and turned to face me. "It's a surprise party."

I agreed to help and we went back to the table and had our cognac and coffee.

It was close to nine when Mr. Hartman dropped us off in front of MacTriff's. It was Friday night and you could tell from the dispirited way the combo was playing that there wasn't much crowd yet. You could hear the bartender, the waitress and the owner applauding.

We took a booth and Jenny came over to take our orders. Jenny was short and bowlegged, with an old face. What she did have going for her was a remarkable pair of breasts: large, jutting forward and hardly sagging at all. Back in the spring, one of the town studs had told me he'd done Jenny a couple of times.

He told me the breasts were real. "The rest of her belongs in a carnival but those, they're first class." You could tell what kind of night it was in MacTriff's by the kind of rush Jenny got put on her around midnight.

If the working girls stayed home, you could see the studs starting hanging around Jenny, buying her drinks and hands on her ass in the dark Aisle between the tables. She'd get frisky then and she'd play them off against one another. One of them might get it that night but he was certainly going to have to work for it.

We ordered beer all around and when Jenny brought it Buzz leaned out from the booth and blocked her while she was putting out the bottles and glasses. "Jenny, I'd like to chew on one of those some night when you're not doing anything else."

Jenny laughed. "Come back on your birthday."

"It is my birthday," Buzz said.

Jenny looked at Rick and me for confirmation. "That's the truth," Rick said.

"You're putting me on," she said.

"Show her your ID," I said.

Buzz pulled out the card file from his wallet and handed it to Jenny. She squinted at it and her lips moved as she read the date. When she handed the card file back, she said," I guess you got me this time."

"I guess I did," Buzz said. "When?"

"Closing time." Jenny smiled, looking at Buzz and probably deciding that it wasn't a bad idea after all. "You might think you've won but I'll break your back."

Buzz shook his head. "All I want for my birthday is a chew."

"That's all?" Jenny didn't seem to believe him.

"That's all."

"Come on." Jenny started down the aisle toward the rear of the bar.

Buzz followed her. "Where?"

"The storeroom." When they reached the kitchen door Jenny called out to the bartender. "Going to the storeroom, Eddie. Back in a minute." When the kitchen door closed behind them, I looked over at Rick. He was trying to drink his beer and choking on it.

"I didn't really think he'd do it," I said. "I thought it was all talk."

"That's the wine and the cognac talking," Rick said. "There's one consolation," I said ... I never heard of anybody getting clap chewing on a tit."

We drank our beer and waited. The minutes went by. Another couple came in and Eddie ducked under the bar and came out on the floor to take their orders. We finished our beer and divided up Buzz's.

A couple more minutes and Jenny came out of the kitchen, followed by Buzz. As Buzz passed the platform where the combo played, Rick and I started singing, "Happy Birthday to you, happy birthday to you ... " and the piano player who was taking a break and having a drink stepped over to the piano and backed us up with a few chords. Rick held up three fingers to Jenny and she turned and went to the bar.

"How was it?" Rick asked.

Buzz looked at his empty bottle. "Amazing. Beautiful. I've never seen anything like it."

"How'd it taste?" I asked.

"Like an armpit," Buzz·said.

Jenny brought the three beers Buzz had ordered and braced a fat hip against the table, smiling down at Buzz. "That was a goodie, wasn't it, honey?"

Buzz agreed that it was.

A little after ten, Rick and I split up the tab, telling Buzz it was his birthday drink.

"You leave the tip," Rick told Buzz. "You were the one who got the taste,"

Buzz left a couple of dollars and we crossed Chapel heading up Park Street toward Buzz's apartment. It was two and a half blocks. After the beer, the wine and the cognac, we were all feeling it and Buzz was saying over and over, "What a fucking birthday, what a goddamn birthday."

Outside the apartment building, I took a quick look in the parking lot but I didn't see Mr. Hartman's car. There were a number of other cars that didn't belong there and before Buzz could see how packed the parking lot was, I took him by the arm and pulled him past it, saying, "Come on, birthday boy, let's see what you've got to drink in your place."

"A little gin and a lemon that's turning green."

"I'll have a drink of that," I said. "Heavy on the green lemon."

"Make that two," Rick said, taking Buzz's arm from the other side.

Buzz stopped at the foot of the stairs. "That godawful lemon. Why don't we go back to MacTriff's for one more drink? Look, as a favor, I'll get Jenny to let both of you chew on a tit. She'd do it for me."

"I want to see the lemon first," I said.

"Shit, yes," Rick said, "and if it's really green and it's not a lime we'll turn right around and go back."

Buzz nodded. "I think it's a lemon."

At the door to his apartment, key out, he hesitated again. "Are you sure?"

"I've got to see that lemon," I said.

"I wish I'd never seen that damned lemon. There I was in Pegnataro's and I was walking through the fruit section and that damned lemon saw me and jumped a foot in the air." He inserted the key and turned it. "It might even have jumped three feet ... "

A blast of sound from the dark room stopped him. "Surprise! Happy birthday, Buzzi," the cries overlapping each other in a kind of confusion.

Buzz was so stunned and speechless, that I reached around him and turned on the overhead light. They were all there, his friends from the school. As soon as the lights went on, they started tooting toy paper horns and throwing confetti.

Buzz mumbled, "Jesus Christ." He left the doorway and started for his father.

A couple of girls stopped him to give him a hug and a kiss and some of the guys shook his hand.

Mr. Hartman was standing near the rear wall of the living room, beaming, his arms locked across his chest. To his right, along the wall, there was a caterer s table, white cloth covering it, overloaded with food. Nearby, on a smaller table, there must have been around two cases of assorted hard stuff, bourbon, scotch, gin, and vodka.

Rick pushed me slightly to get me out of the doorway so he could close the door. He turned back to me and whispered, "You ain't seen nothing yet."

"What?"

"The real surprise is yet to come,"

"Huh?"

"Wait and be surprised with Buzz," He took me by the arm. "Let's find a drink."

By the time we reached the table Buzz had worked his way through the well-wishers and he and his father were hugging each other. They were both a little wet-eyed. While Rick mixed himself a scotch and water, I went looking for the beer. I looked in the refrigerator but I couldn't even find the green lemon in there. Finally, I asked a guy I didn't know and he pointed me toward the bathroom.

The bathtub was full of beer and ice and there was a bottle opener hanging from a string tied to the shower curtain railing. I was opening a bottle, partly obscured by the door, when a girl I'd seen around the school but didn't know stormed into the bath-room, slamming the door closed behind her. She stopped herself in time, fingers caught in the elastic of her underpants, about to skin them down. She saw me then and yelled at me, "What are you, a peeping tom or something?"

I shook my head and smiled. I left and closed the door behind me. Back in the living room, Buzz's stereo was up at full blast and several couples were dancing. I drifted by the food table and helped myself to some rare roast beef. I was a couple of feet away from Buzz and Mr. Hartman when the door bell rang.

I heard Mr. Hartman say, "It's your party, Buzz, you answer the door." I turned around then, remembering what Rick had said, and watched Buzz cross to the door.

The doorbell rang once more and broke off abruptly when Buzz opened the door.

A beautiful woman stood out in the hallway. She was tall, five-ten or so, with black shoulder length hair and dark skin. Either there was was Spanish blood in her or she had a great tan. She was wearing a bright red mini dress and long beautiful legs showed beneath the short skirt.

She smiled and said something to Buzz and he stepped out into the hall and pulled the door closed behind him.

I looked at Mr. Hartman and he was smiling to himself. I found Rick over at the bar table and tapped him on the shoulder. "Is this it? What is it?"

Rick grinned. "Wait and see. Let Buzz tell you about it. I don't want to spoil his fun."

I turned and looked at the door when he did and watched Buzz come in with the girl on his arm. She was almost as tall as he was and she moved with the grace of a dancer. There was a swing to her hips but it was so mild and modulated that her small and plum round belly didn't seem to move at all.

Buzz stopped first in front of his father. "Dad, I'd like you to meet a friend of mine, Beverly."

Mr. Hartman took her hand and held it. "Buzz, this is a beautiful girl, but is she Jewish?"

There was a frozen moment, when I wasn't sure what was going to happen next, and then Mr. Hartman and Buzz put their heads back and laughed.

Beverly pulled her hand away from Mr. Hartman and stood watching them.

It was, for me, a harsh, gut chilling moment because I could see how much she hated both of them. It was on her face, passing over it like a shadow, and then it was gone and a blandness just this side of amusement was there instead.

Buzz patted his father on the back and then brought the girl over to where Rick and I were standing.

I didn't wait for the introduction. I put out my hand and said, "Nice to meet you."

There was also, without meaning to, the suggestion of a small, abortive bow from the waist. I was standing close to her and I could almost see how she saw me reflect off her face. I didn't like what I saw, so I asked if I could mix her a drink. She said yes and I went over to the bar table and mixed her a scotch on the rocks.

I got back and was about to hand her the drink when Rick said, "Buzz, you owe me," and took Beverly by the arm and they moved out onto the dance floor.

She danced with a flair, a kind of showmanship, as if to say this is the way we do it in New York and only in select parts of New York at that. What Beverly was doing looked like it had been choreographed for a musical.

Beside me, Buzz said, "Look at this," and handed me a small white card about the size of a calling card. The raised black lettering read HENRY A. HARTMAN and under that FURS and an address,

I pushed the card back at him. "So what?"

"No, look at the other side."

I flipped the card and saw the bold block printing, HAPPY BIRTHDAY, SON. I still didn't understand and the puzzlement must have shown on my face, Buzz leaned toward me. "The girl gave me the card when I went to the door. She's my birthday present."

"The shit you say."

"She said so in the hall."

I understood then and I handed back the card. "My birthday's in November, the twenty-first. Tell your old man."

While he was laughing, all that laughing was getting on my nerves, I went into the bathroom and dug another beer out of the bath tub.

It was getting drunker and drunker and I got so I didn't know what time it was. It had been a little after ten when we got to the apartment. The next time I looked my watch it was one a.m. and it seemed to be going double time and triple time.

A while after that, I'm not sure exactly how long, I found myself sitting on the sofa next to Beverly. I think I was there first, drinking what I hoped was my last beer, trying to muster up the energy to walk the four blocks back to my room. She'd just finished dancing with Charlie Basnight. There was a beaded mustache of perspiration on her upper lip and an oily film on her forehead.

After flopping down next to me, catching her breath in short audible gasps, she noticed me. "Didn't you fix me a drink when I first got here?" I said I had. "Would you fix me another?"

I nodded and went over and poured a good double shot of scotch over ice and brought it back to her. She took the glass and looked down into it. "No twist of lemon?"

"I'm sorry. I…"

She smiled. "That's all right. It's good scotch." She lifted the glass to drink and stopped. Her other hand made a grab for her left eye. She lowered the glass to the floor carefully, the hand still cupped under her eye. "Oh, shit."

"What?"

"These fucking contact lenses. I think I just lost one." She blinked the eye and felt around the lower lid. "Yes, I did." The left hand remained cupped under her eye while she slid her right hand down the front of her dress. "This is the second time tonight. One popped out on the train and it took me fifteen minutes to find it. It's all that goddamn trash in the air."

Remaining in the same place, without moving my feet, I squatted and looked at the floor in front of her. I tried looking at the floor from an angle so I'd see the dull glint of the lens if it was there. Nothing showed and I worked my hand slowly across the floor to see if I could find it by touch. Still nothing. I was straightening up, about to look on the sofa beside her. When I saw the flash from the tip of my right shoe.

"Is that it?" I lifted the shoe toward her, pointing, until she saw it, wet her finger and lifted it deftly from the shoe tip. Beverly cleaned it in her mouth and replaced it. Then, when she was sure it wasn't going to pop out again, she got her drink and took a long swallow.

"Thank you," she said. "You're very good at finding lenses."

"Thanks."

"You wear them too?"

"My wife does." Then I was sorry I'd said that. It was like inviting people to ask the whole series of questions that usually followed.

"Is your wife here?"

I shook my head ... We're getting divorced." Then, because I knew the other questions and the other answers, I turned it around and pointed it back at her. "You ever been married?"

"I was once ... almost. We changed our minds at the last minute. It was just as well."

"You said you were from New York." When she hesitated, I added, "You said you took the train in tonight."

"I could have come from Boston," she said.

"You're right."

Then, when I aid nothing more, she offered in a low voice, "I'm from New York... She tilted back her head and drain the glass. "I model there. Clothes and furs."

"You know Mr. Hartman?"

She looked across the room at Mr. Hartman who was dancing the jerk with one of the young girls. "I'm a friend of a friend."

I nodded and I guess she thought the nod meant more than it really did.

"Look," she said, dropping her voice to a whisper but with an edge to it, "it's just a joke and it's a favor I'm doing a friend."

"I never thought it was anything else," I said.

"The hell you didn't."

"Boy Scout honor," I said, holding up the Scout signal of three fingers.

She ignored that. "I mean, probably most of the people here think I'm going to sleep with Buzz."

"I doubt that."

"I mean ... what kind of girl do they think I am?" There was a growing harshness in her voice. "I might sleep with somebody but not as a joke."

"Sure," I said, "everybody knows that"

"What?"

"What you said. That everybody sleeps with somebody but nobody does it as a joke."

That calmed her down a little and we talked about restaurants in New York while I finished most of my beer, It was past time and I said goodnight to her and then said my goodnight around the room, Mr. Hartman got emotional and said that it was nice of any older person like me to take an interest in his son, He blinked back tears when I said that Buzz was a good man and a good friend.

Buzz caught me at the door. "Shit, man, don't leave. I might fuck her on the living room rug and you can watch."

"Watching isn't one of my sports...Then I needed to soften that a little. "Now, if watching is one of your sports...."

I left him laughing. After all, as they say in the farm country, it's no read licked off my candy one way or the other.

BOOK TWO

CHAPTER TEN

NEW HAVEN, 1966

WHAT TO DO UNTIL
THE KILLING STOPS

The young man was standing at the point where the bar at MacTriff's hooks left and runs on four or five feet before it terminates against the side wall. He was around six feet tall, blond hair cut short, with the thick hard body of a professional lineman. There were several men at the bar and two women seated at the small tables near the bar.

What made me notice him first was that he was wearing a short sleeve shirt and that both arms were heavily tattooed, I hadn't seen that many tattoos on anybody that young in a long time.

It was late afternoon and fairly quiet at first. After a few minutes he began to talk to the men on both sides of him. I could hear enough of what he was saying to know that he was talking about Vietnam and the Green Berets. I picked up my beer and moved down the bar closer to him so that I could listen. He noticed my movement and, as if playing toward a larger audience, he backed up one step and raised his voice a bit.

I·gave up counting after fifty. Maybe I should have kept on. I shoulda known as soon as I got back stateside some groundhog would ask me how many I'd killed,11

That stung one of the men near me, a man in his late forties.

He said he'd been in the Marines when the young man was probably still in diapers.

"That might be but it was a different kind of war. You took some place and killed all the gooks there and it stayed took and then you moved on to the next place, all the time moving closer to Germany or Japan. And when you got there the war was over. Shit, in Vietnam, you kill all the gooks in one place and you go away and you come back in a week and there's another bunch of gooks you got to kill. Shit, 'Nam aint nothing but one big killing ground." He looked around at the face close to him. "You ever kill hogs? That's what it's like." He nodded his thanks to the ex-Marine who'd bought him a drink and said, "Cheers" before he drank off part of it.

The bartender, Fred, got interested and stopped off to listen. "Were you in the Rangers?"

"That bunch of pussies?"

"I thought they were supposed to be tough." Fred looked offended. "As tough as the Coast Guard." The young man turned slightly to face the tables where the women were. "No, I wore the green flat hat, the beret."

"You just out?" I asked.

"Yeah, I did two tours there and decided it was somebody else's time to do the killing."

He was answering me but I could follow the line of his eyes and see that he was watching the young brown-haired waitress from the Toddle House who usually came by for a couple of drinks after her shift ended at four o'clock.

The ex-Marine asked how the women were.

The young man held his nose. "Let's just say it's good to be back in the land of the round-eyed women." He grinned. "Or should I say ladies?" The men around him laughed and the brown-haired waitress smiled.

It was time for me to leave but I had one more question. "How long is the war going to last?"

"At the rate it's going," he said, "I'd say about a thousand years."

I went to the other end of the bar to get my briefcase. When I passed him on the way out, he was asking Fred to give the waitress a drink on him.

Around ten o'clock that evening, I ran into Rick and Buzz in front of the Yale library. Often that was as far as they got. The girls from a small Catholic college in town trooped in on some evenings to use the reference room. Rick and Buzz would sit on the steps in front, wearing their most expensive tweed jackets and faded jeans, and try to meet the pretty ones. Sometimes it worked and sometimes it didn't.

I'd been in the graduate library since I'd left MacTriff's and I'd timed myself, spending exactly four hours, and then I'd put the books back on the shelves and walked out. As I walked out the front door, I saw Rick and Buzz talking to two girls down by the bicycle racks. It was a fairly animated conversation but when I got closer, I saw that Rick wasn't interested. The pretty girl was listening to Buzz and the other girl had bad skin. Rick was just going along with it until Buzz found out what he could do. So, knowing I'd have at least one companion for a drink, I turned and went back up the steps and waited under the shadow of one of the columns and smoked a cigarette. By the time the foursome split in half I'd finished the cigarette. The girls passed by me on the way into the library. The pretty girl was saying how cute the two of them were and the girl with the bad skin looked a little flushed and unhappy. As they went through the door, I could hear the girl with the bad skin say, "I wasn't that interested ... "

I angled down the steps and caught up with Rick and Buzz.

"Given time," I said, coming up behind them in the darkness, "you two are going to be great nasty old men."

They stopped for me and moved apart so that I could walk between them.

"That girl probably had a great personality," Buzz said.

"Maybe so," Rick said, "but what if we were in the dark somewhere and I miss her mouth and kiss her on one of her pimples?"

"Enough," Buzz said.

We crossed the street and passed by the Yale Station post office. "You two going anywhere in particular?" I asked.

"Thought we might have a drink," Buzz said. "The life of a graduate student is not an easy one, all that mucking around in dusty libraries, eye strain and sore tailbones from sitting all day on hard chairs."

"MacTriff's?" Rick asked. "Why not."

"I was thinking about chewing on Jenny's other tit," Buzz said. "But this time I think I'll ask her to wash it off with Dial soap."

"That'll make the hair fall off," I said.

"All for the better," Buzz said, "because last time a handful got caught in my teeth."

"Enough." Rick reached around me and popped Buzz on the shoulder. "You'll ruin my appetite for it."

We decided on a booth far enough from the juke box so we could talk if we wanted to. Jenny took our orders and said that she was talking to a friend at the bar but that she'd join us for a drink in a while. As my eyes got used to the dim light, I saw the young man who'd been talking about Vietnam earlier. He was sitting with the waitress from the Toddle House in a booth across the aisle and down and away from us. About the time I recognized him he saw me and waved.

"Who's that?" Rick asked.

I explained how I'd met him and what he'd been talking about. "He's a big mother," Rick said. "Look at those shoulders." Buzz looked, "No neck. He's one of Williams' no neck monsters."

I said, "I wouldn't say that to his face, he might not understand literary allusions."

We'd turned back to our beers when the noise at their booth increased sharply. They were arguing but I couldn't hear much of it. Bick shifted nervously in his seat, "I hope he doesn't kill her."

"He's probably more civilized than that."

Buzz shook his head. "Green Berets are supposed to be trained to kill on reflex."

"Bullshit."

"No, that's what I read in a magazine."

The ex-Green Beret raised his voice another notch. "Why don't you take that five and stick it up your ass. Maybe it'll turn into a twenty dollar bill,"

There was a sputter and a hiss from the waitress. Almost with a leap she was out into the aisle and moving toward the front door. She clacked past us on wobbly high heels. Behind her, in the booth, the big man's booming laugh chased her out of the place.

I was canted toward the front door, watching the girl leave, when Rick said, "Here comes your friend."

I turned back as he stopped in the aisle by our booth. Seated, looking up at him, he looked as big and wide as a brick wall

"I was talking to you this afternoon, right?" I nodded,

"Mind if I sit with you?"

I looked at Bick and Buzz and they didn't object so I nodded toward the empty seat next to Rick, across the table from me. He eased himself into the seat and placed his drink on the table in front of him. I did the introductions and waited while he seemed to be trying to remember his name.

"Burt McElveen," he said finally.

Next to me, Buzz smiled and said, "It looks like your girl's mad at you."

"Fuck her," he said. "A fuck and a blow job and she thinks I'm a loan company."

"She any good?" This from Rick.

"Naw. She felt like she had warts on her tongue." Burt laughed. "Maybe they were warts."

I was listening to his voice, trying to place his accent. There was a twang in there somewhere. Being in the service might have smoothed it out some but it was still there. "Are you from around here?"

"Kentucky," he said. "I wouldn't live up here except I had the offer of a job."

"What kind of job?" I asked.

"Test firing M-16's over at the Winchester plant."

Buzz started to laugh and then thought better of it.

Burt saw the smothered laugh and looked at him hard, as if he didn't allow anybody to find humor in his job. "Shit, but I can make those babies talk. The old farts on the range they never shot at anybody in their lives. Or it must have been back in World War One. Me, I was killing gooks up to a month and a half ago."

Buzz flinched a little next to me. "How does it feel to kill somebody?"

"With a rifle, at a distance, it's like killing rabbits." He shrugged. "You don't feel anything after the first one or two. Hand-to-hand's different. You never get used to the smell of hot blood and guts and shit." Burt placed his hands on the center of the table, with the palms up. "See those? They kill too."

There was a ridge of callous along the bottom edge of his hand. The fingers seemed square and jammed back until they were all about the same length. The hands looked hard and heavy, like steel or stone.

"I did six years in 'Nam and I spent an hour every day practicing with these hands. Shit, they're quicker than a pig-sticker or an M-16."

"Karate?" I asked.

"That and some other stuff. All those gook ways of killing in unarmed combat. With just these hands I can kill you 803 ways in five seconds or less."

"That's a lot of ways." All that talk about killing was getting to me, making me edgy. It wasn't just the killing, it was the bland way he talked about it, the way some people talked about cars or the relative merits of beer.

"You ain't just bird-turding," he said.

An hour went by. We got off the subject of killing but he didn't seem as interested as he'd been before. When Buzz mentioned a book, Burt said, "Ain't read a book in ten years and I probably won't read another one in the next twenty years." About movies: "John Wayne don't make enough of them." About plays: "I never been to a real one and I doubt I'd spend my money that way."

"What if it was free?" Rick asked. "I still wouldn't."

"Why not?" I asked.

"I saw one once when I was in the 6th grade. It was about this boy who didn't eat the right things and he didn't feel good. Then as soon as he started eating right, he felt better and his grades got better and he made first string pitcher on the baseball team." Burt shrugged. "It was silly."

"Maybe now. But it wasn't silly for the 6th grade."

"It was silly even then. All the rest of the kids knew it was silly too. When you're living on dried beans and skillet bread where're you supposed to get the quarts of milk, all those green vegetables and the meat? It didn't say a thing to me except that I was shit-poorer than people in other parts of the country." He stepped into the aisle. "Back in a minute. Got to bleed my lizard."

The men's room door closed behind Burt. Buzz looked over at me. "I don't think I can stand much more of this."

"Me either." This from Rick.

I nodded. "When he comes back we'll take off and go somewhere Else."

"We ought to leave now." Rick poured off the last of his beer.

"Like they say in those English movies, that man's crackers and there's no way of knowing what he'll do next."

Then it was too late to leave because he was bouncing down the aisle toward the booth. Before he was seated, I said, "We've got to go. Got early class in the morning." That was a lie. The class wasn't until noon.

"Naw, look. I was going to buy us all a round." He turned and yelled toward the bar. "Jenny, a round over here." He sat down and pinned Rick into the booth. "I've got to go myself. One last drink. Hate to drink by myself. And I don't drink past midnight except on Saturday night. I got to keep my eye sharp for test firing those M-16s, right?"

"It's late," I began, "and we ... "

"One drink. That can't hurt."

Jenny came down the aisle toward us, carrying a tray on which there were three beers and a bourbon and water for Burt. "See?" Burt said, "they're already opened."

A little grimly, defeated, Bick and Buzz and I settled back to drink the beer on him. We did it grudgingly, in silence. After a few minutes the silenced weighed at us and Rick decided to break it and try to be civil. "Are the Green Berets a part of Special Services?"

Innocent mistake or not, this angered Burt. "Special Services? You trying to shit me? They run movie projectors and most of them are queers. I was in Special Forces."

"I'm sorry," Rick said.

"Sorry don't mean shit."

"Come on," I said, "he didn't mean anything by it."

"You guys in college think you're so goddam smart. You think your shit smells better than ice cream."

"Come off it," I said. I was getting angry. I knew it was all crazy, that I shouldn't be ushing him, but it was one of those scenes you know is bad even when you're in the middle of it. The strange part is that you feel like it has to be finished, as absurd as it is. "We didn't want these beers in the first place. If we have to take shit with them…"

"You're forgetting something." Burt showed me the hands, the hard ridges at the bottoms.

"Yeah, I know," I said, "you can kill me 803 ways in five seconds."

"You better believe it."

"The only thing I don't understand is whether you kill me one of those 803 ways or all 803 ways."

Next to me I could feel Buzz tense up. I looked at him and saw that he was trying to decide if he could get over the back of the booth if the fight started. Across from me at an angle, next to Burt, Rick said, "Now, wait a fucking minute. This is crazy."

"You better watch it," Burt said, ignoring Rick, "you get me started and your ass is mud."

"I've heard that before. I did my time. You won't get any cherry."

"Let's drink our beers and forget it," Rick said.

"I don't want any cherry," Burt said. "I just want about ten pounds of your ass."

"Forget it," I said. "Get queer for somebody else." Then, slowly, without an abrupt movement, I put my hands palm down on the table and slid out of the booth. "It's my bedtime and I've talked enough cheap shit."

Without looking at Burt I turned and walked out of the bar. I didn't breathe until I felt the cold outside air on my face. I could feel the strain, listening for footsteps behind me. When there weren't any, I let the breath out in a long hiss. Maybe the breath was all that was holding me up. My knees were on the point of buckling under me. I locked them and walked stiff-legged down to the corner and across the street. I walked about half a block, feeling the fear slipping away from me, and I stopped and leaned against a brick building. Cars passed, their lights striking at me, and I knew they thought I was drunk. One man even yelled something at me and I used that anger to push myself the rest of the way to the room. I fell across the bed, the lights in my eyes, but I didn't have enough energy to get up and turn them off.

Some time later, when I felt stronger, I discovered that I had a headache. I fixed myself a Bromo and was drinking it when I heard footsteps coming down the hallway toward my room. I thought, oh, shit, and tried to remember if I'd locked the door. There was a knock at the door. "Who is it?"

"Rick. Buzz is with me."

"Coming." I tossed off the rest of the Bromo and opened the door. We looked at each other and then we started laughing hysterically.

When that had worn itself out, Buzz said, "You know what he was doing when we left?"

I shook my head.

He gave Jenny a riddle. He asked her what goes hard and comes out soft.

"If anybody knew, it would be Jenny."

"She wouldn't guess. Finally, he had to tell her. You want to make a guess?"

I shook my head. "If Jenny won't guess I won't either."

"Chewing gum," Buzz said. "He said the answer was chewing gum."

I stayed away from MacTriff's until the weekend. I told myself there were a number of reasons. I'd tick them off once or twice a day but I didn't allow myself to consider the real one. By Saturday I began to feel that I hadn't been that frightened. I left the library and walked down to the bar. I wanted to stop at MacTriff's window and look in but I talked myself out of it and pushed open the door and sat down at the bar. Part way through the first beer I lifted my eyes and looked around the bar. Burt wasn't there. That was a relief and I drank a few more beers, feeling the tenseness and the strain going out of my neck and shoulders.

Around five, while I was having what I'd decided would be my last beer for the afternoon, I'd calmed down so much that I didn't look around when the door opened. I felt that blast of cold air and then that was shut off. A few seconds later somebody sat down on the stool next to me. I looked up and it was Burt McElveen.

He was smiling. "I've been looking for you, good buddy."

"Have you?"

"I wanted to tell you there was no hard feelings about the other night."

"None with me either," I forced myself to say.

"Let's shake then." He put out his hand and I put out mine and we shook. He squeezed my hand hard for a moment and then released it.

"Your hand's kind of soft," he said.

"It doesn't need to be anything else."

He lowered his voice. "You don't know how close you came to getting killed the other night, old buddy. If I'd been a little drunker or a little madder ... " He let that trail off, unfinished.

"When I was doing my time in the Navy we used to say that you can kill me but you can't eat me."

His face was hard, the emotion flat and bland. "I don't know what that means."

"It's just a saying."

Fred, the bartender, came down to our end of the bar. Burt ordered a beer and counted out the forty cents from a small handful of change.

Before he put the change away, he raked around in it, as if making an estimate of what was left. He drank half a glass of beer before he turned to me again.

"There was something else I wanted to see you about." I nodded but didn't say anything. "I'm a little short until payday. I thought you might lend me ten until next week."

I didn't say anything for a long time. I thought about it. I let it roll around in my head. I knew his kind and I knew if I loaned him the money I'd never see him again. He'd stay away from MacTriff's so he wouldn't have to run into me. He'd find himself another bar to drink in, in another part of town, and if I saw him at all it would be an accident.

"I'm a little short myself," I said. I got out my wallet and took out a five. "I can maybe spare five until next week." I didn't hand it to him. I waited until he nodded. Then I placed it on the bar in front of him.

"Thanks," He tucked it away in his shirt pocket and finished off his beer. "Got to go now. See you next week."

He left, the blast of cold air striking me between the shoulders.

I sat there and drank my beer and tried to talk to myself. There was nothing that I could tell myself that I'd believe. After a while I accepted the sour taste in my mouth for what it was.

CHAPTER ELEVEN
NEW HAVEN, 1966
JOLLY SEASON

Just like it was following the wrong script, it rained on Christmas Eve. By the time it got dark, the rain had become brittle small projectiles of ice, dry clacking against each other. I left my room around eight and walked down to DiNicola's. While it didn't seem the proper meal for the holidays, I ordered the fettucine and ate at one of the tables in the bar half of the restaurant. While I ate, the family men were leaving, throwing down the last of their drinks, heading for home. The shouts of "Merry Christmas" floated in the air like banners.

By nine, only the homeless men remained in the bar, some eight of us. The ice and wind scratched against the long windows of the bar, muffled by the drawn drapes. There weren't many customers in the restaurant part and the waitresses took turns standing in the doorway that separated the bar from the restaurant, looking at the owner, who sat at one of the small tables drinking coffee and sipping cognac from a shot glass. At exactly nine-thirty the owner, let all the waitresses but one leave. The waitresses who were leaving stopped off at the bar to receive their good night-Merry Christmas drink, drinking it standing up, back two or three feet from the bar according to the state regulations.

"Merry Christmas, Bud," they called to the bartender, pulling their collars high and ducking their heads as they went outside. Turning on my bar stool, I could see the thick swirl of snow just beyond the door.

"It's turned to snow," one of the men said.

"Looks like a blizzard," another said.

At ten o'clock, the owner came out of the kitchen with a pewter pitcher and a tray of small glass cups. He poured an eggnog for each man at the bar and one for the bartender and himself. "Gentlemen," he said, lifting his cup, "Merry Christmas to you all."

"Merry Christmas," we shouted back at him and drank. I felt the eggnog bounce off the top of the Hull's Export and I thought for a moment I was going to be sick.

"Now, gentlemen," the owner said, "we're closing in ten minutes so that our employees can get home and get ready for Christmas." And he put his cup down and daubed at his mustache with a handkerchief.

The wind was driving the snow down the street toward me when I left the bar and turned up Park toward Chapel. The force of the wind staggered me and I thought, so this is the way it was with Nanook of the North, and I grabbed at a brick wall to steady myself on the iced over side walk.

Piss on you, Nanook. I left the sidewalk and went out into the street where the tire chains had smashed the ice, dodging the slow moving cars, leaving the street only when I reached the building where I had my room. The building was dark, except for the entrance hallway light. I was the only tenant left there during the holidays.

Up in my room, I put on coffee and water and plugged in the electric coffee pot. I tore the Christmas wrapping from the bottle of Remy Martin cognac I'd given myself for Christmas. When the coffee was perked, I poured myself a cup and rinsed out the toothbrush glass for the cognac. I took the coffee and the cognac over to my desk and cleared off a corner by pushing the books and notebooks back into a jumbled pile.

It was time to think about the letter. It had been bothering me for two days, since it arrived. I'd tried pushing it aside, tried to forget it in the bars and the movies. In the books, the cheap novels I read when I wanted to blot out my mind. Now it was time to think back over the letter and see what had bothered me.

Something had and it was there, just at the edge of my mind, nagging, pushing out at me.

I had a sip of the cognac and followed it with a gulp of coffee. I got the letter from the top of the dresser and studied the envelope first. It was addressed in Elaine's handwriting and the postmark showed that it had been mailed from Raleigh on December 20th. The time was blurred. Nothing there. Putting the envelope aside, I unfolded the letter. The letter was written on a piece of tablet paper. Someone with a ruler had drawn lines on the paper with a pencil, two heavier lines cut through the center with a lighter line. The lines were there so that Evadne would know how large to write the letters. A capital letter went from one heavy line to the next. The lowercase letters only reached up as far as the light center line.

Although I knew the letter by heart, I read it again.

Dear Daddy,

I am having a good time. It is not cold here. Thank you for my Japanese doll. It is very pretty. I love you.

Evadne

I finished off the cup of coffee and had another, adding some cognac to the glass to bring the level up. It was there in the letter somewhere. It was there but it eluded me.

Around one a.m, I put out the light and got into bed. I moved my pillow to the foot of the bed so that I could turn on my side and look outside the window. The snow was swirling around, puffing up, and diving in the narrow passageway between the buildings. It was a kind of dance and I watched it until I was tired enough to sleep.

Then.

It was morning and the wind had stopped. Snowflakes as big as quarters drifted down. What awoke me was that suddenly the room was unbearably cold. It looked like the furnace was out again. It had happened earlier in the fall, back when it hadn't mattered much and it had taken the repair men two days to fix it. Now it was Christmas day … there wouldn't be many repair men willing to work. I resigned myself to a cold holiday, to sleeping under my blankets and my topcoat. Still, on the chance that something might be done, I dressed to go outside, to the phone booth across the street. At the door, I stopped and took off my topcoat. It was too early. The landlord wouldn't be awake yet. In the whole city of New Haven, I was probably the only adult awake who didn't have to be.

I made a pot of coffee and sat down at my desk to wait for nine o'clock. When the coffee was ready, I folded the letter from Evadne without looking at it and put it back on the dresser top.

Nine o'clock at last. I tugged on my overshoes and my topcoat and went down the hallway and the two flights of narrow stairs to the main entrance hall. I walked down the steps to the side walk, holding onto the railing because there was ice under the snow drift. Then, after I'd crossed the sidewalk and stepped off the curb into the street, I was more certain of my footing and I could lift my eyes and look around me.

The houses on the block were old and they faced, in the future, the threat of urban renewal. They needed painting and they'd weathered quite a bit. Now, in the snow and ice, in the still morning street where nobody moved, I thought, God, it almost looks like Japan that winter.

I was there stationed at Atsugi. In that little town of Otsuka-Mammachi where the houses hadn't ever been painted, where they'd weathered to the colors of driftwood. That winter it snowed several times and I'd stand at the second floor window and look out across the bare winter fields at the weathered houses and the winding road passed beyond the courtyard. I'd compare the real life in front of me with the Japanese prints I'd seen and I'd think, yes, yes, that's the way it is, that stillness caught by the artist in a way that a photograph couldn't.

At that moment a police car, chains pounding down against the ice and slush, rounded the corner and passed me while I waited. The driver looked at me, turning to face me and I put up a hand and waved and they went on past. So, it was not Japan after all. It was New Haven and it was Christmas.

Of course, that was it. What had been bothering me about the letter. *Japanese.* That, with the carefully lined out paper. Flashing across my eyes, held there for the moment it took me to register the images, I knew how the letter had been written.

An afternoon in Raleigh. Elaine asks, "Wouldn't you like to write your daddy a letter and thank him for the doll he sent?"

"Yes, Mommy." But Evadne has no enthusiasm.

Her mother does. She lines out the paper, one sheet for the letter she will write and one for the copy Evadne will make.

Laboring over the letter, the unaccustomed ballpoint pen awkward in her small hand. "What is this word, Mommy?"

"Japanese."

"It's a long word."

"Yes," Elaine says.

And there are shorter words. *I love you.* Evadne writes the words without questioning, without protest. When the letter is addressed and sealed and stamped, placed on the table near the front door, Evadne sighs like a child who has suffered.

"My hand hurts and I don't like writing letters."

Crap and snow fall on my head. The snowflakes smaller now. Like ice needles. A wino who's probably slept in a doorway all night rounds a far corner and moves toward me, old overcoat without buttons flapping in the wind like wings.

I closed the phone booth door behind me and dialed the landlord's number. It rang ten times and no one answers. Merry Christmas, Mr. Landlord, where ever you are.

The wino caught me as I left the booth. His voice holding me like claws. I took out the handful·of change and gave it to him, saving back a dime for a later call to the landlord.

The wino was old and almost toothless, the gray tongue raking around the place where the teeth were missing.

"Merry Christmas," the wino said, holding the change in his balled hand as if it will fly away.

CHAPTER TWELVE
NEW HAVEN, 1967
AND WHO IS HELEN
TWELVETREES?

Morning now. I have been alone all night...which is fine when you consider that my bed sleeps no more than one without difficulty. At least I comfort myself that way when I awake to the stillness and the cold sheet beside me. The pillow with the scent of my own winter sweat, overpowering the perfume, cologne, and hair shampoo that Sylvia wore. Under the sweat somewhere but lost.

Morning. From my window, I see that there is little sun and the day is dark and overcast.

A womb-day, a friend of mine used to call it back in the Chapel Hill days. Reach out and grab the edges of it and pull it down around you like a big pink womb. But he'd been smoking some dope that morning while working on his (he said) massive novel that would expose the root causes of drunkenness in West Virginia. When completed. Nobody had ever seen any of the novel so it was possible that conceits like this one about the overcast day and the womb were his way of reminding us that he was a writer. Or it was the dope.

His name was Miles. He was a thin, gangling boy who'd dropped out of the University to write his novel and, in some special way of knowing who was balling and who wasn't, the rest of us on the Alley had decided that he was probably a virgin. Not only that but there was some feeling that he was trying to decide whether he liked boys or girls. So, the fragment from Robert Frost had become a kind of catchword: " ... miles to go before I sleep ... " which meant that it was better not to go to sleep around Miles just in case he decided to jump off the wrong side of the fence.

Fences. I found my shower shoes and went into the bathroom, leaning on the wash basin and trying to decide if I wanted to shave. A different fence. Sylvia had jumped off the night before. I'd known for a long time that it was coming, so maybe it shouldn't matter now that it had happened. Somehow it did matter and it bothered me that she'd jumped to the far side of the fence where I couldn't see her anymore, where I had a lot of trouble ... here at the bathroom mirror staring at the reddish glint of a day's growth of beard ... remembering exactly what she looked like.

I'd met her a month or so before, a week or two into January. Now other news had been added to the original word I'd spread around the school: the divorce proceedings were underway. That brought another flood of invitations, some of them more absurd than others. Several times I found myself expected to charm some plain or utterly ugly girl. This match-making for losers defined me in their eyes. Still, a couple of times I'd been so charming, had tried so hard, that it was all I could do to keep from going to bed with them.

The party where I met Sylvia ... that was the most absurd party of all. Bud Guess, one of the third-year actors, had rented a cottage in North Haven and he decided to have a cookout. It didn't seem to matter to him that it was near freezing that Sunday afternoon. It only mattered that the cottage came with a cinder-block barbecue pit and he wanted to use it.

It was some indication of the winter boredom in New Haven that fifty people showed up, to stand in overcoats and gloves, either drinking or holding franks on straightened out coat hangers over the charcoal bed of the pit.

I'd come early to help set the party up and I'd been busy for a time so I didn't notice her at first. To this day I don't know which of Bud's friends brought her or invited her ... and then ignored her. I was busy getting the fire hot enough to cook the franks, choking from the wind shifted smoke. Then I turned around and saw her. She was sitting in one of the low children's swings that the occupants before Bud had installed and then declined to take with them when they left. Sitting there alone, long legs pushed out in front of her, she looked quite cold and lost and left out. I must have some special affinity for the cold and the lost because from the moment I saw her, I wanted to touch her, to discover the texture of the skin in the small of her back.

Of course, in time I did discover the texture of the skin in the small of her back. The graying now, but bluish red tissue of old stretch marks. That first day very little happened. I introduced myself and we talked about theatre as a beginning point and then about books until we agreed that *The Idiot* was the greatest novel ever written.

Afterwards, I mixed her drinks from my bottle and once I smoked myself well cooking her a frank over the dying coals. She ate the hotdog with her eyes on me, as if I'd given her the greatest gift in the world and with such relish and gusto that I had to stop myself, saying *quit that, everything is not a symbol.*

The party didn't last as long as Bud had thought it would. The temperature seemed to be dropping with the sun, the long shadows moving across the yard. The guests left for warmer places, the chills and shivers in their voices as they said their goodbyes. Sylvia remained to help clean up and, when we were almost done with it, Bud left to drive the last of his guests into New Haven.

For one moment, one static moment, she stood.in the kitchen door-way, eyes locked into mine, until neither of us could breathe. And said, "I wish you'd hug me."

Which I did, but so well, I found out two days later, that I cracked three of her ribs.

At that moment, I didn't know and her thin rib cage pressed against my chest gave no sign of pain, only the thump and ruptured lurch of her heart. Because I am slow, unable or unwilling to know what comes next, I stood with my back hard against the door frame, holding her like I might a frightened or angry child, until the moment was past and we both stepped away at the same time, a bit shamed by what had happened and what had not happened.

I waited two days before I called and Sylvia met me at MacTriff's for a couple of drinks. Early in the week, MacTriff's was nearly empty and dull. It wasn't hard to suggest that she drive out to Bud's cottage with me to pick up a part of a bottle of Irish and some beer I'd left there. I knew Bud wasn't there. He'd started work on a major production the Monday after the party and he'd be tied up until around one a.m.

He'd said I could use the cottage for anything I wanted to, stressing the *anything*. He'd seen my room once and knew why I didn't want to take a girl there. He'd said that a girl could go to my room with one purpose in mind and end up, instead, talking about slum landlords.

It was as if, in the days between meetings, I had decided what I wanted to happen and she had decided what she wanted to happen. Every move we made from the time we entered the cottage until we stood naked beside the sofa seemed sculptured and choreographed so that there was economy and beauty in it all. Then I could discover the texture of the small of her back but not before I saw the wide overlapping band of adhesive tape on her left side, extending from the center of her back to a point just beyond the tips of her ribs in front.

"Did I do this?" Touching the tape, sticky where the edges were, the smell of it on my fingers.

Nodding. "But it doesn't hurt now."

"I'm sorry,"

"Don't be. I asked you to hug me."

I said, "I forget how strong I am at times."

"You are strong." The chill of wonder in her voice.

Still not touching, the red flare of light through the window of Bud's old oil heater wrapping around her body in the dark room, like a photograph burning from the edges inward.

"You are strong enough not to touch me." No censure in her voice, only a shading of regret.

"That," I said, "is not strength," and touched her. Gently, tenderly where the tape was.

The precarious beginning. The precarious continuing. Later that night, oppressed by the dry heat in the cottage, we dressed and went out into the dark yard. Above the elms and the judas tree the ice frost of stars. Sylvia took my hand and led me around the side of the cottage to the cinderblock cooking pit. "You were here the first time I saw you," she said.

"Yes, here."

"I thought you looked very kind and very distinguished," Then she stepped up onto the narrow ledge on the near side of the cooking pit. It was a ledge only six or eight inches wide and she stood, still holding my hand, until I climbed into the ledge in front of her. Close together, our heads back, dizzy with the star distance and the bare limb patterns of the trees, the Irish whiskey we'd been drinking. I was afraid we'd lose our balance and fall.

"Careful," I said.

"You'll take care of me, won't you?" Of course. Nodding only. "I knew you would."

But somewhere in my right shoulder, a tired and not often used muscle began its nervous pulsing and I knew that I was not young enough to be climbing towers with young girls, not strong enough to withstand the winter chill without a topcoat and a scarf.

"I'm cold."

"Yes," she said, " I can feel you shivering."

It was Saturday night, near midnight, at her apartment. It was the same week and our second date. Her dinner guests had just left: a one-legged city planner and his wife. The wife had a flat round face, a face like a Moon Pie. Just looking at her, all evening, I could feel how it was as a child, with the waxy chocolate of the Moon Pie stuck to my teeth. The city planner was thin, a body that seemed to be one long connected bone. He'd had the bad taste to wear ankle length socks so that when he crossed his legs, a section of the artificial leg showed. It had been a pale tan leather at one time but now the oily splotches of use stained it.

I helped Sylvia stack the dishes in the sink, there for the maid when she came in on Monday. I stood beside the kitchen window, drinking cognac, feeling the late winter snowstorm shake the pane against my right elbow.

Sylvia, at the kitchen counter, back to me, went on putting the leftovers away. "I put clean sheets on the bed."

Then behind her, looking down past her shoulder at three artichokes. "Is that an invitation?"

"Yes." The artichokes ladled into the storage bowl, the snap of the plastic top.

Hours later, pillows doubled behind our heads, we faced the window that looked out over the street. Dark in the bedroom and beyond the thinning, slowly falling snow there was the glow of a single street light. Sylvia shifted her weight and placed her head against my collar bone. "Beautiful."

"Yes. When I was a child in Georgia it never snowed. I had to wait until I got to Chapel Hill before...."

"No, I meant us. It was beautiful, wasn't it?

"Beautiful and tragic and full of soul."

The head lifted from my collarbone. "Why is it tragic?"

"No," I said, "that's only a catchword, something I heard a coed say one night coming out of a movie."

"Please don't use catchwords." The weight against my collarbone once more.

"All right. No more catchwords."

The taste of cognac on the rough edge of her tongue when we kiss. "It wasn't ugly, was it?"

"Don't be silly."

"I couldn't stand it if it got ugly," she said.

A single drop of sweat begins in my right armpit and races down my side. "Why should it?"

"It usually does."

Usually. I filed that word away. *Usually.*

A Sunday afternoon, days gone by, seated now by a fireplace where a huge log burned. After a cold, frozen hike around the block, a large shot of cognac in a snifter warmed my hand.

"Your drinking bothers me," she said.

"Really?" I said.

"Yes, it does."

"I don't drink that much."

"But you drink all the time."

"You're exaggerating."

"No, you've always got a bottle or a glass in your hand."

Nag. Nag. I smiled and shook my head.

"The drinking covers up something bitter in you."

I sniffed the cognac fumes but didn't drink yet.

"The real you, I don't know the real you."

"It's not important."

"You're somebody else when you drink."

"The monster comes out?"

"You cracked my ribs…"

"That was passion."

I took a swallow of the cognac, letting it trickle down my throat. "There." Sylvia pointed at the snifter. "See what I'm talking about."

For her, that was the proof, the point nailed to the wall forever, and I could only shake my head and look away from her while the log snapped in the fireplace and the brandy soured in my stomach.

At her bedroom door a week ago, a movie and a late dinner behind us, reading the time after midnight while I waited for her to finish in the bathroom. She came out dressed in pajamas and a robe. I turned in the door frame to let her pass and at the same time I put out an arm to stop her.

"I don't feel like it tonight," she said.

I said nothing, allowing myself only a minor shrug.

"Women are different from men. Sometimes they don't want to."

I said I'd better go home then.

"You'll call me?"

I said that I would.

Out in the hallway, only two steps away from the door, I heard the whack of the night latch. At the bottom of the stairs, I turned off the stairwell lights and closed the outside door quietly behind me.

It all led to the night in MacTriff's. It was a Friday night, the night for the hawks and scavengers, when men prowl the aisles, eyes upon the girls who sit alone or in pairs. In the back far corner, on a low platform, a gay piano player with curled hair and a drunk bass player frill and lace and staggered their way through *Green Dolphin Street.*

Sylvia wasn't happy. Hardly the first drink placed in front of us and across the aisle from us a drunk woman did something to offend her. The woman, gap teeth showing in a slack mouth, wore a sheer white blouse. Suddenly, defiantly, as if on a dare from the two men with her, the woman reached behind her, unbuttoned two or three buttons, unhooked her bra, and slipped it out of the back of her blouse. She balled the bra up and dropped it into her purse. Then, while the two men laughed and applauded, she threw back her shoulders and thrust out the small breasts which had flat round nipples the shape and color of oyster crackers.

"It's so common," Sylvia said.

"Yes," I said, "Tacky."

But in a corner of my mind I rolled, one of the nipples between my thumb and forefinger until it creaked and crumbled like an oyster cracker. Dust falling into my palm.

I decided that it was best to leave, the drinks paid for but hardly touched. We made the short walk to my room and there, on my last clean pair of sheets, we began to make love. Deep in her thighs, feeling wild and happy, I wanted to believe that the distance had gone away and that everything was fine again.

"I'm sorry." Her words choked by my lunges. "I don't know what's wrong but I don't feel anything from the waist down."

The gentleman that I think I am I stopped what he was doing and poured each of us a splash of cognac and sat on the edge of the bed beside her, waiting for her to say something.

Which she didn't. Until the silence grew around us as solid as setting concrete and the filtered light from the street beyond burned us in shadow against the walls. Until she moved past me and dressed in the bathroom. At the partly opened door she said goodnight and left.

I waited for an hour, the curtain drawn back on one side of the bathroom window, looking out at the street past the dirty ice crust the street crew had piled on the side of the walk. While I watched an old wino stopped by the snow mound and after looking in both directions pissed while billows of condensation floated around him. It lasted a long time, it seemed to me.

When the hour was up, I took a hot shower and then a cold shower and then a hot shower, followed by another cold shower. Not that it made me feel any better. Maybe it was worse really, knowing that it was supposed to ease the groin ache. At least, I remembered someone telling me that it would. But maybe that was back in high school and I'm too old for that to work now. Anyway, the hour was up and she hadn't come back. I poured the two untouched cognacs back into the bottle and got myself a beer from the outside window ledge where I kept them in cold weather. For February, the room seemed awfully cold but after a while I got used to it and I turned on the TV set to watch part of the late movie.

I think it starred Helen Twelvetrees but I wouldn't swear to it.

CHAPTER THIRTEEN
NEW HAVEN, 1967
AND ONE MONTH I
PLAYED WORD GAMES

March is the bad month, not April, no matter what banker-poets or poet-bankers tell you. Not trusting the banker part of him, can I trust the poet part? No, and for me, March seems to have a special kind of chemistry, just the approach of April at a distance and there is a unique pollen in the emotional air. In brief, I catch my first and only cough and cold of the year. It is a violent one. It racks me with harsh spasms. It splatters the walls, the doors, and the floors with mucous.

Just the thought of all that mucous and I vomit violently, the remains of careful breakfasts and black strands and ropes of coffee. And then ... after a week ... it is gone and I have prepared myself for April.

This March was the same and yet quite different. The illness was the same: I coughed and retched and blew my nose until it was crusty and the inside tissue felt like somebody had strapped a straight-edged razor on it. I waited out the week patiently, marking off the days in my mind, saying four more days and then three more and then two more and one. And then it was over.

I woke up the eighth day to a bright March morning, the wind swirling down the narrow alley by my window, the sound like somebody whistling between their teeth. I was weak but I knew that I could have breakfast now without the danger of having to see it again an hour later. Still, as I shaved and showered, I knew that it was different this time. I didn't look forward to the day.

Maybe that was the aftermath of Sylvia. I hadn't seen her since that night and I hadn't called ... though a couple of times I'd dialed the first three or four numbers ... standing in a street booth or at MacTriff's bar phone ....before I put the receiver back on the hook and talked myself out of it. More than once I'd shamed myself out of the call by making up the conversation, I knew we'd have.

"So it's you?" she'd say.

"Yes, it's me," I'd say.

Hard silence while we both breathed deeply and coughed politely into the receivers. "I thought I'd call and see how you are."

"I'm fine."

I'd wait, knowing that her proper upbringing dictates the proper question.

"How are you?"

"Lonely, very lonely."

Surprised at myself, snapping at the words as if to catch them in my teeth and chew them up and swallow them.

"I'm sorry about that, but I don't feel that we ought to start ...."

"Oh, I didn't mean to ... "

I'd let the words tail off as if it meant so little that it wasn't worth finishing.

"Well, I've got something on the stove and if I don't ... Sure, well I'll see you."

"Goodbye."

"Goodbye"

And I'd try to hang up before I heard the click from her phone. Somehow it seemed important that she hear my click instead.

So I didn't call her and the days when I was sick I didn't call her...I told myself...because I didn't want her to see me that way. It was too much like being a male version of *Camille*. Me coughing my life away and a last minute reconciliation. Hugs and tears and some sad and hopeless balling in my narrow bed until everything was right again...and I died.

Just thinking about Sylvia took some of the edge off my breakfast hunger. I was at the bathroom mirror, combing my hair so that it covered the bald spot on top, when on impulse I took the thin bar of soap from the dish and wrote, using the wet edge, *LOVE SUCKS* in large letters on the mirror. Then, in some odd way satisfied, I went off to look for my friends to see how they would react to my resurrection.

The next morning, after shaving, I wiped off *LOVE SUCKS* with a wad of wet toilet paper and replaced it with *WITHOUT EXCEPTION*. That remained on the mirror until the next morning which I erased it and wrote *EVERYTIME*. Then, *IN TOTO*, not really sure that it followed, but I was in a hurry, about to be late for a class and I didn't even have time for a shower.

Though no one saw them except me, I began to call them futility statements and I'd spend a part of each day trying to decide what the statement for the next day would be. As I moved away from the *LOVE SUCKS* sequence, away from the series into the single statement, I have a choice of three or four and I'd polish and hone them, withholding the final selection until the morning when I was under the shower.

While the futility statements grew bleak and dark, I found that the depression within me seemed to ease. It might have been the approach of April, a certain brightness that overshadowed the usual ugliness of New Haven. The wind had a green scent and I thought about the ocean often, about catching a bus down to the beach and looking at the waves for a while.

So, without knowing it was coming to an end, I did my last two futility statements. The first one popped into my head one morning and I didn't, at the time, remember where it came from. I wrote *SEX IS HOPE*.

I left that on the mirror for a week, partly because I liked what it said but also because of the realization that HOPE had somehow worked itself into one of the statements. That appeared to be a go sign and I felt I needed all the good signs I could muster.

After the first three days or so I wasn't reading it anymore. I shaved with part of it blocking my face or I splattered it with tooth paste or hunched over below it as I arranged my hair ... all without seeing the statement. It was, therefore, surprising when I realized where it came from. It had been years ago, when I'd been an undergraduate. I'd had two courses under Dr. Earl Holcomme in the English department and I thought he was God. I'd asked him to read John Bell Clayton's *Six Angels At My Back*, not to test him, but to have him reaffirm that he could walk on water. A few days later, at a chance and hurried meeting in Polk Place, Dr. Holcomme said, "That book you loaned me ... in it, Sex is Hope." Then he'd rushed off to some meeting or other. Now, looking back at it, I realized that it wasn't a pointless, curt remark or a scholarly dismissal of the book. It just seemed that way at the time.

When the week was up, I wiped SEX IS HOPE from the mirror with the wet end of a towel I was sending to the laundry that day. Just on impulse, without trying it out first, I turned it around and wrote HOPE IS SEX. But as soon as it was on the mirror, I knew that it wasn't the same thing at all. But, just in case, on the chance that it might assume a meaning, I left it on the mirror for the day and went down to Marty's Cafe for breakfast.

CHAPTER FOURTEEN
NEW HAVEN, 1967
THE FIRST TWO
COMMANDMENTS
AND THAT'S ALL

I hadn't intended to write my own decalogue. It just happened and there wasn't anything I could do about it. I was doodling in the theatre history class, writing over and over again, *just because you want something*, while I was thinking of Sylvia. I wanted to see her but I knew that too much time had passed. March had ended with the futility statements and April suffered my attempts at resignation. Maybe it was the result of the two months of introspection, as if knowing myself would help me accept it, that gave me the final half of the first commandments

… doesn't mean that somebody else has to want it.

That seemed so much to the point, so right, that I copied it down on a clean sheet of paper and marked it #1. I didn't know at the time how long it would be before I'd write the second one. And I had no idea that I would have to see Sylvia gain to find the inspiration for it.

✤   ✤   ✤

It had been a terrible war movie. I left my seat and went into the lobby several times to smoke a cigarette. When I returned, I found that I hadn't missed much: the nurse was still mad at the hero because he was too cynical about the value of 11fe … not having seen him cry when he had to write the letter back to the family of his radioman … and the black from New York City and the southern poor white grit (from an unspecified part of the south) were still carrying on their own personal war in the middle of the other war and the cowardly young soldier from the Midwest was cracking up because he secretly believed that he'd caused his best friend's death. I sat through the last twenty minutes while they tied up all the loose ends, using the time to pick the wax out of my ears. The cowardly soldier … his name was Bert … died doing something brave, going out into the jungle against orders to try to rescue a wounded man from his outfit. With all that pain, after the sniper got him, he managed a smile that meant he didn't have to worry about being a coward anymore. The black from New York and the poor white grit got caught in hand-to-hand combat with six or eight of the enemy and saved each other's lives a time or two and after it was over they were seen exchanging addresses so that they could visit each other after the war. The hero, wounded and flown back to the States, leaves his hospital bed to go out to that little town in the midwest for the funeral of the cowardly soldier, Bert, who'd received the Medal of Honor. The nurse is at the funeral too … though it's never explained why she's there … and after taps and the rifle salute she's standing behind him and he doesn't know she's there. He turns around and she sees the tears and he's ashamed and she says something like, "The smog's terrible out here … so bad I just lost a contact lens," and he blinks his eyes and sniffs a couple of times and agrees. The last shot is one of those extreme high angle ones that shows us the whole cemetery and all the people going in all directions away from the fresh grave and the hero and the nurse are heading toward his car and you just know that they're headed for a motel where they're going to ball all day and night and drink ice cold good American beer and then live happily ever after. For the first year, at least.

It was around par for the usual afternoon movie. I could have stayed home and watched one pretty much like it on television. But that wasn't what I wanted. I needed to be out and away from the room, the distraction that spending the bright afternoon in the darkness watching absurd images gave me. I picked the films carefully. I saw only adventure, war, murder mystery and detective films. I avoided the New Wave films and the ones with obvious social messages. I didn't want to care, I wanted those flat, wallpaper thin characters that I'd spent my childhood caring about. The caring without really caring, concern while still being sure that it would all work out.

I headed away from the theatre, blinking into the near four o'clock slanted sun and feeling a little disoriented as I often was after going to an afternoon film. As I turned onto Chapel Street, I found myself face-to-face with Sylvia. She was coming out of a dress shop and blinking herself, into the sun and we stood for a few startled seconds blinking at each other. For a hysterical moment, I thought she was the nurse character out of the movie, that she was going to say something about the smog and her contact lenses. Instead, while she searched in her purse and took out a pair of sunglasses, she said hello.

I said hello also.

Then, as she concealed herself behind the glasses, I asked if she'd like a drink.

The Captain's Chair is a bar I'd passed on the way to Chapel Street. It's a mishmash of fish nets and mounted fish and portholes with painted blue-green water and the suggestion of a perspective horizon off there somewhere in the distance. The waitress brought our drinks, a gin and tonic for Sylvia and a beer for me, and then stood at the far end of the bar, painting her nails with a metallic gray polish, blowing on the polish and then waving her hands around in the air as if warding off trees.

"I thought I might run into you sometime." I said and looked away from her, engrossed in the correct adjustment of the head on my beer.

"It's nice that we did." The tone was so neutral that I could read nothing into it.

"I just thought we might." That lame and crippled remark rolled off the edge of my tongue while she looked at me and nodded slowly, calculatingly.

"I've been thinking about you," she said. I sipped at my beer, waiting.

"I think you might need help." She paused and then with more certainty and forces "No, I've decided that you need help."

"I'll take all the help I can get."

"I knew you'd say that."

"It's my southern background," I said. "I agree to almost everything a lady suggests."

Then, while I choked on my beer, she suggested that I make an appointment with the Yale University psychiatrist. "After your treatment's underway, there's no reason why we can't see each other two or three times a week." She dipped her finger into the gin and tonic and trapped the wedge of lime against the side of the glass. "We'd start once a week … perhaps a weekend night … and then, if your therapy's going well, who knows?" She smiled, the smile surfacing all the thoughts of bed that I'd tried to keep away, the jerky stop-motion, freeze frame of being inside her, the coarse stiff hair that cut me sometimes, the liquid sheathe of her that could scald me if I let myself be surprised, and the sometimes when she went down on me, her tongue with the changing texture that could be as rough as hemp twine or as delicate as still, slow breath. "I'm not sure I want to."

"It could make all the difference in the world." She lifted the wedge of lime and bit into it. "For you and for us." The lime meat bitten away she dropped the rind into the ashtray.

"I'm not sure what I'm supposed to tell the psychiatrist."

"Why, the truth."

I looked at her. "I'm not sure what you think the truth is."

"It's not a matter of what I think." She sounded exasperated. "It's what you know to be the truth."

I shook my head. "Like what?"

"Well, first of all your drinking," She said. I agreed. That was a safe beginning. "Then there are all those scars from your marriage. Your inability to love,"

I nodded. That wasn't as safe. True or not.

"Also," she said, lowering her voice and leaning toward me, "there's the problem you think you have with your manhood, the way you're always demanding oral sex." She made a little face. "It's disgusting."

"I'm supposed to tell him that?"

"That first of all. Most of all. That'll give him something to work with."

"But it's not true."

Eyes level with mine, face serious, she nodded several times emphatically. "It's true. It's all too true." Her face set in concrete, saying, oh, how you have made me suffer, what you have made me endure. What I have had to put up with.

After we'd said goodbye outside the bar, walking through the afternoon crowds, I realized that I'd promised to call the Infirmary and make an appointment. The realization was something like walking into a door in the dark.

❦ ❦ ❦

Two afternoons later. A sunny cool day. I thought about stopping at MacTriff's for a couple of beers on the way to the Infirmary. I talked myself out of it on the grounds that alcohol on my breath might register on some scale the psychiatrist used for first impressions.

As I'd promised, I made the call the morning after I'd seen Sylvia. The secretary who answered had seemed abrupt. "Is it urgent?"

"What do you mean by urgent?"

"Dr. Vastellin is very busy. If it can wait a week or a month … ?"

Visions of thighs and breasts. "It can't wait that long."

"Then it's urgent?"

"To me it is."

She gave me the two o'clock appointment with the implied thrust of "it had damned well better be."

Dr. Vastellin's secretary was young, not more than twenty. She looked like one of that legions of girls right out of high school and shorthand and typing classes who find jobs at hospitals with the hope of meeting and marrying a doctor. They're usually a fraction overdressed and overgroomed and finally a little pathetic a few years later when they find out it hasn't worked. The body they thought they'd bargain with while it was young has now grown a few years older, the skin tone's fading, and then they settle for a blue-collar worker and the bitterness that goes with that.

This girl had a few years to go and the arrogance of someone who spent her days typing the case histories and really knew you inside out. I could tell that she remembered me and we sat staring at each other for a few minutes, me trying estimate how many years it would take before the realization hit her and her trying to diagnose my special kind of sexual perversion. Until the intercom buzzed and I was told that the doctor would see me now.

I was surprised to find that there wasn't a couch in the room. Only a large desk and two comfortable chairs and floor to ceiling bookcases overflowing with books and journals. There was a large double window directly behind the desk and I sat and looked out at the gothic nightmare of the campus skyline. At first there were only the standard questions and answers and I think we both took that time to study each other.

Dr. Vastellin seemed to be in his late thirties or early forties, going a little toward weight now though he'd probably been athletic once, with incredibly blue-black hair and a five o'clock shadow that seemed to be pigment rather than rapidly growing beard. He had a long horse face, with a feminine mouth and small, even and almost delicate teeth. His voice was pitched a little high, though when he seemed aware of it, he made an effort to lower the register somewhat.

The basic facts out of the way, he put the legal pad aside."What seems to be the problem?"

"I'm not sure."

He tapped the desk top impatiently. "Is it sexual?"

"I guess some of it is."

"What part?"

"I'm not sure."

"Men or women?"

"Women ... That is, one woman."

"Your problem is with this one woman?"

"Yes."

"A sexual problem?"

"It seems to be."

"Impotence? Premature ejaculation?"

"None of those."

"Sexual demands she won't gratify?"

"She says I demand she blow me all the time. "

"I see."

"But I don't think I do."

"No demands at all?"

(The first time it happened with Sylvia, it had been early morning and she's been holding it and saying how wonderful it was and then she leaned forward and run her tongue around the foreskin ridge. She felt it jump in her hand and she looked at me and asked "do you like that?")

"I like it ... if that's a demand?"

"More than other intercourse?"

"As much as."

"But you didn't say do this, do that?"

"No, but sometimes she asked if I wanted her to."

"And what did you say?"

"I said, yes, please."

"And now something has happened?"

"She thinks it's ugly now."

"Your a sex organ?"

"No, screwing, everything."

"And that's your fault?"

"It must be. She thinks so."

"How is it your fault?"

"I don't know."

"But she believes that it is?"

"She says so."

"Do you hurt her? Do you try to hurt her?"

"No."

"How is it ugly?"

"It just is ... for her."

"Fine, except ... "

"When she thinks it's ugly?"

"Yes."

"I see."

"There are other things I'm supposed to tell you."

"What?"

"Things she told me to tell you about."

"She *told* you to tell me?"

"Yes, my drinking she says is to cover up some bitterness."

"What else?" Dr. Vestellin made a note on his legal pad.

"My inability to love. That's what she calls it."

We spent a few minutes talking about my drinking and the marriage, and what I felt about it. Mainly it seemed that I was talking, prodded by him now and then when I slowed down. He listened without making any notes, and once or twice looked out of the skyline, but it was obvious that he was still listening. When I finished, he waited for a long count of 10, as if to be sure that I wasn't going to add something else. Then he nodded and stood up.

"I can't help you. You've just got one of those human problems."

I shook my head.

"It's something you are to discover for yourself."

"Discover what?"

"I can't tell you."

"Tell me what?"

"That's not the way therapy is supposed to work."

"Go ahead and break a rule."

"It might not be your problem."

I thanked him and left his office. As I passed through the waiting room, I heard him telling the secretary that there would be no case history on me. I could feel the secretary's disappointment strike between my shoulders just before I closed the hallway door behind me.

I went to MacTriff's. I thought about calling Sylvia. I kept putting it off until later, and then some of the guys from the school came in during the early evening, and we sat around one of the booths until around midnight. At 1 a.m, I left and started home. About a half a block from my place, I vomited against the side of a red brick building, the force of it splattering my pants cuffs and shoes. Then I went home and passed out.

The stain was there the next morning when I passed by, dried now, a kind of yellowish-red kidney shape with a texture of lumps and strands. It is the new art, I thought, holding my breath until I was past it. New art out of new materials. Out of my gut, the artist might say. And then I gave up the whole metaphor as being absurd.

I waited another two days before I called Sylvia. I reached her in the late afternoon at her apartment. I told her that I'd been to see the Man. She sounded pleased about that but not too pleased that I wouldn't tell her over the phone what the Man had said.

"That's childish of you," she said.

"It's kind of complicated." I hesitated, to give the hook time enough to set. "And a little difficult."

The hook was in. She said that she had to go out for a while but she'd be back between nine and nine-thirty. "If you get there before I do, you can let yourself in. You know where the key is, don't you? Make yourself some coffee or a drink. Now I've got to run. There's something on the stove and it might burn." And she said goodbye and hung up.

I don't know where she'd found that "something on the stove" excuse, but I'd been there several times when she'd used it on people as a way of getting them off the phone. It bothered me that she didn't vary it from time to time, a bath she was running, someone at the door or ... or, as it had been with me when I was there, someone in bed with a hard-on that might go away. One night she'd held onto it, stroking·it, moving the foreskin gently back and forth … and at one point when the girl at the other end of the line was talking at some length she'd leaned over and taken it in her mouth and gurgled. Like a baby. Receiver still at her ear, listening until the girl had stopped, then she'd straightened up and let me slip away and gone on talking about clothes and the party the girl was giving the following Saturday. To say a minute or so later, "And now I've got to run. I've got something on the stove and it might burn."

It was after ten when I heard the key in the lock. I stacked my theatre history notes in my briefcase and zipped it closed. I reached the front door about the time she entered and reached past her to put my briefcase on the table beside the door.

"You're here. Good." She dropped her purse on top of my brief case. "Sorry I'm late. I couldn't help it." She gave me a brief hug in passing and stepped away from me, unbuttoning her blouse as she reached the bedroom door. "I'm so tired and it's late and I've got to get up early in the morning and catch the train to New York."

I was still near the front door, watching her "I can come back another night."

Now from the lighted bedroom, her voice muffled some by the partly closed door. "No, we can talk while I wash my hair."

I waited in the hallway, seeing the complete bedroom in the back of my eye, reconstructing her movements by the sounds of drawers opening and closing, the closet door's squeak, the metallic tingle of bed springs, the thuck-thuck of shoes dropped on the floor. "I won't be a minute …

She was wearing only a bra and a half slip when she came back into the hall and walked toward the bathroom. Her eyes glided past me as if I weren't there. But, from the bathroom, she said, "Come talk to me."

I leaned in the doorway, shoulder against the frame.

"Tell me what he said." Not facing me, looking up into the open medicine cabinet, moving the bottles around until she selected a jar of shampoo.

I hadn't planned to do it. It just happened. One moment I was in the doorway and the next I was pressed up against her back, one hand sliding along her hip and the other dipping past the elastic band and brushing against the pubic hair.

"I don't want to. Not tonight."

I backed away from her, until I was against the door frame again.

"I've got a bacterial infection of some kind." She placed the bathmat under the sink and began to shampoo her hair. "Tell me what he said."

I told her, almost word-for-word. By the time I finished she'd rinsed most of the soap out of her hair and had wrapped a towel around her head.

"And that was all he said?"

"That was it."

"He doesn't sound like a very good psychiatrist to me."

"I thought he was pretty good," I said.

She pulled the plastic shower curtain down the full length of the tub, leaving an opening at the end near me. "Because he said what you wanted him to?"

"Maybe."

"Because you want to believe what he said?"

"I guess so."

"You weren't honest with him. That's why he couldn't help you" Facing me, she unhooked the bra and dropped it into the wicker clothes hamper. The small breasts shook free, creased and deep red where the bra had cut into the flesh. "No wonder he said what he did." The half-slip and the panties followed the bra and the hamper slammed shut. The pubic hair had been trimmed, the triangle smaller, ready for her swim suit. "If you'd told him the truth …" She crossed in front of me and stepped into the tub, taking the towel from her head and dropping it on the floor. Just before she turned on the shower she continued, "… he'd have said some things you didn't want to hear."

I watched her shower. At first, she seemed to concentrate on rinsing the shampoo from her hair. But after a while, she went on to shower the rest of her, luxuriating in the process of soaping her pubic hair, stroking the soap into her breasts. After she'd rinsed completely I handed her a towel from the linen shelf and waited while she dried herself. "But I guess you don't want help."

"If all you say is true, I guess I don't."

From the bedroom doorway, puffing on a cigarette, I watched while she dressed in her pajamas and turned back the bed covers.

"I've got to get up early in the morning," she said.

I nodded. "I'd better leave then."

I was part way to the front door when she called me back. "I couldn't do that."

"What?" I asked.

"What you just did. I couldn't stand there and watch somebody I wanted … naked and in the shower … and just stand there. I'd have to do something. I just couldn't stand there like you did."

"You might be right."

"Maybe you ought to tell that to the psychiatrist the next time you see him."

I shook my head. I got my briefcase and left.

At the bus stop a block away, staring down the street for the first glimpse of the bus headlights, the second commandment began to form inside me. By the time the bus arrived I had it worked out. It was really simple after I'd worked at it for a few minutes. *Just because somebody else wants something.* … I got on the bus and found a seat near the side door, Except for a drunk sailor and an old black man the bus was empty,... *doesn't mean that you have to want it.*

That seemed to cover everything, every situation. I decided that I didn't need to make up the other eight,

CHAPTER FIFTEEN
NEW HAVEN, 1967
THE VOYEURS DON'T
LIVE HERE ANY MORE

It was an afternoon in late May and it was all done. All except the dissertation. Exams over, term papers in on time, and all the final grades in the Chairman's office. It had been a bad two or three weeks but now I was calm again, over the dex and with two full nights of sleep behind me.

The movers had been in my room for only about an hour during the morning. It had taken them that long to box up the books and clothes and load them on the truck. They'd seemed a little disappointed at the meager nature of my belongings and they'd seemed unwilling to make any predictions about when I could expect my things to arrive in Millhouse. To be honest, it didn't matter. I had the whole summer ahead of me and I didn't have a teaching job for the fall. The books and clothes could float around in limbo for a year for all the need I'd have of them.

After lunch, I went by my bank to close out my account and stopped by MacTriff's for a beer. It was slow, almost nobody there, and I'd have left if Mason and Robert hadn't come in. They were both in the class behind me and I didn't know them well.

Mason was a theatre tech, big and fleshy with a receding hair line. He always wore high cut shoes with steel reinforced toes and

he always carried a slide rule in a leather holster on his hip. I'd
seen him at the Christmas party the year before and he'd been
wearing the slide rule then to. Maybe he slept with it under his
pillow.

The other student with him, Robert, was English, Oxford
educated, in the PHD program in theatre history. Thin, pale
skinned, with bright red hair and a bushy thick mustache. We
ordered beers and carried them to the front window booth. With
the blinds up we could look out at the people passing by. Not that
we did at first. There were classes to talk about and rumors to
pass around and Robert, in his clipped accent, kept saying, "You
lucky bastard" to me, meaning that he envied me because I was
through with the course work. At first, I didn't mind, but after
the fifth or sixth time I began to feel that Robert didn't really like
me very much. I'd have left ... I was considering it ... but something shifted our attention outside.

Mason stood up and said, "Look at that."

Robert and I pushed back our chair and stood up. A beautiful blonde woman in her thirties was walking two boxer pups
past the bar front. When the woman was directly outside our
window, both pups suddenly decided to take a crap. One pup
made it to the curb but the other one didn't. When the embarrassed woman dragged the two pups away there was, on the sidewalk outside our window, a mound of fresh dogshit that must
have weighed a pound.

"This might be fun," Mason said, stopping me, when I started
to sit down again.

For around an hour we stood at the window, drinking beer,
and watching the reactions of the people passing by. Now and
then, a man or a woman would miss the mound narrowly and
walk on without being aware they'd been lucky.

Other times a man or a woman would step directly into it
and walk on apace or two before they noticed that the traction

had changed. They'd turn and look at the mound and their reactions ranged from disgust to amusement. Several people looked down at the last moment. Their last second adjustments to avoid it looked like some kind of grotesque ballet.

By the time the hour was up, the mound was flattened and Mason and Robert weren't as amused anymore. It was clouding up directly above the University to my right. A good heavy spring rain would wash it all away. The dogshit certainly... and, at times, I almost wished it would wash the town away too. Town that smelled of garlic and rancid olive oil, of roasted peppers, of whiskey sweat, the scent of rotten beaches when the wind blew in from the coast.

And then I saw Elaine. I hadn't seen her for several months, not since the day when Evadne and I had walked on the beach and I'd carried home the sad talisman of her tiny white socks.

"There's another one," Robert said. "Let's see what this lady does." That was no lady, that was...

Elaine wore a summer print dress, tight across her ass and open low above those breasts. Head up, 1 eking away from MacTriff's as if she knew I'd be inside.

"Squish!" Robert banged-his beer bottle on the table. "Dead center."

Not pausing, not noticing, gone past the scope of the window and out of sight.

Mason laughed. "She's going to get home and think she needs to wash her feet...

But I knew better. It wouldn't happen that way. There were special rules for Elaine. In the next block or so, she'd step into a small puddle of water where someone had just washed their windows. That would rinse the dogshit away. At the next corner, a laundry truck would take the turn a little too fast and a nice white fluffy towel would float out... as the rear door banged open... and land on the sidewalk just one moment before she stepped onto it … still not noticing … sank into the deep nap and walked on with a clean and perfect shoe.

"That was one of the best," Robert said.

She was all right in her time, I thought, and went and bought another round.

CHAPTER SIXTEEN

CHAPEL HILL, 1967

THE MORNING LOOKS
DIFFERENT SOMEHOW

The party was at Whit Brownlee's log cabin off the Old Durham Road. He lived there with Dottie George. Whit was a sort of modern version of a remittance man. The story was that his family in south Florida sent him money each month if he'd stay away. I'm not sure of the story but he had money and he didn't work. Dottie had come down from New York to do graduate work in Sociology. After the first semester, she moved in with Whit and not long after that she dropped out of school. Not that I knew this much at first. I didn't know them at all when I went to that party the Saturday night I arrived back in Chapel Hill.

I flew into Raleigh-Durham Airport at five-twenty and took the limousine in from the terminal to town. It rained off and on all the way, the fields to the left and right looking like small lakes at the low water mark. We seemed to drive into one storm and out and then into another one. I checked into the Carolina Inn and showered and walked the one block into the main part of Franklin Street. It was drizzling and I crossed to Sloan's Drug store and followed the awnings until I reached the middle of the block where I ducked under the Tempo Room Arch and down the dark stairs.

At first, it was too dark for me to see if I recognized anybody and it was a time before I got used to the stale odors. I sat at the bar and was halfway through a beer when I recognized a voice and turned on my stool and saw Max Pilgrim at one of the tables at the dark front end of the bar.

Max is a potter from Durham, a heavy meaty man going to beer belly. Everybody said he was a great potter, that he belonged in a larger city, but the only time I'd had anything to do with his pots it had been a big disappointment. I'd had him throw a teapot for mama for a Christmas present and he'd done a beautiful job, except that he'd experimented with the glaze and it hadn't worked. The tea Mama had made in the pot had had a kind of clay taste and, after a time, Mama had given up on it and made a flower pot out of it. It was an expensive flower pot.

While I was trying to decide whether I'd go over and sit with him, he brought an empty bottle up to the bar. I said, "Hello, Max" and he blinked at me and said, "Jesus H. Christ" and grabbed me by the shoulder with one of his square fingered hands.

"You back?" he asked. I said I was passing through on my way to Georgia, "Staying awhile?"

"A day or two." Then when the bartender brought his beer I said, "I'll sit with you if it's all right."

"There?" He jerked his head in the direction of the table where he'd been sitting. "That pig, I'm not going back over there." He perched on the stool next to me and leaned on the bar. "There's a party tonight. You up for a party?"

Up. That word again. "I might be. How about the girl over there?" I nodded toward the table he'd left.

"The dogs can have her." He tilted back the beer bottle and let it run down his throat. "In fact, you ask me tomorrow and I'll tell you the dogs did eat her."

I strained into the bad light. From the vague shape of her, she seemed to be a large girl. "What's wrong with her?"

Max shrugged. "Sometimes I don't know if she likes boys or girls. I'm not sure she knows either."

"A problem."

"You bet your ass it is."

I signaled the bartender for another round. I was telling Max about some of the bars in New Haven when I looked up and the girl was standing just behind him. She was a big girl, maybe an inch or so over six feet, and she must have weighed close to a hundred and eighty pounds. A pale face without makeup or lipstick. Brown hair cut close and short, to the shape of her head. Small, almost pointed ears pushing against the fringe of short hair.

"Max," the voice thin and a little hurt, "am I still going to the party with you?"

"Does a dog have wings?"

"I don't know what I did."

"Can a dog fly south in the winter?"

Her eyes whipped toward me and away and I got up and said, "Bathroom" and left them to whatever their trouble was.

The bathroom was the way I remembered it: the floor about an inch deep in piss and water, dark cigarette butts floating in it. I didn't have to piss, but I stood and looked down into the john for a minute and then flushed it. Outside, I sighed like somebody who felt relieved.

Max and the girl were still at it, heads together, the low rumble of their voices under the blast of the juke box but still there.

I didn't want to listen to them, so I put a dime in the Student Prince pinball machine and played it badly until the five balls were gone. Then I thought, piss on them, and went down to get my beer.

Max looked up. "There you are. Thought you got lost."

"I considered it."

"This is Marcia. She wants to know if we're taking her to the party."

"Up to you," I said, but I knew that was too abrupt and I grinned at her to soften it.

"Take a look at her ass."

"What?" I thought I'd misunderstood him.

"Take a look at that great ass she's got," Max said.

I shook my head. "No thanks."

"Go ahead," Max insisted. "She's proud of it. She knows it's made out of vanilla ice cream."

"Oh, shit." I stepped away from the bar a pace and looked down at her and then walked around her to my place at the bar.

"Right?" Max said.

"Grade A fantastic," I said.

"You better believe it. Does a dog have fleas? Does a girl suck and fuck?"

I looked at Marcia and her face flushed and she closed her eyes for an instant before she forced them open again.

"Right, Marcia?" Max moved over and offered Marcia his bar stool and took the one on the other side of her.

There were cars packed in the driveway bumper-to-bumper and others along the drainage ditch that bordered the highway. The house where Whit lived had been one of those old-style, high raftered tobacco barns before the government quotas came in. After the quotas it hadn't seemed worthwhile to keep the barn up and the owner had rented it to Whit at a low monthly rent, with the agreement that Whit would make certain improvements. He was supposed to add on a bathroom and partition off the one large room into a bedroom, living room and kitchen. The partitioning was mostly completed but the bathroom was yet to be done. There was a little shed to one side of the house and in one corner of the shed there was a crude outdoor privy.

Carrying a bag of beer, I followed Max and Marcia up the driveway and around the house into the backyard. It was somewhere after nine and the backyard was dark except for the glow from a shallow pit fire forty or fifty yards from the back steps.

There were small groups spread around the yard, some sitting on blankets and other standing. When I passed one of the groups, I got a whiff of grass and turned and looked at Max.

"Some law-breakers in every group," Max said. He led me up to the back steps, looking for Whit so he could introduce me. On the way, Marcia left us and stopped at one of the groups. Max noticed it and said that it didn't matter. He could find her in the dark by the smell. "She's got a crotch like a sewer." We stopped at the back steps and Max looked around for Whit. "Hey, maybe it is a sewer."

We didn't find Whit until two hours later. It turned out he was showing a visitor his grass patch. According to Max, it was some distance from the house and some of the stalks were eight or nine feet high. "If Whit don't watch out, the cops will spot it from a fire tower or a spotter plane."

Instead of Whit, we found Dottie George, the girl he was living with. Max introduced us and wandered off into the darkness, laughing and sniffing. I followed Dottie into the kitchen and put my sack of beer on the kitchen table. I took out a six-pack and offered her one.

"Real, honest to God Bud?" She thanked me and poured off some of it into a jelly glass. "We've been drinking Red Fox for so long I'd forgotten they made any other kind."

If I had to guess, I'd have put her age at the late twenties, maybe even edging toward thirty. It was hard to be sure because Dottie was the plainest, sexy woman I'd met in a long time.

Swarthy, with crooked teeth that needed cleaning, dark eyes without eyebrows and hair the color of coal.

"You smoke?" she asked.

"Sometimes."

She was pigeon breasted, the breast bone jutting out above the low-cut blouse.

"How about now?"

I nodded and she brought out cigarette papers and a spice jar from the rack above the stove. She rolled it well, thin and tight, so tight she didn't need to twist the end. Then she swept up the droppings and swallowed them. "Ever have hash candy?"

I said I hadn't.

"Tasty."

I lit it for her and we passed it back and forth, the hot smoke burning me as I tried to hold it down.

"Relax," Dottie said. "Don't fight it."

I shook my shoulders a few times, trying to get my back loose. I took a couple of deep breaths and after that it seemed to go down better.

We rolled a couple more. Now and then, somebody would pass through the kitchen and intercept it and have a couple of puffs and say something like "Good shit" and go on where they were headed.

It was a good high coming on, the best high I'd ever felt and it scared me a little because I didn't know exactly what to expect from it.

"You like to fuck?"

I gagged on the smoke. "That's some question."

"Do you?" She took a short puff and held it in while she passed the joint back to me. "I believe in being direct. Do you?"

"Yes," I said, "but sometimes I don't think I'm very good at it."

I expected her to laugh, braced myself against it. When it didn't come, I looked at her. She nodded a couple of times and said, "I think I'm going to put you in my good book."

"What does that mean?"

"I hate those walking cocks. Whit's one but it's too late to do anything about it, I hate the ones who tell you they'll curl your toenails and cure your toothache." She shrugged. "All that, when all you asked is if they liked to fuck."

We were down to the butt quarter inch. Dottie pinched it out and shook the grass out and swallowed it. "I mean, I like to fuck and I like men better who don't try to blow smoke up my ass." She helped herself to another Bud from my sack. "Let's see what the party's doing."

I followed her from cluster to cluster for a few minutes and then I lost Dottie when I left to find the bathroom. I found it but there was a line forming, so I settled for a short walk into the field to the left of the house. I'd just started to piss when I heard somebody coming up behind me. I assumed it was one of the guys from the party but when I looked around, I saw a blonde girl squatting a few feet from me.

"Hi," she said. "Hi."

"I did this over poison ivy two years ago. I caught a hell of a case."

"Get it cured?"

"Sure."

I heard the snap of elastic. When I'd finished and zipped up, she was gone. I spent a few minutes moving from group to group looking for her. Maybe it was all for the best that I didn't find her. I wasn't sure what I was supposed to say to her. That we'd shared a piss or something like that, I guess.

I got what was left of my sack of beer and settled down with my back against a tree and watched the coals in the pit fire ash and whiten over. I could tell that it was late but it seemed too much trouble to look at my watch. I drank a couple of beers and I was almost asleep when I heard Max calling me. I found him over by the back steps. There was just enough light from the kitchen for me to see that Marcia, standing just beyond his shoulder, was crying.

Max looked mean and drunk. "You drive Marcia back to town for me?"

"I don't ... want to go," Marcia said.

"I don't give a shit what you want." Then to me: "Will you?"

"I'm afraid I'm not up to it," I said.

Max looked at me for a long moment. "It happens. I'll see if Charlie Snead can."

He went away to look for Charlie and I stood there, looking at Marcia and feeling foolish. She was trying to choke back the crying and sniffling, gasping for air like there was enough left for her.

"I don't ... Want to leave. You could ... Ask him ... To let me stay." I shook my head. "That's between you and Max."

"He's mad at me because he wanted me to do it out in the Haybarn and I didn't want to. She was gasping for air. "And he said he hit me if I didn't" she was choking and coughing "so I did now he says he's sick of me." Her voice rose to a whine. "And I want to stay at the party."

"None of my business either way," I said and walked back to my tree.

When I looked back, I saw Max and another man leading her down the driveway toward the highway where the car was parked. I heard the car start up and drive away. I was watching the coals again and I didn't know that Max was back until he flopped down beside me.

"Built your nest here, huh?"

"It seemed a god idea at the time," I said. I offered him one of my last two beers.

And threw the tab in the fire pit. "Do you know what that shit told me? You know what you tried to pull on me?"

"No, what?"

"That bitch. She said she'd rather fuck women than men. She said bowling Mia convinced her of it."

I didn't say anything, I just looked at the ashes.

"I felt like pulling her inside out like a pea coat sleeve."

I knew he was waiting for me to say something, so I said shit, I felt the same way. That seem to satisfy him, and he left, after saying, he looked for me before he left for town.

Some indeterminate time later, I awoke and found that Dottie was kneeling in front of me, kissing me. The bark of the tree was cutting into my back, and it felt like my own skin peeling off when I pulled away from it.

"Sleep tight," Dottie said

"I was."

We kissed again, and then broke out laughing right in the middle of the kiss, because Max started calling me and Whit started calling her and it was time to go.

CHAPTER SEVENTEEN

CHAPEL HILL, 1967

AND THEN THE MORNING AFTER WHAT YOU DO IS

"**I** 've felt better."

I was seated at the bar at Pop's. The Falstaff clock over the cash register showed that it was 2:05, but I knew it wasn't the correct time. The shape I was in, I couldn't remember whether the clock was fast or slow.

"Slow," I said.

Pop your two construction workers were drinking a late lunch. "Exams are over. Graduation is next week. First summer session is 10 days off. No wonder it slow."

"You could close."

"Used to," pop said. "No reason to close now."

There it was I know we'd reach it given the time. Mom had died in November, 2 ½ months after I passed through on the way to New Haven. He'd sent me a telegram, and I phoned him within an hour of receiving it. There wasn't much I could do to comfort him, but I had run up a big phone bill trying. It had been midterm exam time and I hadn't been able to attend the funeral. I'd sent flowers and I'd written him a long letter. Still, I had a feeling he had been hurt that I hadn't been at mama's funeral.

"Used to go to the mountains," Pop said.

I remembered I had gone with them once. He'd rented a house in Blowing Rock in the Mayfair Manor section for a week. They looked across the valley toward grandfather mountain. We even had our meals on the porch. Breakfast, while we watch the missed blowing up the side of the valley, obscuring the face of the mountain. Lunch, watching the sun walk across the porch toward us, inch by inch. Dinner in the cooler evening, so cool, coffee and Metaxa were needed to ward off the chill. Mama had cooked all the meals, over Pop's protests. "Whose vacation is it?" Mama would ask. "Not mine. I'm always on vacation."

"Why not Miami?" I waited for his puzzled look, and then added, "All the Greeks go to Miami this time of year." He still looked puzzled. "They go there for the sponge fishing," I said.

He shook his head, regarding me with the large still eyes. "Now is the best part of the sponge fishing season." Then, in desperation: "It's supposed to be a joke. A bad joke."

He went back to the kitchen to prepare for the dinner meal.

Stretched out on my bed at the Carolina Inn, laying on my left side, so I could watch through the window the lights of Cameron Avenue smeared in the pit-pit of the slow late spring rain, I thought of my life, the dark tunnel going toward no light, and for the first time in years, I remembered, my brother, Jerry.

Jerry, who was dead. Who walked on the thin blade edge of being charming. Who found that having to be charming, was not charming. That it was a poor paying job with bad hours. Back to dust where the worms are not charmed. *I am to Jerry as Jerry is to … or Jerry is to me as I am to …*

Until I fell asleep.

CHAPTER EIGHTEEN
MILLHOUSE, GEORGIA 1967
SOMEDAY I WILL THINK
ABOUT JERRY AGAIN

From the spiderwebs in the stairwell, it looked like nobody had been in the attic for years. I went downstairs and got a broom from the kitchen, and cleared them away before I went up. There was only one light fixture, against the back wall, opposite the dormer windows, but the wiring had gone bad of the bulb and burned out. It didn't seem worth another trip downstairs.

I found the trunk I wanted and pulled it over to the right dormer window. It was one of the old metal, footlocker types, the corner, smashed and rounded off, the lock broken, and the two wide cloth straps buckled around it to hold it together. The buckles on the straps seem fused together it took me a long time to work them free. I don't know what I expected to find inside. There, on top, was a leather-bound copy of The Argonaut Yearbook for John H. Rogers High School, Milhouse, Georgia, class of 1945.

Near the back of the yearbook, in the senior section, I found what I was looking for: a picture of Jerry. The face looking out at me, was laughing, this in contrast to the solemn faces in the pages around him. It was a square, rather blocky face. It had been retouched. As I remember, there had been a mass of blue acne scars on both cheeks and a pepper and a pits on his forehead. Do you have been airbrushed away. Jerry, his hair done in the style of the period, the flat top, the squared, office head, the hair, about 2 inches long, standing up like grass stubble. The hair seemed lighter than I remembered it. There was a caption under his picture:

Call him laughing boy. He'll answer to it. Practical Joker. Remember the baby black snake in the teacher's lounge? Intelligent but says he doesn't know how to use it. Most likely to succeed as a standup comic. Watch out, Jack Benny! Football 1,2,3,4. Baseball 1,2,3,4. Track three, 4. Monogram club 2,3,4.. Radio club 3,4.. Speech club 1,2,3,4. Student body VP 3.

I started back at the front of the book and worked my way through slowly. I found several more pictures of him. In a dinner jacket at a production of *Clarence*. Fears faced in a three-point stance in a football uniform. At a table in the school cafeteria, having lunch. Eyes closed in the back row of a classroom. Dancing at the Junior Senior, his arms around a small, dark-haired girl.

The pictures didn't tell me that much more about them. Except, in those pictures, you could see the acne scars. I reached the senior pictures again, and I began reading the notes that his classmates had written beside their pictures. Then I noticed something odd. I didn't see it at first, and had gone past it, before the realization hit me, and I flipped back. It was under the picture of a pretty girl named Beverly Archer.

In green ink, in the thick ropy hand writing, there was her note: "It's been great knowing you, Jerry! I'll never forget those great afternoons at Second Mill Lake! Don't you dare forget either!"

Below that, in a tight, thin hand, that I recognized as Jerry's:

"Screwed her the first time at the country club, on the 14th hole, green, 4 July 1944. Four or five times after that. Had bad breath. Squealed like a stuck pig every time." Then, below that, in a different ink, "Married to Bo Kearney in 1948. Divorced 1955. Died in a car accident in Atlanta, 1958. That peace at rest at last."

Then I understood it. He had carried the yearbook with him until his death. It was even with him when he died. The trunk had arrived by Railway Express the day after the funeral. Mama couldn't bear to open it and she had them put it in the attic, with the idea of going through it later. And the trunk had been pushed further and further away, like the memory of Jerry, until was forgotten completely. Covered with dust, like the chair that needed re-upholstering, the lamp base that needed a new shade, the baby crib that wasn't needed anymore.

Often the notes Jerry added were short, to the point. Under Robert Bass: "Died in Korea: 1951." Beside the photo of John Marsh: "Put in the pen 1950 for armed robbery. Didn't know he had it in him." Below the picture of a plain, flat-faced girl named April Zune: "Heard from Bobby she was working for a house in Savannah. Remember her as being too shy to say screw, much less do it."

Two of the notes were much longer, showing the result of constant additions, the handwriting, at times sprawling out of control. Maybe he'd been drinking. The first of the lengthy notations was under the picture of a girl named Rebecca Clark. She had short, blonde, hair, thin and wispy, large, hyperthyroid eyes. She'd written: "love you, Jerry. I'll never forget you, ever!"

Jerry had written: "never screwed her. Wasn't sure that I could, and wasn't sure that I wanted to. I thought I loved her. The whole four years of high school. Loved her desperately, hopelessly, painfully. Dated her a few times the junior and senior years. Never could talk to her, found myself tongue-tied, knew I bought her. Did foolish things to try and impress her. Instead, I must've convinced her I was crazy. Saw her the last time at the party at Second Mill Lake, graduation night, at the cabin that belong to Benny's family. Everybody there with their steady date. She danced all night with Sonny Mason while I danced with

Mary Lou. At dawn, drove back to town, the four of us, and had breakfast at the Railroad Café."

Added later: "Went to Agnes Scott. Called her once and try to make a date. Think she didn't remember me at first. Married a marine captain in 1951."

An arrow was drawn to a facing page. Written there in a shaky hand: "last heard from item on the society page of *The Southerner*. Living in Alameda, California. Husband a colonel. Two children, both boys" below, that, and careful, black lettering: "bad ass world that doesn't keep its promises."

It took me a few minutes to find the Mary Lou he'd gone to the graduation party with. Her last name was Maron. I recognized her as the girl in the junior/senior dance photograph. Mary Lou had written under her picture: "those nights at the BBQ shack! Those classes together! I'll never forget you, Jerrie! Never!"

Jerry's first note read: "could've married her. Even considered it a time or two. But knew that it would bury me. Would root me. Believed there was somebody better ahead, just around the next corner, the whole dream and promise of love. But that didn't work. Like the time I bought a pound of jellybeans and found they had bit or licorice centers."

There was a note added later. "Moved to Atlanta in 1948 when I was in the army. Never tried to find her again. Knew what I'd find."

After I finished with the yearbook, I went through the other contents of the trunk. On top, there was the monogram sweater, moth holes in the back and the right sleeve. The sweater was purple and white, with four white rings around the left by sept. It was his letter sweater from his senior year. Next, I took out a pair of green pants with a broken zipper, a tweed jacket with leather reinforced, elbows, a bundle of paperback books –- westerns, and mysteries mostly— a rolled up dark suit with shiny knees and a dark stain on the jacket that might've been vomit or blood, several pairs of boxer shorts, and far at the back of the trunk in a tied up bundle of letters.

The letters on top were from mama. I didn't need to read them to know what they said. I'd had the same letter from time to time from her. What the weather was like, lady-like forwarding of local scandal, and pleas to find ourselves before it was too late. Always that, the last paragraph that you didn't need to read. You knew it was there, the words hardly changing from year to year.

Some of the other letters were bills: a loan company he owed $110, hotel rent past due, a notice that *The Riders of the Purple Sage* was overdue and the late fee of five cents a day was being charged, a letter from the Internal Revenue Service inquiring bluntly why he hadn't filed for the years 1962 and 1963. Near the bottom of the bundle, there was a letter for me, the announcement my marriage.

Finally, at the bottom of the bundle, there was a letter addressed to me at the Chapel Hill address. It was stamped and sealed, but it had not been mailed. That bothered me, and I sat there, smelling the dust and the mold and not sure I wanted to read the letter, not sure that I ought to read it. Maybe it answered the question and I wasn't sure that I wanted the answer.

But then I said to myself, oh shit I might as well. The letter was dated January 3, 1964. Ten days I thought, that was ten days before he died then I didn't want to read the letter but I did anyway.

I've been meaning to write you for a couple of months, really for a year or two. I've written you for five times, but haven't mailed any of them. I make the mistake of reading them over the next morning and they don't make much sense. I end up deciding that a phone call would be better. But I never seem to be near a phone booth.

I was in Durham last spring, riding a bus through on the way north, and I thought about breaking the trip for a side trip to Chapel Hill to see you and Elaine and the baby. Maybe I should have at the time, I decided that I better go on north, and shine up my penny a little ... So I wouldn't be the bad penny when I did turn up. I knew that, why didn't want to meet Elaine the way I was, didn't want her to see me the way I was.

Maybe I'm better this year. I hope so. I am in Chicago this year ... For the skiing season. At least that's what it looks like when I try to walk on those ice and snowed-on streets here. Or maybe it's the ice-skating season. One or the other, I guess it's even funnier when I've had a few drinks. It won't surprise you to know that I've had a few tonight. In fact, I got 86'd at one of the bars tonight — that's a polite term for being thrown out — and I'm back at the hotel drinking about a gallon of black coffee so I can go out and try it again. I don't like staying here in the hotel. I don't like it in the bars either. If I had any sense, I'd settle for chair out in the lobby, but nobody ever accused me of having that much sense.

Let me tell you something that happened a few days ago. I'm staying in one of the better hotels in the low rent district — all the best of the low rent people live here. You can buy them for a quarter, but the resale value is pretty low. Something was wrong with the toilet. The water kept running out after you flushed it. I decided to fix it myself instead of waiting for the repair man. I took the top off the water tank and guess what I found inside? A big beetle kind of bug. Big as a quarter and black and shiny. I don't know how long it had been in the water tank. Maybe it was born there, spent its whole life, swimming, treading, water, swimming to stay where it was. I fixed the toilet ... The bulb was disconnected from the arm ... And now the toilet is flushed. The beetle drops out of the side as the level drops and then when the tank is full again, there it is, still struggling to stay afloat, to be where it was yesterday. I've watched the bug for several days and several times I thought about taking the bug out. But there's always the chance of the bug belongs there, that it wouldn't know what to do if I took it out. I looked in the tank a few minutes ago and it was still there. Treading water, floating with the tides that we can't see.

I hope you had a good Christmas, your second as a respectable married man. This might be a bad time to ask… And feel free to ignore me if it is… But I'm a little short now and I could use $50 if you have it. Until I get back on my feet. I could pay it back to you in a month or so. But like I said, if you're short, just forget I asked at all understand.

I folded the letter. That was why he never mailed it because he had trouble asking for money. Knowing that he could get money from mama, but a lecture came with the money order. Thinking he might get the money for me, without the lecture, but afraid I couldn't afford it now that I had a wife and child.

And 10 days later, he either fell or jumped from the 15th floor of a hotel in Chicago. Mama and the rest of the family had decided that he fell, probably while drunk. As if God had told them one Sunday at church. Above the organ, above the choir. The whisper that only a select a few people here.

CHAPTER NINETEEN

GEORGIA, 1967

SUNDAY MORNINGS WE SWAM IN THE RAIN

I was fooled by the cloud cover at 9 o'clock that Sunday morning. I thought it might burn off as the sun moved toward noon. There was a breeze from the east, from the direction of the coast 120 miles away. If I tried hard enough, I could believe that the breeze had the scent of salt spray in it, they carried the sound breakers, like the muffled roar from the inner curls of conch shells.

By the time I reached Billie's house, it looked like a big mistake. The clouds look darker now, like it would rain in the next few minutes. Like it might rain all day and then all the next week. The rain might be good for the tobacco and the cotton and the truck farmers but it was going to be hell on a Sunday picnic.

Billie came to the door before I could get out of the car. She wore a brief two-piece bathing suit under her loose shift. She carried a beach bag and a beach basket . . . the lunch she packed for us.

"I won't hear of it."

I waited until she was in the car, with the door pulled shot behind her. "Here of what?"

"Calling the picnic off."

I backed out of the driveway and turned east. "I didn't say anything."

"But you were going to."

"Maybe."

"I've been planning this picnic for a week."

I knew.

"I've been cooking for two days … Two whole days."

I knew.

"So, it can't rain."

We drove through the large Lake View housing development. A mile past it, the road banked sharply to the left and followed the curved boundary of Second Mill Lake. The new residents of Millhouse preferred to call it Cypress Lake, because it sounded fancier, unless rustic. They got so you could tell the old-time residence from the newer ones just buy what they called the lake. Of course, looking at the lake you can understand why they called it Cypress Lake: the submerged, wet, gray spikes of cypress trunks dotted the western half of the lake.

The bathhouse and the swimming area were the south end. The bathhouse, built out of the scrap pine and unpainted, wouldn't be open until after church. I parked in the spot nearest to the bathhouse and turned to look at Billie. Unless there was someone in the children's play area, directly behind the bathhouse, we were the first to arrive for the day.

"Are you sorry I talked you into it?"

"Of course not," I said.

"There wasn't any way to know it might rain."

I rolled down the window and stuck out my hand. It wasn't raining yet, but there was a damp coolness to the breeze that blew in against my face "Maybe it will blow past, Billie." I didn't believe it. It seemed more likely that the rain clouds were going to be with us for the rest of the day.

"A beer?"

I reached behind the seat and lifted the cooler that I'd filled with beer and ice the night before at Fat Jack's.

Billie shook her head. "I brought some fresh coffee."

"That sounds even better." I returned the cooler to the backseat. I held the plastic cups while she poured the steaming coffee from the thermos. Far in the distance, there were the first rumblings of thunder.

By the time I'd sipped half a cup of coffee, all around us it was as still and dark as twilight. I could feel myself, pressing, grunting, saying, come on, come on, turn it loose. Then the lightning, the brief scar tissue, sliced through the near darkness. The whiplash cracked.

"I'm afraid." She said. I put my cup on the floorboards and pulled Billie toward me, until her head was under my arm. "Afraid of lightning since it hit the tobacco barn ... I was out in the field ... I was five ... "

"It's all right."

"I feel like ... I can't breathe."

"Sure you can." I kissed her. "The worst is over."

Then the deluge hit, the rain pouring over and past us like waves, breaking, bursting against the car. The windows blurred so you couldn't see outside.

"Are you sure ... It's over?"

I got my coffee from the floorboards and took a sip. "The only thing I'm really sure of is that this is one hell of an interesting picnic."

When it slackened to a thin, driving rain, I eased Billie away and took off my shirt and T-shirt. "Weren't we going swimming?" I kicked off my loafers and stepped outside the car to strip off my pants. I hitched up my swim trunks and leaned into the car. "How about it?"

"Is the rain cold?"

"A little, but the water will be warm."

"You sure?"

I swore to it and she slipped the shift over her head and stepped out of the car into the rain.

"It *is* cold. I've got goose pimples."

Closing the car door, I said, "that's better than those other kinds." And pulled her flat against me, running my hands over her roughly until the goose pimples disappeared. "Last one in … has to pick up the chicken bones." I whirled and ran down the grass to the sandy beach and into the lake. I had to wait for a distance before the water was deep enough for me to make my dive. When I hit the water, there was a freezing shock to it, and I came up, swimming, knowing that the chill would go away. I felt strange because, as far as I could see, the lake was pitted by the rain and I could hear the flat tap-tap of the single drops striking around me.

I reached the guard rope about 150 yards out before I stopped. I swung under the rope, usually the restricting limit for young swimmers, and came up on the other side, holding onto the rope. Billie was a few yards behind.

"You … You … You," she was saying.

I waited until she reached the guard rail. "I what?"

"You lied to me. It's freezing."

I laughed. "Is that all?"

I pushed away from the rope and struck out for the first diving tower. It was another 150 yards away, and I was puffing hard when I reached the ladder. I hung on, waiting for my breath to ease. Then, legs shaking a little, I climbed the ladder to the platform. I sat on the edge of the platform legs dangling, looking back at Billie. She waited at the guard rope until I was on the tower before she began dog paddling after she swam a short distance, tread water for a minute or so, and then swim on. It took her a long time, and when she reached the tower, she crouched with her feet on the bottom rung for a time while she recovered.

I pulled her the last few feet onto the platform and we sat in the warm rain, warm after the swim, and looked out over our private lake. For the next hour or so, all the cars have passed on the road, bordering the lake we're headed toward town people bringing their children into Sunday school. Some of them waved at us, and we stood up and waved back.

It was a good morning, and we were both happy when the rain stopped, and the clouds blew past the sun was warm on us when we swam back to the guard rope and from there into the shallow water. When we reach the car, I dried off and put on my T-shirt. We took the picnic basket around behind the bathhouse to the children's play area. We sat side-by-side in the low, children's swings and ate an early lunch. She had fixed fried chicken, a mound of thinly sliced roast, pork, potato salad, and pickles, and olives. For dessert, she baked an apple pie with a lattice top crust.

On the way back to town, all the cars were headed away from Millhouse. People coming back from church.

That night, Billie asked me if I was ever going to marry her. She didn't mean right away. She meant ever. If I'd been at all perceptive, hadn't been tired from the morning swim and the afternoon screwing, I could've seen it coming. It had been too good a week. What goes up must.

"I don't know."

"Don't know or won't say?"

She was at the kitchen sink, drying the supper dishes. Earlier, watching her move about the kitchen, I thought it was an interesting domestic scene. Now, sitting at the table, drinking a final cup of coffee, I realized it what had been a scene for me, had been real world to her.

"Which one?" She insisted.

"A bit of both, I guess."

"I'd make you a good wife."

"I'm not sure I want a wife."

"I guess that's all then." Her back to me, she stopped with a plate and towel pressed together. Now the towel moved again, and she put the plate aside.

"Be sure," I said. "Be very sure."

"I'm sure."

I waited a long minute or two to see if she changed her mind. When she didn't, I left the table and went to the bathroom and got my damn swim suit from the peg and the Depp kit I'd left there a week before. By the time I passed the kitchen door, she'd finished the dishes and was sweeping the floor. She didn't look up when I stepped into the doorway.

"Sure, Billie?"

"Yes."

On the drive back to town, I said to myself screw it, fuck it, what did you expect? I said it so often that I must have convinced myself. At least, I like to think that I did. Of course, it's always hard to be sure.

BOOK THREE

CHAPTER TWENTY

CHAPEL HILL, 1967-69

AND TWO
CHRISTMASES LATER,
IT DIDN'T SNOW

My first fall back in Chapel Hill, the weather was mild until the middle of October. For the next two months, into the winter, it was cold and windy. One weekend there was a rain and sleet storm. The bare trees creaked in their quarter inch coating of ice. For the three days that the ice remained on the trees, I'd wake in the night to the crack, crack, crack of the ice and think the sky was falling. Chicken little is back in town. Older but the same.

During the Christmas break, I flew down to Georgia for the holidays and returned on December 27. It had snowed on Christmas Eve while I was gone and there was so much snow and ice in my driveway that the fuel truck wouldn't back in until I shoveled off the snow and chipped up the patches of ice.

The second Fall, there were a few mild flurries but the snow didn't stick. It melted the moment it touched the ground or the street. During the winter, there were forecasts that snow was expected ... It seemed to happen about once a week ... But none of the predictions came true, and I moved toward Christmas without a real snow that I'd count. I didn't spend the holidays in Millhouse that year, pleading term papers that needed grading and a group of lectures that had to be reworked. Looking back on it maybe I spent the Christmas in Chapel Hill expecting snow. That and the fact that I wasn't sure I could stand another Christmas in Millhouse. Billie, if I wanted to see her, wasn't there. Fat Jack said she left for Atlanta and he didn't have her address there. Maybe that was true. Maybe it wasn't. Fat Jack, whatever else you thought of him, could keep a secret if he was asked to. So, I spent the Christmas in Chapel Hill and it didn't snow. A dim sun warmed the Christmas day winds in the places where there weren't shadows and I found myself forced to pass the afternoon and evening with a young faculty couple who believed that nobody should be alone on Christmas day. I ate too much, and I drank too much, and on the way up to my front door late that night, I vomited out all their cloying hospitality.

The next morning, I was out early, spreading sand over the frozen vomit peels. My lawn after that, the grass, dead and brown anyway, looked like moles have been digging in it.

And so, into the new year 1969. A lot happened that first year and four months I was back in Chapel Hill, since I'd taken the job as an instructor in the Department of Drama. That first semester, in October 1967, I took two days off from class and flew up to New York. From there, I took a train into New Haven. The next morning, I met my lawyer, James Butten, Junior at his office and we were walked over to the courthouse, building to wait our turn in divorce court. The grounds we settled upon was the standard one: mental cruelty, and Mr. Butten led me around to talking about the things Elaine had done to hurt me, ending with what I understood later must be a stock group of questions and answers.

"What happened to you as a result of the unhappy relationship between you and your wife?"

I wasn't sure that I understood the question. I said "I couldn't sleep and I didn't eat well and I lost some weight."

"How much weight?"

"Fifteen or twenty pounds."

The judge, who was bored, and hadn't been listening very closely, leaned over the edge of his desk, and looked at me. As if estimating my weight.

"And since your separation, what have you noticed about yourself?"

"I feel much better."

The judge nodded at the lawyer, is it to say that that covered it to his satisfaction. I was followed on the stand in rapid succession, by three witnesses, who still lived in the student apartments. Prompted by Mr. Butten, they told dark stories about how Elaine had mistreated me, and how I was unhappy all the time. Each witness answered the same final question: "And since his separation, what have you noticed about him?"

Answer one: "He seems better adjusted."

Answer to: "He seems to be getting along better."

Answer three: "He doesn't seem to be unhappy anymore."

It took about 20 minutes, and the divorce was granted. Elaine wasn't there, but a lawyer was there to represent her. Child support for a Evadne was agreed-upon at $160 a month. Visitation could be worked out later through the court. Everybody seemed happy about it.

I left the court a single man. I didn't feel any different than I had the day before, or the month before. I guess I expected to, and that was the disappointing aspect of it all.

The first winter back in Chapel Hill, I was looking for a used sofa. I'd been in the furniture stores and to the Trading Post out in Carrbere. I didn't find anything I wanted at the prices they wanted and I'd about giving up when I saw the ad in the *Chapel Hill Weekly*: used sofa, dark green, excellent condition reasonable price.

There was also a phone number that I called a few minutes later. The woman who answered said that she was Agnes Black, and that I could see the sofa any time that evening. Her voice was low, with the suggestion of a southern accent that had been educated away.

Her apartment was one of the duplexes on Rosemary Street. It was set fairly far back into the lot, off the street front, and I had trouble finding it. I couldn't find the number and I was about to look for a phone so I could call and get better directions, when a Ford turned into the horseshoe driveway. It parked in front of one of the duplexes nearby. There was a young girl in the car, and she jumped when I called her. She turned on me defensively, so I stopped walking toward her and kept my distance. I asked if Agnes Black lived in one of these apartments.

"Her?" There was a brief hesitation while she seemed to be measuring me. "Last one over there." She nodded once in the direction of the last duplex on the far right. When I turned back to the girl, she was moving quickly up the steps my Thank You was lost in the noise of the slammed door. From the way, she acted, I assumed that she locked the door, too.

"Come in."

The woman I followed into the living room, was probably around 30, though she looked much younger. She walked like people do on a tennis court, springy on her toes. There was only a slight sag of skin along her chin line, a loss of skin tone, to convince me that she wasn't eighteen. Agnes Black was tall for a woman, 5'10' or so, and a little thin for my taste. That pelvis,

I thought, if she turned in the living room to face me, would scrape and cut like the edge of a knife.

"This is the sofa." Looked at the sofa. It seemed ordinary enough. It was in good condition, almost new. I couldn't see any signs of wear.

"There's nothing wrong with it," she said. "It's just that I moved to this apartment recently and the sofa doesn't fit the color design here. I need something brown or tan."

I looked around as if I could tell the difference and nodded.

"It clashes."

When I nodded again, she asked if I wanted to drink. We settled on bourbon and water, and I followed her to the doorway of the small kitchen and watched washing mixed drinks. Small breasts the shape of pairs. An ass that I could cover with my spread hands. She turned from the sink where she been adding water and caught me looking at her. There was a fleeting blur of irritation, but she smoothed it over with a tentative smile. I took the drink from her and back to ahead of her into the living room.

"Why don't you try it?" She indicated the sofa and I walked over and sat down.

I leaned back and said, "Nice."

"It opens into a bed, too." When I just looked at her, she put her drink aside and move the coffee table. I got up and stepped away while she been over and pulled up the bottom half until it clicked an open flat. "Try it."

"That's all right."

"No, go ahead."

I felt silly doing it, but I sat on the sofa and kicked off my loafers. I stretched out my head against the armrest, and close my eyes. I felt a shift in the sofa and I open my eyes slightly and saw that she was sitting on the edge of the sofa near my feet.

"It supports my weight better than it does you," Agnes said.

"It's fine."

I pretended that my eyes were still closed and watched her through the narrow slits. She excepted her drink, and then ran her hand along the front edge of the sofa, as a feeling the texture. For a brief moment, her hand lifted and moved toward me, as if she were going to touch me. But something stopped her and her hand dropped to her side, and she stood up. I got up and closed the sofa for her, put on my loafers, and found my drink.

We talked about other things for a few minutes. I found out that she was working on a PhD in math. It was her second year of coursework and, she said, very demanding. She smiled obligingly when I said the numbers were all beyond me, and that I hadn't been able to balance my checkbook for years and years. Then, because it was time, we talked price and settled upon $75 for the sofa. I took out my checkbook and wrote the check.

Taking the check from me: "Are you sure?"

"What?"

"About the balance?"

I laughed with her. "Within a dollar or two either way."

It was time to go. She looked at her watch a time or to in the last few minutes, and there wasn't any reason to hold my empty glass any longer. When I said it might be a day or two before I could pick it up, that I'd have to find someone with a truck, she said she'd have it delivered to my house. She had a friend who had a truck. She'd call me after she had seen him. There was a chance he could bring it to my house by the next morning, a Saturday.

Down the drain. Upped the flue. She had a boyfriend who had a truck and delivered sofas for her. I left with the thin image of her burned in the back of my eye.

Agnes called the next morning and it woke me from a hangover sleep. Her friend John had said he could bring the sofa in the next hour if it was all right with me. I said that was fine and then I couldn't think of anything else to say and maybe she couldn't either because we ended up saying goodbye and hanging up. I showered and was having a 2nd cup of coffee when I heard the truck coming up the driveway.

The sofa was in the back of a pick-up truck with Vinson Construction Company painted on the door panel. The driver, when he got out of the truck cab turned out to be short, stocky with a head of gray and curly hair. He seemed to be in his early 40s. There was a young black man with him. He introduced himself as John Vinson. He didn't introduce the young black man. Over my protest, he and the young black man carried the sofa into the house while I had the door open for them.

The young black man went outside to wait in the truck. John Vinson looked around at the bareness of the living room.

"I just moved to town." I said.

He agreed that it did take time to get settled. And then bluntly: "Did you know Agnes before?"

I shook my head "I just answered the ad."

"Nice girl."

I said that she certainly seemed to be. I sounded as uninterested as I could, and he seemed satisfied, and left.

That afternoon, I went downtown and bought a pair of prints for the living room walls. All the time, I was thinking about the way, John Vinson had acted. There was only one way to read it. With all that smoke, maybe I could find out where the fire was.

I thought I already knew. I thought it might happen, but I wasn't sure. There was a chance that I might be wrong. Just in case, to occupy myself, I bought a gallon of olive-green paint and started painting the bathroom. I finished the first coat when the phone rang.

"Hello."

I said "hello."

"I just called to see how the sofa is," Agnes said. "I like to think of it as a follow up to the adoption."

"Is this Agnes?" I knew very well that it was, but I wasn't about to admit it. "Agnes black?"

"How many sofas did you adopt this week?"

"Well, I did tell a few people I was buying a sofa."

Mark one up for me.

"This is Agnes Black."

"Well, hello Agnes Black."

"I called to see if the sofa got there all right."

Time be blunt. "Is that really why you called?"

Silence. Then a low, bubbling laugh. "I guess not."

"Why then?"

"It seemed like a good idea at the time."

"And not now?" I asked.

"Maybe," She said. "And then again maybe not."

Mark that exchange up as a draw. Points to me for asking the blunt question. Points to Agnes for answering the question and not killing the conversation altogether. It was time for me to shift the conversation onto important matters.

"The sofa got here without a dent. That might be because your boyfriend wouldn't let me help him bring it in the house. I got to hold the door."

"He's not my boyfriend. He's just an old friend."

"Does he know that?"

"Yes, he knows she's just an old friend."

That was time for both of us to win a few points. "Maybe that's what you wanted to tell me?"

"Yes."

End of that part of the game there wasn't any way of knowing who won, and who lost. It was too early for all of that. Then, too, since everybody kept their own running tabulations, there wasn't any way of knowing what the score was at any one given point in the relationship up.

"I'm glad that's out of the way," Agnes said. "You make it hard on a girl."

"I am relieved, too."

We spent a few minutes talking about the possibilities of a few things we might do together. Holding back the one we were both most aware of. It turned out that she wasn't doing anything that night. She was having an early supper with a girlfriend that would be over by 8 o'clock or so. We agreed we meet at Harry's when supper was over. A few beers and a lot of talk. It would be a beginning.

Near midnight. The evening behind us. We stayed at Harry's for an hour or so and then we tried the Tempo Room but we couldn't get in. It was packed to the staircase. We walked around to The Shack. We went in. It was almost empty. Two construction workers were at the bar and two couple sat at one of the back booths. Agnes and I took a booth near the front and talked until the bartender came by the booth and said that it was closing time.

I found out only the basic things about her. That she grown up in Charlotte. That her father was a dentist. That she gotten her undergraduate degree from the women's college in Greensboro. She taught high school for a time, a little defensive about how long she'd taught, and then she come to University of North Carolina to work on her Master's. She's been encouraged to go on for her PhD even before she completed the work on the thesis.

At the same time, she was finding out things about me. What appeared to bother her the most was that I was divorced. Or was it that she didn't believe it I was divorced? It was hard to know exactly what she thought. There's been a break in her composure, but she recovered so fast that I wasn't sure what she'd shown me. We moved on to other things, but I kept thinking about the reaction.

When we were outside The Shack, I asked, "What now?"

"Got any suggestions?"

"We could go over to my house and read my divorce papers."

"Not on the first date," she said.

I left it at that. We walked a block and a half to her apartment. She didn't ask me in, and I didn't ask to be asked in. I said

"I'll call you." I waited until she was in her apartment, the lights on, before I walked out the horseshoe and headed for home.

I didn't call her. I let Sunday go by. Then Monday and Tuesday. I didn't ask myself why I put off calling. I wouldn't be able to answer. At least, not an answer that I'd accept. Late Wednesday afternoon, she called me. "Just checking to see if your phone is out of order."

"I'm the one who's out of order."

"Sick?"

"Only in the head," I said.

"Only in the head?"

"Also, the liver, the light, one elbow, and my big toe."

"Gosh," she said, "that sounds like the Dismals to me."

"I appreciate the gosh," I said.

"Does the invitation to read the divorce papers still hold?"

I said that I did.

"Had supper yet?"

"Not this early"

"I'll be there in a half hour."

When she arrived, she brought a covered casserole dish, a large bowl of salad and a bottle of Chablis. She paused in the doorway and looked at the living room, empty, except for the sofa, and the two prints on the wall.

"I hope they didn't repossess the stove, too."

"Not yet."

While the oven preheated, I gave her a tour of the house. When she saw the olive green bathroom, which I'd painted, she said: "Ugh."

I explained that I'd painted it that color because I was going to move the sofa in there.

"If it will fit."

Then I noticed that she wasn't interested in the rest of the tour. She discovered the old brass bed. It had been in Uncle Bob's attic in Millhouse for the last 20 years or so, since Aunt Ethel had re-furnished the bedroom in Danish modern. I'd tried to pay them for the bed, but Uncle Bob insisted that I just get it out of the house.

"It's beautiful," Agnes said. "The last time I priced one of these, they wanted an arm and a leg for it."

"Try it," I said.

"You don't think I will, do you?" She kicked off her shoes and stretched out on the bed. "I'd almost let myself be seduced to sleep in a bed like this one."

"Now, that's an idea."

"But first she swung her legs over the side of the bed and stood up. "We better spend a few minutes reading those divorce papers."

The dishes washed and stacked to dry, I broke out a bottle of cognac that I've been saving for a special occasion. Agnes made a pot of coffee and we sat at the kitchen table sipped the brandy and coffee. Agnes looked through the doorway into the living room.

"That's a beautiful sofa you've got there."

"But not as tempting as the brass bed?"

"Nothing is as tempting as that brass bed." Still keeping it light: "You said something about divorce papers?"

I nodded. "I did."

I went into the bedroom and rooted around in one of the trucks until I found the portfolio that I kept my important papers in. The divorce decree was on top. I carried it back into the kitchen and dropped it on the table in front of her.

"The proof."

I freshened my coffee and added another half shot of cognac to my glass. I sipped cognac and watched her. She read her way slowly through the document.

"It says here," she said looking across at me, "that it's not final for 90 days."

"That's so she can protest it, if she wants to."

"That it's not final?"

"Not until the middle of January." I said.

"Ha!" she pushed back her chair from the table. "I've been rolling around in the brass bed of a married man."

"By yourself," I said.

Standing, during the wronged woman scene from some old Joan Crawford movie: "That doesn't matter in the bed of a married man."

"That's true."

"And drinking," she looked at the bottle of cognac and read the label "The champagne cognac of a married man." I nodded. "Calling a married man on the phone and practically begging him to take me out."

"That's true ... Begging."

"Alone with a married man in his house at 9 o'clock at night"

"On a weekday," I said.

Her voice rising in the mock histrionics: "is there anything I haven't done with this married man, anything at all?"

"Balled," I said.

"What did you say?"

"You haven't balled married man yet."

Agnes laughed and let the whole scene fall away. She sat across the table from me. "That's the one we're gonna have to think about," she said.

On Saturday night, we had dinner together and returned to my house to listen to music. Around 11 o'clock, in the middle of a Bartek string Quartet, Agnes said, "I think I'll stay here tonight." Then my surprise expression, she added "I haven't slept with a married man for a long time." She walked to the bedroom doorway and paused. "Are the sheets clean?"

"Changed today," I said. "Clean, except for any dust they might have collected since this morning."

"I won't be picky this time."

"Big of you," I said.

"No," she said, a laugh rumbling at the edges, "it's going to be big of you ... I hope."

I woke up very early on Sunday morning, the pillow doubled behind my head, and listened to her snore while I watched the sky beyond my window lighten and go toward dawn. I had the beginning of a headache, still so far away that it almost seemed like the memory of a headache I'd had the week before. It wasn't the drinking, I knew, that caused the headache, but the fact that I hadn't slept well. Part of that was because she'd been demanding, and we'd made love three times. The rest was because I'd slept alone so long that I felt restricted in my new half of the bed.

The amazement, looking back over it, was that I'd wanted her that much, that I'd made love to her three times. I'd felt myself slowing down the last two or three years, the desire weakening. But now, suddenly, I was acting like I was twenty years old again.

What attracted me sexually to some women and not others? Why was I a failure with some women and an insatiable success with others? I couldn't figure it out. And now there was Agnes, curled up in a ball, her back against my hip. Now, thinking about her, I felt myself harden. It seemed a shame to waste it, but I decided to have an Alka-Seltzer in the shower instead.

I edged toward the side of the bed and stood up. At that moment, Agnes turned toward me and opened her eyes. She laughed and kicked the covers away. She stood up and moved around the bed, stopping to lift a glass containing the watery remains of last night's drink from the nightstand and finish it.

She looked at my hardness with mock surprise: "I thought all the great lovers left town."

"I just got back."

"Stay a while then ... and welcome back." She took me in her hand and a shudder shook her body. It was either the chill in the room or something else.

"Thank you," I said.

Her lips brushed my chest, her hand gripping me. "This is big of you."

"I guess so."

Her voice was soft, low and husky. "One before breakfast always improves my appetite."

We went back to bed.

Toward Christmas, the Christmas I had to spend in Millhouse. I came back on the 27th to find the furnace cold, the fuel oil out and almost brought on a heart attack clearing the driveway so the driver wouldn't have an excuse to go away. While the house was warming, I called Agnes to tell her I was back in town and found out that Agnes's mother was visiting for a few days. Agnes said her mother thought I sounded interesting and she wanted to meet me.

"And," her voice low, as if she was alone, "I haven't even told her some of the best things about you."

"Maybe she assumes those," I said.

"My mother," Agnes said, "is a Southern lady, and she assumes no such thing."

I dropped by her apartment around 8:30 and found them still seated at the dining room table, their meal finished and coffee in front of them. Agnes introduced me to her mother and filled a cup for me. While I was getting seated, she brought out a new bottle of cognac and two glasses.

"He's been teaching me bad habits," she said to her mother while she poured out two shots.

Mrs. Black looked at the cognac. "I might be persuaded to try your bad habit myself."

"Mother."

"I think I'm old enough." Mrs. Black was a thin, frail woman in her 60s. Silver gray hair in a neat bun, eyes clear and quick, graceful pale hands with enlarged, milky blue veins. Her voice with soft and had the southern lady's gentile intonations. "I understand that you teach at the University young man."

I said that I did, that I was an instructor, and that I taught theater, history and dramatic criticism. Over the next few minutes, Mrs. Black questioned me closely about my educational background, about my family, and about my prospects in the teaching profession. It wasn't an inquisition. It seemed like the genuine curiosity of an older lady. Still, I felt that she knew more about me after a few minutes than Agnes did.

Agnes said very little. She did insert a word now and then. Mainly she listened, trying to hold a pinched and strained a smile on her face.

When there was a pause in the conversation, Agnes said "Mother, I forgot to tell him to bring his bank statement with him or the stub from last month's paycheck."

Mrs. Black protested that such an invasion of my privacy was the last thing in the world she intended. But the point had been made, and the conversation shifted away from me. We talked about the weather and literature for a few more minutes and then I said good night and left

I was in bed about half asleep when I heard the front door-bell. When I turned on the bedroom light, I saw that it was 12:20. I opened the front door and Agnes stepped quickly in, out of the December wind.

"What's wrong?"

"I couldn't wait until tomorrow," she said.

"Horny, huh?"

"Until my teeth hurt." She took off her coat and dropped it on the sofa. "It's been almost a week."

Later, in bed with the agony gone, a more intense pain than she'd ever allowed me to see, she guttered like a candle going out, her head on the meaty part of my shoulder.

"Hey," I said gently "don't go to sleep."

"I will if I want to."

"You've got to go home."

"I don't know if I have if I don't want to."

"That means I'll have to hide from your mother for the rest of the time she is in town."

"No, you won't." Her hand ruffled my chest hair. "She knows."

"Knows what?"

"I had a talk with her years ago. So she knows and she excepts it."

"Knows what?" I asked. "Excepts what?"

"That I need to fuck."

"That's a strange conversation to have with your mother."

"Isn't it?" The laughter breaking against my chest like bubbles. "But she's very understanding."

"She must be."

"She is." Her voice faded, seeming to move more and more away from me. "I can sleep now. I couldn't sleep for a week."

The December wind fluttered at the bedroom window and I could hear the tall poplar creaking outside. I'd slept well over the last week, as if some of the promises had been kept after all. But I knew I wouldn't sleep well that night. That it would be only fitfully, at the edges of the deep drop off, hanging there against my will, because I was exercising my bad habit of walking around a statement she'd made: *That I need to.*

That seemed reasonable. We all need to. Counter to that the way she appeared on my doorstep. On the other hand, it had been a full week. But ... She told her mother she needed to. That muddied waters a little bit. Of course, part of the time I wasn't sure when she was joking. That might mean she hadn't told her mother anything at all.

The sky was gray and winter cold when the phone rang. I caught it on the second ring. Agnes stirred in her sleep and relaxed again.

"This is Mrs. Black."

"Yes, Mrs. Black."

"I'm sorry to bother you at this hour but is Agnes with you?"

"Yes, she is."

"I was worried about her. I'm sorry to have called. It's just ... "

I said that I understood.

"Thank you. Goodbye." Mrs. Black hung up.

Red eyed, yawning, I slipped on a pair of pants and a shirt and went into the kitchen. I put the kettle on the burner and washed out the coffee pot while the water heated, I washed up and brushed my teeth. The steam was already beginning. It hissed when I came in shivering from my search for the morning paper. It hadn't arrived yet. I measured out the coffee and poured the boiling water through it. Waiting for the coffee to settle, I sat at the table, chair turned so that I could look out the window above the sink. The bare, dark trees were outlined against the gray sky. The chimney smoke from the house next-door followed the roof line like fog.

I poured off a cup of coffee before all the water had settled through. It was black and strong, stronger than it would've been if I'd waited. Blowing the steam away, sipping it, I felt two assessments of me … years apart … converge and butt together.

The first. I'd been thirteen or fourteen that spring, in the seventh grade at the Millhouse Junior High School. In the weekly school paper, somebody decided to create a Mr. Milhouse Junior High, a composite person. There'd been Joe's body, Jimmy's hair, Burns' blue eyes, Russell's clothes, Matt's smile, Bill's wit... and finally, *my* brain. I'd never thought of myself as having a brain that somebody might admire. I remember I took a lot of kidding about that article. "Brain, huh? Say something smart." Maybe the choice hadn't been serious and yet I think I began to believe it. It became a part of me that didn't need constant restatement. It became a part of my flesh and breath.

And now, the second. In danger, becoming nothing but a cock and balls. I thought about Mrs. Black, probably in bed at Agnes's apartment, also perhaps not asleep. If someone mentioned my name to her, would Mrs. Black think of me as a brain or a blood hard cock lodged in her daughter? Now with her wounded pride, the loss that phoning me had to inflicted upon her, I could guess how she'd see me. Because she was older, it wouldn't be a blue movie, but a series of still photographs.

Agnes, too. Asleep now, breath liquid in my pillow, if she dreamed at all, dreaming of the flying cock and balls she said she'd seen on a sign in Naples during a summer that she'd spent in Italy. She'd thought it must have been for a brothel. At the time she'd told me about the sign, she was holding mine, and she'd said, "if you had a little pair of wings here, and here, yours would look just like it." If she dreamed at all.

I left a cup of coffee and went back into the bedroom. I undressed and threw back the covers. She was sleeping on her back, and that made it easy. I was inside her, filling her, when she opened her eyes. Warm hands coming up to grip my shoulders. "That's a great way to wake somebody up."

"Were you dreaming?" Not moving, still, weight balanced.

"I don't think so."

"No flying cock and balls?"

"Not in my dreams," she said.

Moving then. All the time feeling some important and unde-fined part of me, pulling away from her, until that part of me sat in the kitchen, finishing a cup of coffee and reading the bas-ketball scores, while angry blood meat screwed her with harsh abandon until she whimpered and tried to get away from me. Until her head was tight against the brass headboard and she couldn't run anymore.

It didn't die a violent death. It was more like the death of some-one who moved out of town. There were other men, I guess because I ran into her several times at parties, or at the bars around town. Sometime she was with John Vinson, and other times with younger men who are probably graduate students. Now and then, late at night, she called to give me a few minutes notice before she dropped in. At those times, we gave each other purges, like strangers in brothels. With no pretense, no disguise.

Once, a little before midnight, I called her to see if she wanted to come over. I had trouble understanding her because of the heavy breathing at her end of the line.

"Why are you breathing so hard?"

She giggled. "That's not me breathing hard"

I said good night and hung up.

So crippled, limping toward the spring. I hadn't seen Agnes for a month or so when I ran into her that afternoon at the Record Bar. We hardly said hello when she leaned toward me and asked "how is your love life?"

We left the Record Bar and went to her apartment.

Resting, getting our breath. "If it hadn't been you, it would've been somebody else." She said.

"I guessed that."

"I was out hunting," she said.

I told her that I noticed the clean underwear in the fresh sheets on the bed.

"You seem to be available so I settled on you."

"That's me" I said, "A bargain counter, cock and balls."

While I dressed to leave, she remained in bed, sprawl-legged, raw wound crotch open to me if I changed my mind.

"What happened to us?"

I shook my head. "That's a strange question."

"No, I mean it."

I tied my shoelaces and stood up. "Things we found out about ourselves, I guess."

The phone rang, and while she was talking to someone named Roger, I let myself out of the apartment. Just before the door closed, behind me, I heard her say "I plan to stay in tonight and study, but if..."

Done.

The new year, 1969. As school opened again after the holidays and then the pushed toward final exams, I forgot what it was that I'd spent the whole Christmas vacation waiting for. It didn't seem to matter. If anything ever mattered.

CHAPTER TWENTY ONE
CHAPEL HILL, 1969
AND IF YOU ARE
EVER IN ATLANTA ...

I found the letter in my pigeonhole when I came up from the theater history class at 11 o'clock. There was a return address, but no name in the upper left-hand corner of the envelope. I knew a few people in Atlanta, but the address wasn't familiar.

I carried the letter down the hall to my office and plugged in the coffee pot to reheat the drugs from the morning. I didn't open the letter, just put it in a clear space on the desk and waited for the coffee to warm. There was also a departmental memo, announcing a faculty meeting the following week, and a two-day old copy of the *Millhouse Daily Southern*. Mama had given me the subscription for Christmas. Maybe it was her way of telling me that if I came home regularly, I wouldn't need the paper. I taped the memo to the wall beside my desk, and threw the newspaper in the trash can.

The letter. The coffee cooling at my elbow while I read it twice. It was written in long hand, the letters, large, childish, so that it covered several pages back in front.

I've been thinking about you a lot maybe I don't have any right to, but I do anyway. I think I would have put my pride away earlier and written you, but I didn't know your address there in Chapel Hill. I didn't want to write you in care of your mother's house.

It didn't seem proper. I was in Millhouse a week ago and I saw your Uncle Bob out at Fat's place. If you don't wanna hear from me, don't blame Bob. As far as he knows, we are still friends. I wish we still were. Atlanta is too big and I don't know many people here. Two years is a long time to be in a city and still not know your way around. I don't have a car and all I know is the bus route from where I live to downtown and after that I do a lot of walking.

I've had two or three men, but you know the kind of men I meet. And you know what they all I want from me. I don't want that from them unless they try hard to see me as a person. Maybe there's something about me that makes them think they don't have to look at me any higher than my belly button. They think all they have to do is buy me a few drinks to talk about how much money they make and then I'll go to bed with them some don't even do that.

A man came up to me at the bus stop on Peachtree Street the other afternoon and asked me if I still charge $10. I didn't even know him. I'll tell you, if there hadn't been other people at the bus stop, I'd have hit him as hard as I could. It made me feel so bad, it was all I could do to keep from crying.

I don't want you to think that I believe I have changed all together. I guess that's a part of me that I won't ever be able to change. I'm working at the Austin Brothers discount store. It's like an overgrown dime store. I work in the dry goods section: sheets, pillowcases, bedspreads, towels, and such. You know that it would be in a section that had to do with beds, wouldn't you? The pay isn't good and the hours are long. Friday and Saturday nights are open until nine. Most of the people you wait on are rude and it's hard not to be rude back to them.

I live in a kind of boarding house for women only. Mrs. Barber runs it. She has strict rules. No drinking in the house and no coming home drunk. No wearing shorts or tight pants out of the house on dates or for a walk. You can't smoke in the living room, only in your own room or in the bathroom. She says that it's not lady like to smoke in public. Mrs. Barber is almost old enough to be my grandmother and she's teaching me to knit. I think she's smart enough to know about me, so I have never told her anything about what happened in Millhouse. I guess what makes me think this is that we were having a cup of tea in the kitchen one night, and she said out of nowhere it didn't matter what a girl had done before she came to live here. What matters is that the girl tries with all her heart to be a lady now. She's been trying to convince me to go to night school and learn typing and short hand. When I told her I can't afford it, she said she'll lend it to me. I can pay her back a little bit every week.

So far, I'm holding out against borrowing. You can laugh at me and say this is my country upbringing and you might be right.

I have run out of paper and I don't think I've said anything to you that I meant to. Turns out it's harder than I thought it would be. But it was never easy anyway. With you, I always had to chew up and swallow more words than I said. But, anyway, I wanted you to know that somebody was thinking of you, if you're ever in Atlanta, I'd be glad to see you, and I would do anything that you wanted me to do.

Love, Billie.

Drunk that night. Walking home, talking to myself, the whole way, reaching up now, and then to touch my lips to be sure they aren't moving. Girl in Atlanta, I'm not coming there. Don't wait by the phone, don't meet the mailman, there are no telegrams in me. The phone is out of order, the mailman is barefooted, and the Indians have got the telegraph wire again.

Everything else is possible. Carrier pigeons, if I can catch and tame one. But I understand that special breed of bird almost never fly south anymore.

CHAPTER TWENTY TWO

CHAPEL HILL, 1969

IF IT GETS WORSE, WHICH WAY WEST?

began a journal in the spring of 1969. The first entry is dated April 11. The journals were kept in a large business ledger that I bought at Rose's Five and Ten. I took the price tag off but I think I remember that it cost a dollar and a quarter.

April 13, 1969

I went downtown around noon to buy the *Sunday New York Times*. It wasn't in yet, and I walked down East Franklin, wasting time. When I passed the laundromat, I glanced in and Dottie George seated near the front window writing a letter. She looked up about the time I looked in, and we waved at each other. She caught up with me just before I reached Harry's. She said she was waiting for her laundry to dry and I said I was waiting for *The Times*.

We went into Harry's to have a cup of coffee. From the start, it was obvious that she needed somebody to talk to.

Dottie: It's not going to well with Whit and me. Maybe you know?

I said that I had no, that I was sorry.

Dottie: He started balling some of his old girlfriends. Even bringing them out to the house. I can put up with a lot, but not that.

I said I can understand how you feel.

Dottie: I think I might leave and go west. New Mexico, Colorado or California. I'm not sure. Just somewhere.

I said it was funny, but if you looked a lot American fiction, you'd find that leaving and heading west is almost a symbolic journey. Away from the corrupt east, toward the simple and more direct life, a chance to begin your life all over. To start from scratch.

Dottie: No kidding? Here I am in my own personal novel. Why don't you come with me?

I said I couldn't. They had a contract with the University.

Dottie: Throw it over. Screw them. Going west and getting there might be fun.

I asked why me that she might find I was like Whit, but she didn't know me well enough to be handing me invitations.

Dottie: I smoked a little with you at a party once, and I remember being under a tree with you for a few seconds once.

I said that being under the tree with me didn't really tell her that much about me

Dottie: Yes, it did. You didn't put your hand under my dress.

I said, I usually waited to see if the girl wanted my hand under her dress.

Dottie: That's the difference. The other ones, the ones like Whit, know that you want their hands under your dress.

We finished our coffee and walked back toward the laundromat.

"I am tempted" I said.

"But not enough?" She asked, an edge to her voice. Maybe she asked me at first as a joke, but now she felt like I had rejected her.

"No," I said, "I'm afraid, just pure out and out afraid."

We left it there, hanging in the warm April noon sun.

April 18, 1969

I was standing at the front window of Jeff's bar/newsstand, surrounded by books and magazines, drinking a beer. I saw

Agnes Black pass by outside. I heard she was leaving town. She was going to teach in some girl's school up in Virginia. I ducked. I didn't think she saw me. But she might have.

I was at home around nine when she called. She said she wanted to drop by for a drink. I lied and said I had a date. In fact, I was leaving when the phone rang. "Some other time, Agnes."

I was in bed reading later that night. Soft, spring rain like a whisper on the roof. The doorbell rang. Before I could find my slippers, I heard the front door open. I had forgotten to lock it again. I knew who it was before I saw her.

Agnes was in the doorway. "A date, huh?"

"A short date," I saw there were spray drops of rain in her hair, sparkling in the back lighting from the hallway.

"Some date. I've been sitting outside in my car for an hour."

"Working up your nerve to come in and rape me?"

"Almost." A smile. "I haven't raped anybody for a long time." A plea buried in her voice. "I need it. You know I need it."

"If you said you needed *me*, instead of *it*, I might buy it"

"You," she said "I meant you."

I got back in the bed and found my place in the book. Not looking at her, but I heard her clothing coming off, zippers, the rattle of buckles and ornaments as piece by piece as they struck a chair back. I felt her weight on the side of the bed. I smelled the scent of her perfume. I felt a hand on my chest that I pushed away.

"Look at me," she said.

"There's still time for a pick up at the New Establishment."

"I can't wait that long." She said, her hand on the zipper of my Bermuda shorts, fumbling for the tab, finding it and then pulling it down. She reached her hand inside the opening of the boxer shorts and found what she wanted. My dick began to quiver and harden in her hand.

She smiled. "You see? You wanted to."

I couldn't help it. I was becoming what I didn't want to be. My balls had no sense at all. Or my head was crooked.

May 8, 1969

I went to a party at Johnny DeWitt's big sprawling house. Dottie was there with Whit. Rather, they came together and seemed to split and go in opposite directions as soon as they passed through the front door.

Dottie hadn't seen me for three weeks or so, but started in right where she left off. "What are you afraid of?"

"Of caring one way or the other" I said.

"An emotional chicken, huh?"

I nodded.

"I'm leaving next Friday and going to Aspen first."

I said I hoped that she'd find what she was looking for.

"I may not find it," she said, "but I'm going to look."

She said she'd give me the address in Aspen before she left. I had to promise that I'd write.

May 13, 1969

A letter in my mailbox when I got home in the late afternoon. No return address. Inside, on blue perfumed paper: "You are a son of a bitch. To make me beg for it when you wanted it as much as I did."

No signature.

It was time to read *The Idiot* again. The fifth or sixth or seventh time? Maybe I can find some part of me there, in Prince Myshkin, that I can't find it myself anymore.

May 15, 1969

A Friday. In Jeff's front window again. Late afternoon, the shoppers thinning from the street outside. Then Dottie stopped outside the window and looked in. I put down my beer and went outside.

"Change your mind?" She asked.

I shook my head. "Maybe next year."

"Next years too late for me."

Time to shift the ground. "How are you going?"

"In a Volkswagen bus with Bob and Mary Alice Klein."

"How soon?" I asked. "You got time for a beer?"

She shook her head. "They're waiting for me now ... In the lot behind the Intimate Book Shop." Dottie opened her purse and took out a scrap of paper and a pen. She wrote out her Aspen address. "I'll be here for three weeks to a month. Write me."

I promised that I would. She reached up, I reached out, and we kissed. A suggestion of her tongue, pushing into my mouth and then withdrawn.

"Goodbye," she said.

I returned to Jeff's and found my beer. I placed the Aspen address in the card case section of my wallet, with all the other names and addresses that I don't use. The accumulation of years, turning brown, and yellow from the leather dye. Shifted in a mass from each old wallet into each new wallet. The Aspen address will become a part of that mass, in time dyed as brown and yellow as the others. Knowing that I won't write.

CHAPTER TWENTY THREE

CHAPEL HILL, 1969

BLUE MOVIES
ARE BETTER

I read the letter first, slipping it from under the twine that held the brown wrapping around the small package. The envelope had Uncle Bob's law office address but the letter inside had been typed on a yellow second sheet. The typing errors and strike-throughs suggested that Uncle Bob had typed the letter himself.

I'm sending you, in the attached package, two reels of 8 mm film that I've had in my possession for a number of years, since the last time, your brother Jerry was in Millhouse.

He left the box of things with me, to be mailed to him when he got settled. A few days ago, Ethel was cleaning my study and found the box. Mostly, there are just some books, textbooks are used in high school, and high school football programs.

These two reels of film we're in there, too. And Ethel brought them to me.

I said I'd see what they were. I borrowed a projector from Marr's Camera Shop and, luckily, it turned out, viewed the films alone, one evening in my office.

To say that I was amazed by the films is an understatement. I have told your Aunt they were old practice films from when Jerry played football. I have told her that I'm sure you'd want to see them. See if you think this is Jerry and then lose the film.

Your aunt wants to see them and it might be best for the family if they were carelessly lost up there in Chapel Hill. Blame it on the janitor and she'll forgive you in a year or so. I have to live with her or I'd lose them down here.

The next day, I checked out a projector from the A/V department and set it up in my living room. The living room walls were light enough, so I didn't need a screen. I started the reel marked number one, drew the shades, and started the projector.

The print was of a surprising quality, good definition, with sharp contrast between the darks and lights, not like most dirty films, which are so carelessly printed and developed that often it's difficult to know what's going on in the film. Other dealers make prints from a print, instead of the master print, and the picture quality becomes even poorer. Then prints from that print and on and on until the people seem to be burned out white shadows moving against a gray background. But not this film.

The first reel ran about 12 minutes. I rewound it and threaded in the second reel, put on the lights and sat down at the sofa. It could be. That was what hurt me, shocked me. Even past the mustache in the dark classes, there was a good chance that it was him.

One scene especially. About midway through the first reel, a naked man stood in a bathtub. A woman dressed only in black stockings and a garter belt, sat on the edge of the tub, blowing him. The early shot showed the man only from the stomach down. The emphasis was upon the woman's head and the man's groin. After a minute or two, the camera angle was widened so that we could see another man, dressed in a robe into the bathroom. He tapped a man in the tub on the shoulder and motioned for him to leave. He took off the robe as the first man stepped out of the tub and passed the camera on the way out of the bathroom. That first man smiled as he passed the camera. For that brief moment, even behind the false mustache on the sunglasses, I would swear that it was Jerry. His smile, loose, easy, a little sardonic, as if the smile and the situation that provoked it had been turned back onto itself.

The rest of the film was a jumble of arms and legs and vaginas and cocks and mouths and breasts, a stew of parts and pieces. In the circumstances, the mustaches and the dark glasses were absurd modesty. There was so much revelation of their dark selves. That love was a fuck. The bodies were just so much meat. Function and use. Violate and ravage. All without feeling, either passion or discussed. Then, when it was done, maybe a shot of bad whiskey, while the cameraman packed it all up, the camera and the lights packed away in suitcase, everyone dressed, the money man having passed the folded cash around. To leave with the promised that another film would be shot in a couple of weeks, not more than a month. So, keep it up, we will be in touch. To limp away into their separate lives. All the wounds old, no new ones to show.

That night in bed, trying to force sleep, feeling the solid core that won't dissolve. And what if it is Jerry? The clear spring night behind my dark window, the wind, fresh and high along the rooftops. Now still pillow pole behind my head, I try to empty out the moments of the day. The girl in the theater history class, Marcy, who is trying to con me into letting her take the midterm exam a week late so she can attend a friend's wedding. The faculty meeting that took two hours and didn't accomplish anything. A blonde young girl riding a bike on Cameron Avenue, a clear, spring sun, and her whipping hair. A fresh motorcycle exhaust pipe burn on the inside of a girl's leg as she passed Jeff's bar. Dogs humping on Polk Place as I passed on the way to the library.

These images whip past at first, then slower and slower. Choking to a stop. Jerry is the camel that won't go through the eye of a needle. Jerry ... If it is Jerry ... Awakening in a hotel room in New York or Detroit or Chicago. Probably with the oppressive weight of a hangover, but the body with 10 hours sleep behind it feeling rested and strong. Assuring himself perhaps that he is always horny when he's a bit hung over after shaving a shower, dressed in his best suit, he leaves the hotel and has a late breakfast. Juice, three or four eggs, sausage, toast, and coffee. Knowing that he will need the nourishment before the day is over. After breakfast, he has a slow walk around the area, until the stuffiness of the unaccustomed heavy breakfast is gone. Minutes later, a short bus ride or subway trip behind him, he arrives at the cameraman's apartment. The producer is there, as well as the other male actor.

"How is your hammer hanging?" The other actor asks him.

"Like a wet noodle."

They carry the suitcases that contain the camera and lighting equipment down to the car and stack them in the trunk. On the way out, the producer explains that the girls will meet them at the motel.

"Anybody we know?" The other actor asks.

"I don't think so. One is a whore. The other says she's a dancer."

"What's the difference?" Gerrie asks

"None I know of," the other actor says.

At the motel, the producer parks in front of the end unit, the last one. He already has the key to the door. After letting the cameraman, and the two actors in, he leaves to go to the motel office. The lights are up and in place when he returns and says that everything is set, that the two units next to them won't be rented until they've checked out.

"But that doesn't mean we're making a sound movie. We've got to hold the noise down."

He turns on the radio and sets the level so that it will cover the usual noises. From the outside, it will sound like an afternoon party.

The two women arrive. The knock at the door is tentative, but as soon as they see the producer, they are relaxed. The producer introduces them to Jerry and the other actor, but they don't show any special interest, one way or the other.

"Any plot to this?" The younger woman, the dancer, asks.

"Just fucking and sucking," the cameraman says. "That's all the plot you need."

"Ask a silly question ... " The producer says.

The cameraman is digging around in the bottom of the camera case. "Anybody want a mustache?" He holds up a tray that contains four mustaches. The other actor selects one and sniffs at it.

"The last time I used one, it smelled like a rotten crotch."

"They've been washed."

Jerry selects one and holds it up to his upper lip.

"Do you want spirit gum, or Elmer's glue? The cameraman as

"Spirit gum is better," Jerry says to the other actor.

"Nothing is better than Elmer's glue," the whore says, laughing.

"Who is Elmer?" The cameraman asks.

"The bit is this," The cameraman saud. "You two girls think you're alone in the apartment." He motions to the dancer. "You're on the bed, in your underwear, playing with yourself." He indicates the other actor. "You're under the bed hiding, just in your shorts. You come out and surprise her and she's so hot to go that she takes you on, right?" The camera is on a tripod at the side of the bed. "We'll shoot this one first."

The other actor strips down to his shorts. He's careful when he's taking off his T-shirt, stretching the neck band so he won't touch the mustache he stares at the foot of the bed and watches the dancer as she underdresses.

"Do you want a mustache, chickie?" He asks.

"She's already got a beard," the cameraman says.

At the last minute, just before the shooting begins, there is an argument between the producer and the actors. The actors want to wear dark glasses, and the producer doesn't want them to. He thinks it's cheating. Finally, the cameraman who is ready to go and in patient, settles it by saying that he's not going to shoot any more of their ugly faces that he has to. That's not what the movies about. Dark glasses are taken from the case and had it around. The shooting of the first scene begins.

Jerry leans against the wall and watches. The whore walks over and stands beside him.

"You nervous of these things?" She asks.

"At first," Jerry admits. "I'm afraid it won't come up."

"Relax," the horses. "With me, it'll come up."

Jerry thanks her and turns back to watch the couple on the bed. There is no excitement in the coupling no passion Jerry watches it with the same detachment that he watches TV in a bar.

"Where up." The whore says and she begins to address.

There is a harsh grunt from the other actor, and he arches into a frozen moment, spending himself.

"Take a break," the cameraman says. He moves the camera and the tripod over to the bathroom doorway.

As Jerry and a whore cross to the bathroom, he hears the dancer say to the other actor, "You got to be that rough?"

"That's gentle," the actor says. "You ain't seen rough yet."

Jerry stands naked in the tub, the shower curtain drawn around him. Outside, behind the curtain, he can hear the camera motor running. The bit is that the whore is in the bathroom, about to take a shower. She undresses and strokes her breasts, she plays with herself. That is the show that she's ready. Then she draws back the curtain and discovers Jerry is there. It is time now and it is not all the way up yet. He whips it a couple of times, eyes closed, trying to think of a young girl he knew once, young, tight flesh on the grass of a golf course.

"Ready, Jerry?" The cameraman shouts.

"Sure." The memory has worked to some degree. It is almost up and he knows that it will be all right. The rent will be paid and there will be money for the bars.

When the curtain is pulled away, the whore pretends shock but only for a moment. The cameraman calls for Jerry to shake it at her, insisting. She gives in finally and leans toward him, taking it in her hand and then after she is seated on the edge of the tub, taking it in her mouth. The wet warmth and flick-flick of her tongue and he feels himself pushing out, hard now. When she releases him to take a breath, she says softly, "You see? I told you it would be all right."

The morning seen through red eyes, the sun barely up when I get out of bed and put on the kettle. While the water was heating, I got the two reels from the living room and brought them back to the kitchen. I emptied a metal trashcan and lined it with tinfoil. Then, slowly, taking my time, I cut the film into short pieces and dropped them into the trashcan. By the time I'd finished the first reel, the water was boiling, and I poured it through the coffee. The water settle through the ground, while I chopped up the second reel.

Then, with a fresh cup of coffee in one hand, I carried the film out into the backyard. As an afterthought, I went back into the house and got a can of lighter fluid. I soaked the film with the fluid and stood away when I tossed a match into the trashcan. There was a high flash of flame at first, then it died down so that

I could stand over the can and watch the film turn into white ash and smoke.

I drank my coffee. There went his immortality, up in smoke and down into ash.

If it was Jerry.

CHAPTER TWENTY FOUR

CHAPEL HILL, 1969

DROPS AND
OTHER MATTERS

School was over for the year. All the grades were in, the complaints handled. I spent two or three evenings a week at the New Establishment. If I arrived early enough, I'd find a window table near the front of the bar. There, with the darkness of the bar covering me, I'd look down upon the people passing on Franklin Street. Or, Tyring of the street below, I turned in my chair and watched the young people entering and leaving.

I was the oldest person in the bar, and I sometimes felt that the young people were looking at me with suspicion. Is he a cop, a narc if they'd ask me, I would've been happy to identify myself. But that might make just as many problems. Him a teacher? Him? That beer set, that's stumbler, weaves, and wobbles his way to the men's room every few minutes to relieve his worn out kidneys? I imagine the comments and try to walk a little straighter, to squaring my shoulders and suck in my stomach. To tell the truth, I was certain that they had better things to talk about. It was an odd kind of vanity on my part to believe that they noticed me at all.

I noticed them. Especially the girls. Many of them, shaggy, with an almost unwashed quality, the promise of easy conquest, instant promiscuity. There's one girl in particular that I watched for. She was a blonde, small and slender, almost delicate, neat to a degree that many of the others weren't. I overheard one of the bartenders called her April. One night I asked a couple of people her last name, but nobody seem to know. Once, coming out of the relative darkness of the rest room area, I confronted her, blocking her way for a moment. Maybe she'd seen me in the New Establishment before, or on campus, and I thought there was a moment of recognition, before she smiled at me. Maybe it was there, and maybe it wasn't. Still, after that, each time I went toward the men's room or away from it, I had a "hello, how are you" loaded in the back of my throat, ready to spill out of her. The "hello" remained there, building its fizz and gas, unused. If I did meet her now, I knew that it would explode out at her and frighten both of us.

Then the Greek came in. Nobody ever called him by his real name. He was tall and muscular, with pale skin and dark curling hair. The first few times I saw him, I put his age at around 25, if not on the far side of 25. Actually, someone told me he was really only 19. He was probably the oldest 19-year-old I'd ever met. I met him a year ago and it was some indication of balance on both of our parts that we didn't end up hating each other.

At that time, a couple I knew from New Haven, passed through Chapel Hill on their way to visit her parents in Tampa, Florida. Ace called me and I met them at Harry's. His wife Barbara was back in the restroom when Ace leaned across the booth table toward me.

"Any chance of scoring here in town?"

I must've given him a puzzled look because he leaned closer to me "Weed, grass, pot."

I noted that I understood. "I'm not sure."

"Could you ask around?"

I said that I wasn't sure. I didn't know anybody to ask.

Ace leaned back. "I've got to spend a week with her family, and that means I need at least an ounce to take with me." He laughed. "The last time I was there, Barbara's mother, thought my cigarettes, smelled funny, and I convinced her that it was a special blend for my sinus condition."

I turned in my seat and looked around. It was the early supper rush at Harry's. Of the few people I knew, I didn't know any of them well enough to ask. Then I saw Earl in one of the back booths. I didn't know him well. Slightly, if at all. But I'd done one of his friends a favor once and I've been invited to a party where I was fairly certain they were smoking in one of the rooms. I'd left early because I could see the headlines in the newspapers all across the state: "University of North Carolina, professor arrested in drug raid." No matter what your real rank, you were a professor if you were arrested.

Earl looked up from his grilled frank sandwich and nodded to me as I slid into the seat across from him.

"A favor," I said. "If you can't stand to do it, just say so, and we'll forget I asked." I told him about the friend passing through town. "Do you know some dealer who might sell to me?"

He looked at my tweed jacket and tie and almost choked on his sandwich.

"Not many," he said. "You look like an academic version of a cop." He swallowed, the lump of partly chewed sandwich almost lodging in his throat. "That is, some cop, who went to East Carolina one semester before he flopped out."

I was about to leave, when he stopped me. "There's a guy named the Greek. Tell him I said you were all right. He can call me at home if he wants to check."

He told me two or three places where the Greek spent time when he was dealing. I thanked him and went back to the booth where Ace and Barbara were. I told Ace I'd help him look around.

"For what?" Barbara asked.

"Smoke," Ace said.

We'd about run out of places to look when we found him. It was in a new bar out on W. Franklin St. The bartender pointed out the Greek to me at a table near the pinball machine. Ace and Barbara waited for me at the bar. The Greek looked up at me when I stepped beside his table.

I told him who I was, and asked if I could sit down.

"Sure." He nodded at the chair across the table from him, but I passed that up and sat in the chair to his right.

"Earl told me to tell you that I was all right. You can call him at home if you want to."

He stood up. "You know his number?"

I said that I didn't.

"And Earl is a friend of yours?"

I said I knew him through other people. I didn't know him well enough to call him a friend.

The Greek went to the phone at the far end of the bar. When he came back a few minutes later, he slept in his chair and grounded me. "Teacher, huh?"

"It's a way to make a living."

"What do you want?"

"An ounce of grass," I said.

"I don't deal," he said. "I want to make sure you know that." I nodded. "But I know somebody who does. I'll have to ask around. It might take half an hour or so."

I slipped out my wallet, keeping it under the table, and took out two tens. I wadded them into a small ball and passed it over to the Greek.

"What's that for?" He looked around quickly.

"It's twenty right?"

"Yes, but … "

I told him I didn't want to be seen passing things back and forth with him on street corners. It wouldn't help my reputation much. Or his, either.

"You trust me, huh?" he said.

"It's only money," I said.

Ace and Barbara gave up after an hour of waiting. I drew them a map and gave them the key to my house. They were going to spend the night there anyway. I sat at the bar, drinking beer after beer, feeling foolish. The grass wasn't even for me, I didn't even want it, and here I was spending the whole evening in the thick smoke and loud rock of a bar I didn't like much. I stayed until 11:45, when the bartender gave last call.

Ace and Barbara left the next morning. Ace wanted to make up the twenty to me but I argued that I'd see the Greek in the next day or two and get it back. I didn't believe it, but I tried to make it sound like I did.

It was nearly two weeks before I saw the Greek again. I almost forgot, and the 20. I was walking home one afternoon, and the yellow Mustang pulled up beside me at a stoplight. The horn honked and I turned, and I saw the Greek.

"Do you wanna ride?" He said.

I nodded and got in.

"Sorry I stood you up that night. Somebody was following me and I thought maybe you'd fooled Earl, that you were a narc."

I said there seemed to be problems with most professions.

"I'd have brought it by a day or so later," he said. "But I caught mono and had to spend a week in the hospital."

I gave him directions, and he pulled up into my driveway. He turned and looked through the rear window. Then he opened his shirt down around his belt and passed me a plastic bag. I'd been expecting the twenty back and I didn't want the pot, but it didn't seem cool to say so.

"Any time," the Greek said.

He backed out of the driveway and I went in the house and spent an hour trying to find a good place to hide the grass. I'd put it in one place, and then, a few minutes later, I'd decide that was the first place the police would look. Finally, I put it in a sock and buried it in a mass of socks. After that, every time I'd reach into the drawer, I'd end up with a sock with the ounce of grass in it.

The Greek got himself a beer at the bar and came over to my table. "Is this going to hurt your reputation?" He asked. That became a joke with him, and from that moment on, he'd say that every time before he sat at the table with me.

"What reputation?" I said. "Do you see any other faculty members hanging around a place like this?"

When he was seated, he asked, "Do you know Pete Franklin?"

I said I wasn't sure, that the name didn't mean anything to me.

"He overdosed last night or this morning."

"Is he dead?"

The Greek shook his head. "He's in North Carolina Memorial. I heard he was all right."

"On what?"

"Smack, I heard."

I looked at him and he must've known what I was thinking.

"Not me," he said. "If it was me, I'd be hauling ass over the Virginia Maryland line about now."

"Lucky," I said.

"I don't deal with it." He grinned. "Not because I'm too moral or anything like that. Like any other business, you get to keep turning the dollar over. No matter what people tell you, there aren't that many people on smack here. No profit in it." The grin broadened. "Now, grass, even the middle class are buying that."

Someone approached the table and stopped just behind me. I turned in my chair and saw that it was the blonde girl I'd been thinking about. The Greek smiled at her. "Hello, April."

"Can I see you for a minute?" She asked.

"Sit down," the Greek said. He pushed out a chair with his feet and, after hesitating, she eased into the chair, sitting very straight on the edge of the seat, waiting for the introductions.

"I've seen you around," April said, looking at me.

"Me too," I said. "But I wasn't sure you noticed me."

April nodded. "I did."

The Greek leaned toward her. "Do you want an ounce?"

April looked at me.

"He's all right," the Greek said.

April shook her head. "I want a $10 bag."

The Greek said he'd quit splitting up the bags.

"All I can afford is $10."

The Greek asked if she knew anybody who'd split an ounce with her.

"Nobody who is here."

"I'll take the other half," I said. The Greek looked at me and smiled. He was reading my mind, seeing my interest in April.

"Done then." He finished off his beer. "I'll meet you out front in 25 minutes."

While we waited, I bought another beer for me, and one for April. We watch the street below for the Greek's Mustang. I learned that she was out of school, but that she was trying to get back in during the summer sessions, to see if she could lift her grades and get re-admitted in the fall. The last year she'd been working as a secretary at the hospital.

"My mother likes that. She thinks I'll meet a nice doctor, and get married," she said. "I haven't met a nice doctor yet."

"I'll be a doctor, if I ever finish my dissertation," I said, feeling a little foolish, a little too bold. "Would that count?"

"I thought you looked a little too dignified for up here."

"Me?"

"Yes," April said, "very distinguished."

The Greek's Mustang pulled up by the curb, and we left our unfinished beers on the table and went down to the street.

We paid the Greek, and I suggested that he drop us by my house so we could split the ounce. I was afraid that April might bulk at this, but she didn't. The Greek didn't need directions this time. He turned onto N. Columbia St., passed the fire house, and then pulled into my driveway. I asked the Greek in for a beer, but he said he still had business to do. When April opened the car door, I could see him in the light, smiling at me.

"Take it easy," he said.

"Is someone waiting for you to bring the stuff back?" I asked when we were in the kitchen.

"No."

"How about some coffee?"

She said coffee would be fine and I got out my grinder and ground up a couple of handfuls of coffee beans. I put the kettle on, and while the water heated, I tore off a piece of tinfoil. She divided the ounce into two parts. And looked at me. "Does this look right to you?"

I told her that it was fine with me.

April rolled up the plastic bag and taped it closed. She put it in her purse. I poured the water into the coffee grounds and went into the bedroom and got a pipe I've had for years, since the time I had worn one with my tweed jacket.

"Let's smoke a little of mine."

"Why not?" She said

After we'd smoked one pipe and were passing around the second, April said, "you're very generous with your stuff."

"I really didn't want it," I said. "I wanted to meet you."

April smiled. "I knew that." She drew in the smoke and held it until it was absorbed. "That's good stuff."

"You knew?"

She nodded. "You don't scare me a bit."

"That's reassuring."

The coffee forgotten, I went to the refrigerator and got two beers. Taking the beer from me, April asked, "are you feeling it?"

"Some," I said.

"How does it feel?"

"Loose, easy, a little out of myself."

"It makes me horny," April said.

"What?"

"Grass makes me horny."

"I never heard that before." I shook out the ash and put the pipe aside. I drank some beer and looked across the table at her.

"Don't leer at me."

"Huh?"

"You don't look as dignified when you leer at me."

"I didn't know that I was," I said.

"That's the worst kind. The unconscious leer."

"I'm sorry."

"Anyway, it won't do you any good. Not tonight"

I said I didn't understand.

April opened her purse. "Have a cigar." She held out a paper wrapped Tampax.

"I see."

"I can always go away and come back in three days."

I shook my head. "I'm afraid. If you go away, you might not come back."

"Would that be so bad?"

I nodded. "It would break my balls." Then as an afterthought: "my poor, fat, heart, too."

Her small blond head was on my chest, a scent so delicate that it didn't seem to be perfume. A small hand open and light on my stomach, just covering my belly button.

"You know, it's funny, when you're stretched out on your back, you don't have a beer belly."

"The muscles are out of shape," I said.

"Is this hard on you, sleeping with me this way, and not being able to do anything?"

"Ask me in three days and see if I remember," I said.

"A promise?"

"A promise."

Some mornings I wake up, feeling good, like it's worth waking up. Some mornings.

CHAPTER TWENTY FIVE

CHAPEL HILL, 1969

JUNE BUGS AND WHAT
HAPPENS NEXT

hapel Hill was pleasant and mild in early June. There was rain, but not so much that the town seem to be part of a jungle rainforest. Some years it did. It would rain for days, and if you didn't have air-conditioning, your clothing and curtains felt damp, and the shoes in the closet would turn green. Not this June. It was unlike any other June I'd spent in Chapel Hill.

Among other things, April moved in with me two weeks after I'd met her. As I remember, we were in the bedroom late one night, and she was complaining about the girl who shared the apartment with her. She said she was thinking of moving and I said, not really meaning it at the time, that she could move in with me.

That she considered it at all frightened me. When she accepted later that night, I did prepare to laugh just in case she did, to be followed by a teasing "you didn't think I was serious, did you?" Instead, not sure quite why I changed my mind, I put my arm around her and said "When?"

We were sitting on the front steps, drinking ice tea, one Saturday afternoon near the end of June. The front door was open and we were listening to some of her Rolling Stones records.

Sometime earlier, I'd heard the gasoline driven lawnmower in the distance, so I wasn't surprised when Marshall Beatright, came down the sidewalk past the high hedge that blocked my lawn from the one on my right.

He pushed the battered old mower, a yellow gas can dangling from the handles, up the driveway and stopped. He was followed by his little brother, Jason.

Marshall was black, around 14, tall and stringy for his age. His brother Jason was seven or eight, with some of the baby fat still on him. Marshall had stopped by one afternoon in late May and asked if he could cut my lawn. I liked him and I always paid him a dollar more than the price he'd set, just to be sure he'd come back every two weeks.

Now, watching him, I asked, "Is it ready?"

"Close," he said. He squatted and looked down the level of the lawn toward the street. "It might wait two or three days more."

"Still," I said, leaving it open so that he could walk into it.

"Still, I'm here today and I won't be here two or three days from now," he said.

"Maybe we ought to cut it today."

"It won't hurt any" he said.

While Marshall started the mower, I went into the house and got my checkbook and pen. I sat on the steps next to April and made out a check to Mr. Marshall Beatright. I did it and signed the check, but I didn't fill in the amount. I knew what it would be, but I knew that he would want to haggle a bit, and, since it was a routine we'd gone through the first two times, I thought he'd have been disappointed if we'd done it any other way. The second time in our mock argument, he called me a cheap cracker, and I called him a money hungry spade, but I think we both realized at the same time that we were walking on the edge of something and we'd pulled back.

April touched my shoulder. "What's he got?"

"What?"

"The little boy."

Jason was still in the driveway, out of the way of the mower. He was whirling around, turning, as if something were flying above his head, then, bending at his waist as it dipped lower. I couldn't see the thread, but I could make a guess. "I think it's a June bug."

"A what?"

"A June bug." I took her by the arm and we dodged Marshall and his mower as he went past. We reached the driveway and stood beside Jason.

"Let me see it," I said.

Jason nodded and pulled on the string, drawing the June bug in, like an angler plays a fish, until the green backed beetle was in the palm of his hand.

April leaned over Jason's palm and stared at it. "It's ugly."

I took the beetle from Jason and showed April how the string was tied to one of the back legs. The beetle could fly, but it couldn't get away.

"How long have you had him?" I asked Jason, handing the beetle back to him.

"Since yesterday."

"That leg won't last forever," I told him.

"I know," Jason said. "Then I'll catch me another one."

While April was fixing supper, I explained how a June bug was a poor child's toy, one that he could play with when he couldn't afford the ones from the dime stores or Western Auto. But that was only during the summer. The rest of the year, you had to play thought-up games where you didn't need anything but an imagination.

I'd played with June bugs myself. It had been back in Millhouse, before I started the first grade. Jerry thought he was too old to play with me and I've had to find another friend to play with. He was a little black boy about my own age named Blue. He was kind of a genetic freak, with one blue eye, and one brown eye. Some of the kids called him Blue-eye.

It was Blue who taught me how to catch June bugs, and how to tie the thread to their legs. The time I remember, with a special horror, we each had a June bug, and we were flying them too close together, and the threads got tangled. While he was trying to untangle threads, Blue got mad and jerked at the threads, and the leg came off the bug I was playing with, this tiny hairy leg left secure on the string.

"Look what you did," I said.

Blue took my June bug and threw it up in the air, watching the falling away, downward angle, as it flew into a clump of high weeds. "There is more where that stupid bug came from."

He snapped the thread and threw the leg away. He spent the rest of the morning fussing about how I didn't know how to fly a June bug worth anything.

I think I saw Blue a couple of summers ago when I was in Millhouse. I was on South Main Street, just walking around. It was a hot Saturday in August and I wandered too far out South Main until I was in the section of town where the black juke joints were. The unmoving air, heavy with the rancid odor of overused, cooking oil, the smell of frying fish and chicken.

When I turned to start back up South Main, I almost bumped into a black man who must've been walking right behind me. For a brief moment, face to face, smelling his whiskey breath I saw the blue and the brown eyes and lower down on his throat, the knife or razor scar, lighter than the rest of his skin, the scar tissue as textureless and smooth as oil.

I said "I'm sorry," and he gave me an ironic little bow and stepped around me.

I took a couple of steps and turned back, intending to ask if he was Blue, but he stepped into the Red Lantern Café, and I heard the low rumble of his voice: "Fat ass, white motherfucker thinks he owns the sidewalk," followed by the high giggle of a woman.

"Shower anyone?" I asked.

It was going on twelve. April and I had been to a movie, and on the way back, we'd stopped off at The Shack for a few beers. Now we were back at the house and I'd just opened the bathroom window to see if there was a breeze.

"With you?" she asked.

"It saves on the gas and water bill," I said.

"Well, when you explain it that way..."

I undressed first and leaned in past the shower curtain to adjust the water temperature. When it felt right, I stepped in and soaked myself. I was rinsing off when April pulled back the curtain and moved in beside me. She was wearing a pink shower cap with a couple of strands of hair sticking out at her forehead. I put my arms around her and pulled her up against me, the shower water, pouring down over us, feeling her small breasts flattening against my chest, the excitement got to me, and I could feel myself hardening against her, until she reached down and caught me in her hand.

"Is there room for three of us in here?"

"I hope so," I said

"God, you're hard tonight."

"Whose fault is that? I asked.

"In that case..." April put a hand behind her and felt for the rim of the tub, then she pulled me close to her and took me in her mouth. Slow, gentle, pleasure there, but so far away that it might have been happening to someone else. The shower water beat down upon us. Then, leaning away from me, April said "you taste like Dial soap."

✣ ✣ ✣

In bed a while later, passing the pipe back and forth, a coal of Hash, glowing in the center of the grass, she said: "you know, you're the best fuck in town."

"Is that so?"

"Yes, the best."

"How big is the sample?" I asked.

"What?"

I explained that for such a statement to have any kind of scientific validity, she'd have to test a large percentage of the male population of Chapel Hill.

She laughed. "It was a small sample."

"Then there's the possibility of error."

"Maybe, but I'm satisfied," April said. "And I'm through testing for a while."

For a while?

When I finally slept, the last thing I remembered, her head braced against my chest, was the warm, damp breath that flowed across my skin like water. Ruffling the chest hair, chilling, and warming me at the same time.

CHAPTER TWENTY SIX

NEW YORK, 1969

ONE HOT SUMMER
WE STAYED AT THE
HOTEL EARLE

"You're kidding. You've got to be kidding. You are kidding, aren't you?" Joe-John sounded like he'd already had his first two drinks of the day. I could hear hard rock on the radio or stereo at his apartment.

"No," I said, "that's where I'm staying, just like last time." I looked at April who was unpacking her two suitcases, hanging up her dresses and skirts. "That is, that's where we're staying."

"Does the *we* mean that the plot is thickening?"

I said I didn't know what he meant.

"Caught you one of those 40 year old school teachers infest Chapel Hill during the summer, huh? Back for six weeks to take courses to keep their teaching certificates and get laid, right?"

"Wrong," I said. "Nothing like that."

"In that case, how about a drink later?"

"Sure."

"How about O'Henry's?" Joe-John asked. "It's where all the fat tourist go."

We settled on 6 o'clock.

When we decided to fly up to New York for a week or ten days, I thought a long time about the kind of hotel where we'd make reservations. I had even checked through the hotel directories at the travel agency. What worried me was that a good hotel might have a desk clerk, who'd take one look at me and one look at April and asked to see a marriage certificate.

I had the feeling, from the few times that I'd stayed at the Hotel Earle, that they wouldn't care one way, or the other. With that in mind, I had written the Hotel Earle, and received my letter back a few days later, with a pencil note at the bottom that the reservation was confirmed. The fact that they didn't seem to have stationery of their own at the hotel made me feel a bit better about it.

In the cab on the way in from LaGuardia, April opened her purse and put on a plain gold wedding ring. I lifted her hand and looked at it closely.

"It looks real," I said.

"It is."

"It even looks like gold."

She smiled. "The cheapest one the jewelry store had. I've been leaving it in the dishwasher overnight and scratching it with Brillo pads for two weeks." She turned the ring in the light. "I've probably aged it two or three years."

"Where we are staying, it might not matter."

"Now you tell me."

The clerk at the Hotel Earle, young and just passed pimples, registered us without any hesitation. If he looked at April at all, it was with a badly concealed passion. On the way up to the room, in the elevator, she leaned against me and whispered, "That's not as hard as I thought it would be."

In the hallway, waiting, while the bell boy put our bags in the room, I told her that the clerk had looked at her everywhere, but at her ring finger.

A few minutes before six, we left the hotel and walked over to Sixth Avenue. It wasn't far to O'Henry's. We sat at one of the outdoor tables under a sun umbrella. I ordered a beer for me and a gin and tonic for April. Joe-John arrived a little later, wearing striped bellbottoms and a short sleeve denim shirt. He had a deep tan which Meant that he and Rachel had been getting out of the city on the weekends.

"Is this the horny schoolteacher?" Joe-John asked.

April wasn't sure quite how to take that, so I explained that Joe-John was a big joker. "Most of them bad jokes."

"It was a reasonable mistake," Joe-John said,

When the waiter started for the table, Joe-John pointed at my beer. "Remember those summers in Chapel Hill? The first week at the beginning of each summer session we called the running of the school teachers. Like the running of the bulls, right down the main street. All of them with hungry written on their foreheads. Say hello to one of them, and they'd drop their pants on the spot." The waiter came with his mug of beer. "I thought you still liked older women."

I couldn't let that pass. "Speaking of older women, how is Rachel?"

"I'm going to tell her that you said that."

"She won't believe you," I said.

He hesitated. "You're probably right."

"I'm April." She finished her drink and was chewing an ice cube.

Joe-John leered her and then let a smile undercut the leer. "I bet you are. And May and June and July, too."

April blushed and I moved the conversation away from her to the book he was working on. "How is it going?"

"It's crap." Then he looked at April. "Oh, it's probably fairly good crap, but crap anyway." He wiped his mouth with the back of his hand. "Maybe it will shape up during the rewrite."

An hour later, April and I were ready to leave and go back to the hotel, but Joe-John insisted that Rachel was expecting us, that she'd been preparing dinner for us since I'd called. "Something pretty special for you, I think."

We left O'Henry's and walked up sixth Avenue toward 12ᵗʰ St. "If you'd like, you can move out of the Earle and stay with us. I've still got the Dirty Word bed, the one I had in the apartment I shared with Bill and Oscar. Do you remember the bed?"

I said that I did.

One year, Joe-John shared a small house off Rosemary Street with two other students. It was during the year he was courting Rachel. It had been, in his words, fairly heavy courting, and he hardly ever spent a night at the house. It turned out that his bed was the best one in the house, and every time Bill or Oscar balled a girl, they used his bed. He'd come back to the house early in the morning to change clothes and get his books to find that his bed looked like, the way he said it, twenty men had stood around the bed in a circle and jacked off on it. We named it The Fucking Bed, and Joe-John had carried it around all the years since then.

"No, thanks," I said. "Wouldn't want to damage an heirloom like that."

"So much for hospitality."

"So much," I said.

Rachel is really three or four years older than Joe-John and I think she feels it. She's almost 40 but she dresses like she's 20 and, through pain and agony, she keeps herself slim and sleek. Her hair is always changing shapes and colors. This time it was frosted, cut short and molded to the shape of her face. The first thing you notice about her, after you've absorbed the physical externals, is her voice. At base, it's soft and southern, but she's laid over it a brisk clipped manner, how she thinks the real New

Yorkers speak. The disconcerting aspect of being around her for any time is that after she's had a few drinks, she falls back to the southern speech. When she realizes what she's done, she always laughs as if to tell us that she's really putting it on.

"Veal cordon bleu? Again?"

We were in the dining room, and Rachel, with the help of April, had placed the platter and bowls on the table. It took Joe-John about ten seconds to recognize the main course.

"Buddy, don't ever let your wife...oops girlfriend...go to one of those uptown continental cooking schools. They keep cooking the same things over and over until they're sure they've got it right." Joe-John looked at Rachel. "I think this is the third time this week."

"The second," Rachel said.

"All right, the second." He leaned across the table. "And peas...Does veal cordon bleu go only with peas?"

Rachel smiled at April and me. "Joe-John only acts this way when the writing is not doing well."

"This girl knows how to hack a man's hide," Joe-John said

"Anyway," Rachel said, "The peas are fixed with a subtle difference this time."

Joe-John sat down. "As long as there's a subtle difference."

We ate. April told Rachel that it was great, the best meal she'd ever eaten. Joe-John mumbled about waiting until the next time we came over to dinner and had to eat it again and then see how much we liked it. But I noticed that Joe-John seemed to eat with a good appetite. He brought a double martini to the table with him, and he was alternating sips of that with the wine. By the time the coffee came, he'd regained his good humor, that is, if the whole scene hadn't been a joke anyway.

When the table was cleared, April went into the kitchen with Rachel and I followed Joe-John into his study. There were two, ceiling-high bookcases along the walls to the left and to the right and a desk near the single, wide window, placed so that the light came in over his back when he worked. The desktop was too neat, too orderly, and I realized that Rachel had been telling the truth, that he was having trouble. I'd been there before when the work had been going well. The desk had been a mess then.

"I've got a problem with it," Joe-John said. "Maybe it's plotting or it might be just too much plot. Or the wrong plot."

I said that he seemed confused.

"It might be these million brain cells you lose every year."

"Huh?"

"I read that somewhere. Anyway, I can't seem to concentrate. I start out trying to concentrate on how to beat the book and, after a few minutes, I find my mind wandering."

"What's it about?"

"It's about this guy, he's around 30. He's been fucking everything that moved since he was 15 and one day he's walking down by the arch in Washington Square and his cock falls off. He feels something sliding down on the inside of his pant leg and then splat. There it is on the sidewalk by his shoe. He picks it up and wraps it in his handkerchief and carries at home. Sure enough, when he gets home, he gets into the bathroom where his wife can't see him, and takes down his pants and his shorts and discovers that he's got a pussy instead, a sweet, juicy, tender little fragrant pussy with the maidenhead still in it." He stopped and looked at me. "You know, like April has."

"No comment."

"One of those Carolina gentleman, huh?"

"How about titties?" I asked

"What?"

"Does he look under his T-shirt, too?"

Joe-John shook his head. "That's as far as I've gone, to where he's in the bathroom and discovers he's got a pussy."

"The literary shrinks are going to have fun with this book right after you win your Nobel Prize."

"If I finish it," he said.

"Sure, you'll finish it."

Rachel stood in the doorway and asked if we were going to spend the whole evening in there telling dirty stories are come out into the living room and act civilized.

On the way into the living room, I told Joe-John that, of course, he was dealing with Tiresias myth, and if he could find some way to make the myth relevant to our day, he might be able to get away from just the surface, plot premise. Not because I really believed it, but because he needed to hear it. Secretly, I thought it was the kind of plot that belongs in one of those books they sell in Times Square. He could call it *Solitary Swap* or something like that.

Once, when April was in the bathroom, Rachel said, "that's a sweet little girl."

"Lord, is she ever sweet!" Joe-John said.

Ignoring him, letting her voice fall into the parity of a southern speech pattern: "Are you corrupting the child, that mere child?"

"Yes, Scarlett."

Joe-John tamped a cigarette on the edge of the coffee table. "You've already violated the Mann act."

"Not yet," I said, "but I will before the week is over."

It was 11 p.m when April and I reached Sixth Avenue. I stopped at the corner, looking both ways. "Anything else you want to do tonight? Another drink?"

"Not tonight. We've got all the time in the world." She put an arm around my waist, the hand stroking my hip. "I have discovered something."

"What?"

"Traveling makes me itchy."

"What's that?"

"That's the female version of horny."

"I see."

I kissed her, and we turned and walked down sixth Avenue, toward Eighth Street. We window-shopped the whole way, taking our time, knowing there wasn't any reason to hurry. Knowing that it would be there, maybe even sharper, when we got back to the hotel.

"You know you might be right," I said, as I came out of the delicatessen on Eighth Street. "But it might just be change of scene."

I told her about a friend who lived in Chapel Hill years ago and every now and then, he'd take his wife out to one of those fancy motels on the Durham-Chapel Hill Highway for a weekend. They hadn't been five miles from home, but he said it made all the difference in the world.

In the hotel room, I undressed down to my shorts and opened one of the pop top beers I bought at the delicatessen. I sat on the bed and sipped the beer while April was in the bathroom. When she came out, she was wearing a sheer Shorty nightgown.

"Very fancy," I said.

"I bought two things for this trip, the ring and this."

I handed her the open beer and went to the bathroom door. "It's very pretty" I said, "you look very good through it."

I took a quick shower and dried off. When I returned to the room, she had finished the first beer and had opened another. We sat on the bed, with the pillows upright against the headboard by behind us, and past the beer, back and forth. In the room, next to us, there was soft music from the radio and the measured squeaking of the bed springs.

I pointed toward that room. "You see, fucking is not so remarkable. Everybody does it."

"It's remarkable with us."

Maybe. Maybe not.

"I wish you could always be like this with us," April said.

"Yes"

"Do you think it will be?"

I said I wasn't sure.

"What can happen?"

I told her that one day she might look at me and see an old man no matter how long we lasted together after that, she wouldn't be able to see me any other way. "If it happens, that'll be it."

She put her head on my shoulder, hugging me, her head, moving from side to side, making the silent no, no. "I won't let it happen."

I wish you luck.

"You're not old. You're the best screw in the world."

With how many screws left?

"I've never told you, but I love you." Still, silent, holding her, I wondered about the very young. Love is so easy.

In time, we made love.

Next-door, the bed springs had stopped squeaking.

It lasted a long time, April making love to me, as if trying to convince herself and me that she really did love me. I felt like I was trying to claw my way slowly out of some sad fog and somewhere in the center of it there was slippery ground where neither of us knew what we were doing or why, or where we were or where it was all going to end. And in the distance, a clock struck one.

One Saturday, at a football game with her, pushing past knees toward our seats, I heard one of the co-eds we passed say: "He must be her father." I looked at April to see if she'd heard and found that she was blushing.

I guess I am her father, both of us loving the ritual incest. The green rank scent of it. Acting out in gesture and a language neither of us understands the closet drama in which the surface is more important than the depths. Once, trying to explain this to her, I said that I was writing my own Poetics.

"The modern tragic hero is a man committed to something which he knows in her own heart to be absurd."

"What is absurd?"

Incest and oatmeal cookies.

After a moment: "You haven't answered me."

"I guess you're not going to answer me." Pouting, a muscle coils in her back, ending in the rigid little toe of her left foot. On the side of which there is the smooth, centerless pit of a corn.

Words bubble, child, but there is no answer.

"Sometimes I think you think I'm stupid."

"It is your mind I love most," I say finally.

The muscle uncoils and the corn disappears under the twisted edge of the sheet.

CHAPTER TWENTY SEVEN

NEW YORK AND
NEW HAVEN, 1969
AND ROBIN HOOD
LIVES IN CENTRAL PARK

Evadne waited on the porch of Mrs. Durant's kindergarten. She sat perfectly still in the glider swing, not rocking herself back and forth as children usually do. Back straight, hands in her lap, legs dangling. She looked straight ahead, along the plane of the porch, toward the house next door. When my cab stopped in front of the house, it was as if she counted to five before she turned her head and looked at me.

As she came down the steps, she said: "Mama said I'm supposed to be home by five."

I took her hand at the bottom step. "Don't you even say hello?"

"Hello, daddy."

I held the cab door open for her. "It's good to see you, baby."

"I wanted to tell you what Mama said first, so I wouldn't forget."

"Sure, baby." I closed the door behind us and the cab worked its roundabout way back toward the downtown area of New Haven. "Had lunch yet?

"Yes, but it wasn't good." She wrinkled her nose. "It was chicken stew."

"Are you hungry now?"

Evadne hesitated. "I'm not supposed to get fat again."

"You weren't fat," I said. "You were pleasingly plump."

"Oh, Daddy."

"Like a little white rabbit."

"I wasn't."

"You were too little to remember"

"People always say that." The hint of protest in her voice was controlled, a kind of little girl exasperation. "I wish they would."

"All right, I won't anymore"

The cab pulled into a space near the Green on Chapel Street. The driver turned and looked at us. "This where are you want?"

I put an arm around Evadne. "What do you want to do?"

"Could we go to the beach?"

"Sure, baby." I turned the driver. "You heard the lady."

It had been a spur of the moment decision and I'd barely had time for the taxi ride to Grand Central to catch the ten-twenty to New Haven. I'd left some money with April, so she could do some shopping and told her I'd be back in the early evening, in time for a late dinner.

The train arrived in New Haven a little before noon and I caught a cab to DiNicola's restaurant. I got there as they were opening for the day. The bartender didn't remember me at first. I ordered a Hull's Export draft to see if it was as bad as I remembered. It was.

I got out the phone book and called Mrs. Durant's kindergarten. She said yes, that event, and he was there, but she'd have to hear from her mother before she could allow me to take her out for the afternoon. That was a block, a big block. I didn't want to talk to Elaine. I had another beer and got my nerve up enough. I called the office where she worked.

Elaine didn't recognize my voice, and when I told her who I was, she seemed to move away from the phone. Her voice seemed to be coming from down a long tunnel, flattened out with all the lows and the highs removed.

When she balked at me taking Evadne for the afternoon, I reminded her of the visitation rights and she said if I'd bothered to read the agreement, I would have seen that I was supposed to give her two weeks' notice before a visit. I saw that this approach wasn't getting me anywhere, so I shifted ground and said that I was only going to be in New York another two or three days and that I'd like to see a Evadne before I headed south again. Although I didn't use it, there was an implied please in my voice.

She said it would be all right this time, but next time she wasn't going to be that easy to get along with. I think her and she hung up to make the call to the kindergarten. I went back to the bar. I wanted some fettuccine, but I didn't think there was time. I settled for a cold sandwich and ate it while I waited for the cab the bartender had called for me.

It was too crowded when we reached the beach. We went another mile or two until we were in a more rugged area. We could hardly see the beach from the road, but there were V-cut spaces every hundred yards or so the led from the high grassy dunes down to the beach.

I saw a drive-in restaurant ahead and I had the cab pull off the road and stop there. I knew I was going to have trouble getting back to New Haven, so I over-tipped the driver and asked if he could come back for us at 4 o'clock. He said that he could and I watched while he made a note of the name of the drive-in restaurant.

Evadne still seemed reluctant as we walked up to the door of the restaurant. "Are you sure it's alright?"

"Baby," I said, "if you were living with me, the first thing I would do is put a little more weight on you."

"You would?"

"You better believe it and Boy Scouts honor." I opened the door for her and guided her to a booth. "I never liked skinny white rabbits"

"I am not a rabbit." Then, serious, holding herself erect, so that she could see me above the table, "where do you live now?"

"Chapel Hill."

"Do I know Chapel Hill?"

I shook my head. "You were a little baby then."

"Did you come all the way from Chapel Hill to see me?"

"Partly," I said.

"What, daddy?"

I explained that I was staying in New York for a few days and I'd come to New Haven just to see her. "I wouldn't miss a chance to see you."

"I was in New York once."

I asked what she'd seen in New York.

"Central Park."

"Did you see Robin Hood?" I turned and looked out the window. "He lives there."

"Robin Hood lives there?"

"Sure," I said, "in a treehouse near the pond."

"Does he rob people?"

"Only the rich," I said. "And he gives to the poor."

"Oh, Daddy," Evadne said, "you tell funny stories."

"Is that right?"

Evadne nodded. "Mama said so."

That was like her. I changed the subject.

I argued for a full meal, but Evadne insisted upon a hotdog, French fries, and a Coke. I drank a beer while I watched her nibble lady-like at her hot dog, taking small bites, and placing the hot dog back on her plate while she chewed. It bothered me because it was the portrait of a little girl eating in public with strangers. Correct and perfect and well drilled.

Once we were across the highway, we stopped at the top of the dune, and took off our shoes. Evadne didn't want to, but I convinced her by saying that we'd wade in the water. I put her shoes inside my shoes and rolled up my trouser legs. Then, holding her hand, we started down to the beach.

A few feet down the dune, Evadne stopped, pulling back on my arm. "What are those black things?"

I looked and saw that the whole beach was strewn with black clusters, as far as I could see in both directions.

"It must be seaweed," I said. "It washes up sometimes."

When we were at the beach level, I realized that the whole beach was covered with black, oil-coated fish, rotting, swarmed upon by shifting masses of flies.

"Daddy, they're fish."

I said that she was right, that it wasn't seaweed at all.

We walked a zigzag course down to the low tide mark and waded in the froth.

Evadne seemed to be relaxing, enjoying yourself, until a dead fish rolled in sideways in the surf and almost touched her feet. That spoiled the wading, and we left the water and continued on down the beach, hoping we'd pass the area where the fish-kill was.

It didn't clear up, and I could feel Evadne withdrawing from me, getting more and more remote until she was answering me only with a single word, or a nod. We'd gone along way, and I could see that she was tiring. Until, almost as if we'd read each other's minds, we decided at the same moment to walk back down the beach in the direction we'd come, following our own footsteps, so that we could find the V cut where we'd entered the beach.

When we reached the right dune and climbed it, the cab was waiting for us. I lifted her and placed her on the head of the cab and brushed off her feet with my handkerchief. She squinted into the overcast sky, patient and polite, until I put her sneakers on and tied the laces.

"You didn't know they were dead fish?"

"No," I said, wanting her to believe me. "I really thought it was seaweed."

"Why didn't you know?"

There was no answer for that, and I just shook my head.

I thought we were going to be too early and I'd have to wait with Evadne until Elaine arrived. But when the cab stopped in front of the house, I saw Elaine's car in the driveway.

I went to the porch with her and she kissed me and said that she wanted me to come and see her again. But she was far away from me, pulling away, even as she had her arms around my neck.

Then Elaine opened the front door, and we nodded at each other, our lips moving, and no sound coming out. Evadne waved at me before she stepped inside and Elaine closed the door behind her.

There was still an hour and a half before the next rain train back to New York and I had the cab drop me off at DiNicolas. I had a few drinks and tried to empty the afternoon out of my head, but it wouldn't leave and I rode the train back to New York with the beach, running before my closed eyes, like under exposed film, going faster and faster until it matched the sound of the wheels and finally, I got up and went to the bathroom and threw up.

I got back to the hotel around 8:30 and found that April wasn't in.

I brushed my teeth to get the taste of the vomit out and showered and stretched out on the bed.

When I woke up an hour or so later, April was seated on the edge of the bed, smoking a cigarette and looking down at me. She saw I was awake and asked, "how was your little girl?"

"It was pretty bad." I went into the bathroom and splashed cold water on my face and had an Alka-Seltzer. I felt groggy and half awake and my stomach felt raw.

April watched me from the doorway. "You look like you feel terrible."

"I feel like shit."

"We don't have to eat out."

I said that maybe a good dinner at Mother Bartoletti's might save some of the day. I didn't believe it. It was a crock. Still, staying in the hotel wasn't going to help either.

Before we left the hotel, I got a traveler's check from the safety deposit box and cashed it. The hotel clerk didn't want to cash one for $50, but I bitched at him until he did.

The scampi was excellent. We had a good wine with it and by the time the coffee and Benedictine came, some of the day had begun to fog around the edges. It didn't have the clarity and sharpness of a few hours before. April, who'd been wary of me at first, could feel the change, and she put her hand under the table and stroked my knee. She said she missed me all day, dammit, and she'd been thinking of new ways to rape me for the last 11 or 12 hours.

"Rape me?"

"Seduce, then."

"Seduce?"

"Oh, you know what I mean."

It was going toward midnight when we left the restaurant and walked back to the hotel. I got the key from the clerk and sent April up to the room while I went around to Eighth Street. I got a six pack of beer from the delicatessen and I was headed back, only about a half block from the hotel, when a young boy stepped out of a doorway in front of me.

"Got a light?"

I shifted the bag to my other hand and reached in my pocket for my lighter. I heard a scrape behind me, and before I could turn, I felt something braced against my spine.

"That's a gun," the man behind me said.

He patted my hip and I felt the wallet slip out of my rear trouser pocket.

"Leave me the wallet," I said.

"What?"

"Take the money and leave me the wallet."

I waited a moment and heard the wallet drop at my feet.

"You got a watch?"

The young man who stopped me stepped closer to me and reached for my wrist. At that moment, a car turned the near corner, and the headlights swept across us. The man behind me gave me a push, and I fell headfirst against a brick building wall, the impact making me drop the bag of beer. When I got up, I saw them running onto Eighth Street. I knew they were mixing into the crowd, going into a movie or one of the bars on that stretch of street.

I got my wallet and the bag of beer and walked on to the hotel.

The night clerk called the police for me while I washed a cut on my face. I called April and said I'd be up in a few minutes, but it wasn't anything to worry about. Then I went into the hotel bar and had a drink while I waited for the police to arrive.

Three days later we flew back to Chapel Hill.

CHAPTER TWENTY EIGHT

CHAPEL HILL, 1969

LEAVES, MORTALITY AND WINTER IS COMING

It was late in the year for a large party. Usually, the large parties in Chapel Hill were scheduled during the comfortable weather, the spring, or the summer, or the very early fall, so if the party became too large for the house, it could overflow outside.

It was deceptive October weather, anyway, warm and sunny the whole week before the party, and you really had to breathe the night air, deeply, far back into your nose, to smell of the winter ice. The promise of ice, the gray frost you find on the grass one morning when you came out early to look for the morning paper.

I had reservations about the party. The invitation, as April recounted it to me, had been given to her alone. And when she asked if she could bring someone, Mason Armfield had said "sure ... Two or three more girls."

April said he looked like he wanted to take the invitation back when she explained that she wanted to bring the man she was going with.

"Shit," he said, and then, getting his balance he said, "sure, bring him ... to tell the truth, there are some other people who want to meet you."

"How do you spell meet?" I asked as we sat over a late supper. "M-E-A-T?"

"Probably" she said.

"Are you famous for meeting people?" I asked her.

"Probably."

An hour after we got to the party, I lost track of April. I'd gone to the kitchen to get us a beer from the bag I left in the refrigerator. Just as I entered the kitchen, two teenage kids were taking my bag of beer out of the refrigerator. They were stripping the plastic holder from the last six pack when I reached past them and took two of the beers.

"What, man?"

"My beer," I said.

"Oh." One of the kids with a blonde wispy beard looked at refrigerator. "I guess somebody drank ours."

"Sure," I said.

April wasn't where I left her in the living room.

I put one can in my jacket pocket and opened the other. I spent a few minutes wandering from room to room looking for her, but trying to act like that wasn't what I was doing.

There was a penny-nickel-dime stud game going on in the back room, and I leaned against the wall and wash it for a while. I considered getting in, when one of the players dropped out, but I decided against it.

I worked my way through the back living room and went out on the front porch, empty now, and sat on the cold stone steps.

It was chilly in the sky, seeing it through the nearly bare dark limbs of a large oak, was clear and bright. I tried, watching the stars, feeling their distance against my size, as a way of trying to push the anger away, and getting beyond myself.

I'm not jealous, I kept telling myself. Pissed a little, yes. But not jealous. I didn't like to think of myself that way.

It was like Ernest, a guy I'd known years ago, had put it that time. He told me that when he was 15, he and his friend had been balling their housekeeper, a 40-year-old woman who was a little simple minded. His sister, who was a few years older and very proper, found out about it, she confronted him with it, and tried to shame him. But when it hadn't been as easy as she thought, in desperation she'd thrown her final card at him: "What would you think if I did something like that?"

Ernest, the way he told it, had looked at her coldly and said, "it's your pussy, do what you want with it."

And he and his friend had gone on balling the housekeeper all through high school until they went away to college.

So, it was April's and she could do what she wanted with it. That was the reasonable way to look at it. But you could be pissed if a girl cut out on you at a party. That was reasonable, too. I kept trying to convince myself that was why I was angry. Just that, nothing more. I tried to hold the anger down, but it kept bubbling up, the taste of things I didn't like about myself, the bubbles, breaking in the back of my throat.

Later, sometime later, after I finished both beers, a panel truck pulled up in front of the house and April and another girl got out of the back of the truck. Half way up the walk, April saw me and hesitated. When she reached the steps, she flopped down beside me. The other girl passed, staring at me and went inside.

"Your beer got warm and drank it," I said.

Doors slammed at the panel truck, and two young men came up the walk, carrying a case of beer and two gallons of cheap wine. When they reached the steps, the one carrying the beers stepped around us and went inside. The other man, a gallon of wine and each hand, stopped in front of us. He was dressed mod, wearing bells and a pleated shirt. He was a good-looking guy and he knew it. He didn't say anything at first. He just stared at me. April felt the awkwardness of the situation and asked me, "did you meet Mason Armfield?"

"How do you spell that?" I asked.

"A-R-M-F–I–E–L–D." He looked puzzled.

April giggled and put her head on my shoulder.

"That's what I thought" I said.

Mason ignored me. "Are you coming in, April?"

"Maybe after a while."

"See you then." He walked around us and went inside slamming the door behind him. I lean toward April. "Did you meet Mason?"

"He asked me to, but I didn't."

"That's a girl." I stood up and rubbed my rear end. "My ass went to sleep waiting for you."

She stood up and turned so that she was flat against me. "How would you like me to kiss it and make it well."

"When?"

"Now."

"You don't mind leaving the party?"

April shook her head. "I'd rather be at home."

"You sure?"

"I am sure." She took my arm and we started down the walk. "All they can talk about is dope and how good they are in bed." She laughed. "And from what one of the girls told me, they're not that good, unless they're pretty stoned."

I pretended amazement. "Is that so?"

"That's what she said."

"There's just nothing to believe in anymore."

She put an arm around my waist. "I like old men myself."

"Why?"

"They all think the next fuck might be the last one and that makes them try harder."

"Hard?" I asked.

She said yes. Very hard.

The reading lamp was on, and the overhead light off when I came out of the bathroom and sat on the edge of the bed. April was reading *Castle Keep*, a pillow, doubled up behind her head. I stretched out on the bed beside her.

"Are you serious?" I asked.

"About what?" She marked her place and put the book on the floor beside the bed.

"Old men"

"Of course not." Her eyes were level, watching me. "I like mature men. Mature is different from old and you know it is."

Maybe I didn't know it, but it nagged at me. There was a smell to age, a scent of mortality, and I've smelled it on myself. The first time when I was very little. I was sitting on the front steps, and two old ladies passed me going down the steps after visiting Grandmama. I still have a sense memory of how they smelled – like rooms that have been closed for a long time, like damp old newspapers.

"You're a big silly," April said.

If my skin did begin to wear the scent of mortality, would Dial soap cover it?

"Sometimes I think you're more of a baby than I am."

Or English leather?

"A big mature baby" she said.

Would it soak away in a hot tub or a steam bath?

"But, I love you anyway."

We weren't in any hurry. The next day was Saturday and there wasn't class. April read a few more pages in *Castle Keep* and then ran a bath. She undressed slowly, walking around the room, while I watched. She left the bathroom door open while she bathed. Once, when I got up to look for my cigarettes, I stopped in the doorway and looked at her. She was using bath oil and her body was slick and glistening. She looked around at me.

"Want a bath, old man?"

"I'm reading."

I returned to the bed without the cigarettes and tried to concentrate on *Sarah Sampson*. I was re-reading the play so I could mention it in passing on Monday when I was lecturing on middle class tragedy. It wasn't a complex play, but after standing in the doorway and watching April, it seemed obscure and unimportant. I put the book aside and watched as she came out of the bathroom in a fog of bath oil scent and stretched out on the bed naked. She found her place in *Castle Keep* and began reading.

"You always dress like that when you read?"

"It shouldn't bother an old man," she said.

"It doesn't."

"Good."

"It doesn't bother me at all" I said.

"Good."

And then suddenly, a moment before I reached for her, she moved to the edge of the bed away from me, and said "I'm hungry…Maybe there's a bit of roast pork left."

I caught her arms and pulled her back, turning her. I was angry now, so angry, that if she protested, I didn't hear it.

Entering her before she was ready, feeling the drag of friction, the pain, and then I was like a fist, striking her over and over, moving in and out until she was moaning with pain, or with pain and pleasure. I wasn't sure which, and I didn't care.

It was rape or what I think rape must be like and after the shuddering agony, I lay in the breath guttering, waiting for the pace of my heart to slow to an erratic purr.

Then I discovered that I was crying out of anger, out of the frustration and the shame. The shame that I'd found the rapist in me when I thought I'd outgrown that part of the teenage wet dreams.

I tried to hide the tears, moving up to the side so that I could press my face into the pillow and blot the tears there. I must've been too slow. Perhaps April felt a drop fall on her. She tried to push me back gently so that she could see my face, but I used my weight and my strength to remain where I was.

"I know why you're crying." She said.

I asked why.

"Because it was so beautiful."

Which made me wonder.

I got up early in the morning. I looked in the bathroom mirror, to see if my eyes are puffy. They didn't seem to be. But that was only a small blessing.

I was drinking my 2nd cup of coffee and reading the sports page when April slipped up on me and put her arm around me. Her chin pressed down hard against the top of my head.

"Last night ... " She said softly.

"Yes?"

"It was the greatest ever." Her voice choked. "I'll never forget it as long as I live. If I live to be 100."

Me, either.

"Let's do that again sometime ... Whatever it was."

As soon as the rapist comes back from his vacation.

She released me and stepped away. "You know, that was so fantastic that I forgot I was hungry." The refrigerator door opened and closed. "Now I'm starving."

I went on reading the sports page while the kitchen filled with the smell of bacon and eggs. April was so happy that she was humming and whistling and, to me, it looked like Texas had the number one spot in the football polls sewed up.

CHAPTER TWENTY NINE

CHAPEL HILL, 1969

LAST WORDS BEFORE
THE FINAL WORDS

I t was a surprise to say the least. To say the most. To say anything at all. Maybe it was innocent of me to expect anything
else. To expect anything. To expect.

It happened this way. My 2 o'clock appointment called early
and left a note with the secretary that she had a bad cold and
then my 1 o'clock appointment didn't show. Both students were
in the dramatic criticism course and the conferences were to be
about their independent research. So now they were behind, and
I was behind, and I wasn't sure we'd ever catch up by the end of
the semester.

I went by Pop's for a sandwich and a beer. There was a law
student sitting at the bar, telling what he thought were hilarious
stories about the sexual conduct of a movie star he'd known in
Hollywood. He was a loudmouth and I'd heard him before,
so I took my sandwich and my pitcher of beer and moved as
far away from the bar as I could. I settled on the front booth,
and I sat with my back to the bar, watching the late fall street
outside.

The sky was gray and overcast, and it looked like it might
snow. I ate the sandwich and drink some beer and watched the

people moving outside the window, like some kind of formless and unstructured film.

I finished the pitcher, and I was twirling my glass in the pool of condensation, trying to decide if I could stand the loud-mouth until Pop got back from his afternoon break, when I saw April get out of a panel truck across the street. There wasn't any doubt that it was April and the man with her was Mason Armfield.

After he put money in the meter, Mason took her arm, and they walked back up Franklin Street, passed a few shops, and into an open doorway and out of sight. I didn't need to wonder where they gone. I knew. I've been up there a time or two. There was a stairway leading to the second floor, where there were a dozen or so rooms. Some male students, and other hangers-on around the University, lived in them. There was only one business up there, a typewriter repair shop. I doubted that either April or Mason Armfield owned a typewriter.

It was 1:40 in the afternoon when they went upstairs and they came out almost two hours later. During that time, I sat in the booth and drank beer and watched the street. Pop stopped by for a few minutes, and I tried to fake it, made out that everything was fine. All the time feeling the dry emptiness, the energy run-ning out of me, like it was pouring out of my skin with the sweat.

When they came out of the doorway, they were laughing arm in arm. I waited exactly 10 minutes after the panel truck drove off, leaving a part of a pitcher, and then I walked down Franklin Street, under the overcast sky, moisture in the wind against my face.

When I reached the downtown block of Chapel Hill, I kept going, I didn't turn onto North Columbia toward home, until I reached Jeff's.

I had a few beers there and then I went up to the New Establishment and sat with the Greek while he talked about some new girl he was doing.

When I had enough of the Greek, I went to The Shack. Around six, I decided that it wasn't going to get any better by walking around it. So, I went home. Dry and empty inside.

April didn't look any different. Supper was ready and she had been waiting for it. When she hugged me, I could smell the bath she had in the last hour or two. That was a clue. Sam Spade would make something of that. Mike Hammer would, too. If they would, I guess I would, too. For supper, she made a lamb stew in the Spanish way, the way I liked it best. I thought oh, shit, that's another clue, Sam and Mike. How many more to go?

When she asked me about my day, I lied, and said I spent most of the afternoon in the office. When I'd satisfied her, I asked how she passed her afternoon.

"In the public library, reading," she said, and she even had a stack of books in the living room to prove it.

After supper I said I was tired and went into the bedroom and undressed. Before I went to sleep, I could hear the television going full blast in the living room. There was so much gunfire, that it must've been a war movie or a western.

I awoke, and it was dark in the bedroom. April was leaning over me, but she didn't know I was awake, and she lit a cigarette and sat with her back to me until I pretended to groan and shift around.

"Awake, huh?"

I said it seemed that way.

"You seemed pretty distant today," she said.

I said that might be true but I wasn't sure what it meant.

"Something must be wrong."

"Maybe." I got up and went into the bathroom and pissed out the last of the afternoon beer. Looking down into the bowl, the emptiness still there, and feeling that it all turned to shit, that there wasn't much I could do.

"I guess we've got to talk," April said.

"Go ahead." I stretched out on the bed again.

"I guess I'm leaving."

"Guess?" I watched as she put out her cigarette. "Aren't you sure?"

Head nodding, she gave a jerky little tilt of her head. "I'm sure."

"That's funny," I said. "That's really funny."

"What is?"

"I spent most of the afternoon trying to decide what to do with you. You see, I wasn't in the office. I was at Pop's having a beer and looking out the window around 1:40 or so."

"Mason's not a cause. He's a result."

"God, but you've started talking fancy since you moved in here."

She stood up. "I guess you don't want to talk about it, do you?"

"Not really," I said. "I would like to know why."

"Why Mason Armfield?"

"No, the other why."

She sat in silence for a time, filling part of it with a search for a cigarette. She got an ashtray and placed it on the bed beside her. "I don't want to hurt you. You have to believe that."

"No," I said. "That's what somebody says right before they gut you."

"All right, don't believe me then."

"Thanks," I said.

"I guess I just want more."

"More of what?"

"More of the man I live with. More of the man I love," her hand shook when she tapped the ash from her cigarette. "I thought at first ... I thought it didn't matter. Now I think it matters."

"I guess I don't show much of what I feel."

"It's more than that" she said. "it's like you don't care one way or the other."

"All right." I drew the covers up to my chin and closed my eyes, shutting it out.

"I'll move out in the morning while you're in class."

"Whatever you want," I said.

I didn't sleep well. I seemed to be dropping in and out of sleep every few minutes. Like falling off an edge and then catching myself. And then I was fully awake and sleet was falling outside. The dry brittle crack on the unwrapped leaves outside the bedroom window. It might've been a hard rain, except for the scratch and tap of the ice on the window panes.

I was in bed alone. After she left the bedroom, I heard April opening the sofa into a bed. Now, the luminous dial of the alarm clock showed the time to be 4:20 a.m. Three hours before the alarm went off. Too much time to spend reading, too much time to spend it in the kitchen, drinking coffee. Too early, it was too early, and then I heard April's footsteps as she came through the kitchen and into the bedroom.

She stopped beside the bed, and I turned and looked at her.

"It's freezing," she said. "The living room is like ice."

I threw back a corner of the covers. "Get in."

It took a few minutes for the shivering to go away. She crawled up against me, letting me warm her. Her feet, kicking out cautiously until they were braced against the tops of my feet, seemed to freeze themselves to me. In time, she relaxed, and I could feel the warmth passing back to me.

"You all right now?" I asked.

"Yes." Breath bubbling against my chest. Then, gently as if the evening before hadn't happened: "Daddy, you've been on my mind."

I doubted that. "On my mind, on my mind."

But nothing had changed.

"I wish everything was the way it was back in the first of the summer," April said.

I put my arm under her, turning her so she was under my wing. "Child, winter is not only coming, it is here."

"It'll be all right.

Then, leaning forward, she clamped a chest hair in her teeth and jerked her head back pulling it out cleanly.

"What's that about?" I asked.

"Something to remember you by," she said.

She moved her things out while I was in class. I returned to the house around lunchtime, and found that the only possession she'd left behind was a single hairpin, beginning to rust on the back ledge of the wash basin.

WIND SPRINTS

-END-

Afternoon now. Winter light afternoon. Somewhere, some-where between Harry's and the New Establishment, with a gray hair clutched between her teeth like a flower, April has decided to find herself a young man. Daddies are all right, but young men reflect like windows and brightly polished sports cars. Done, enough. Gray flower wobbling in her teeth as she talks to herself.

And let him kick it to death if he can find it.

Winter light afternoon.

A slow rain falls, so slow that it seems to have frozen into a wall. From my window, from my office high above, I watch the students walk through the wall.

It seems much easier than it probably is.

I fancy myself a bit of a recluse now. Aware that it is something of a pose, that I have turned Hope back against myself, like the wolf cub's head. To gnaw at my entrails. Aware, I affect a stoic introspection. Pretending that I am blinded by some inner light that other people can't see. But knowing that it is an eyes-closed darkness, looking hard at nothing, the tunnel blocked at both ends, and nobody has paid the electric light bill. Or knows where the electric light company's business office is. Or what currency the company excepts.

I spend my evenings in front of the television set, the *TV Guide* at my elbow, referring to it from time to time, as if selecting. Still, certain there is no choice. Only time fill, what to do from seven in the evening until midnight. Feeling the accelerating death of brain cells. Death from non-relevance. Death from social and political overkill: the news specials, and President Nixon's press conferences and primetime speeches.

Often, late at night, after midnight, I find myself making grand and hopeful plans. I will spend the summer in Europe. New York is an hour and 20 minutes away by fan jet from Raleigh-Durham airport. Atlanta even less than that. The world is not as small as Chapel Hill, not as rigidly defined as the limits of this house. Telling myself this as I stretch and yawn in my bed, a light left on in the bathroom because I don't like the darkness anymore.

Not sure what to do about Europe, New York or Atlanta. Not sure I will do anything at all.

Sometimes there are women. Not that I seek them out or choose them. The contrary. They choose me, cripples choosing cripples.

Not long ago, the mother of one of my students came by my office to complain about the grade her daughter had received in Theater History 94 for the fall semester. She pursued me to my house, where we had some drinks, and I taught her to smoke grass.

When she took off her girdle, the curdled flesh ran down her legs like melting ice cream down the sides of a cake cone. But I balled her anyway. I felt it was required and expected of me.

Grotesque and absurd that coupling. The grunting and giggling beast with two backs.

Somewhere around midnight, I thought of her driving home, carrying my ashes to New Bern. No coals to New Bern, only ashes.

Agnes Black sent me a Christmas card from Richmond, Virginia. Under the banal, seasonal inscription for a Happy New Year, her careful penmanship: "I hope you never get laid again. Ever. But if you're ever in Richmond…"

I see April now and then. Always at a distance. Once she was crossing Franklin Street in front of the post office. The second time she was standing, one late evening, beside the parking meters in front of the New Establishment. She was with one of the Durham Hell's Angels. They were wearing He and She black leather jackets with the skull and crossbones patches sewn on the back. Scuffed jeans and high black boots with the jeans folded in back and stuffed into the boots. A high and wide hog parked in the space behind them. The New American primitive, I guess.

The image burning from the center out. The gray ashes. Winds will blow them away.

I tell myself that I'm waiting for the spring. The spring will kiss it and make it well. Believing it hardly at all… except as a way of moving from day to day. The winter waning. Each day, leaving my house and returning, I study the lower limbs of the trees in the front yard, examining the bud scabs. Or walking across campus, scenting the wind for the green heat that will blow the spring in. It will be different then. When the buds bleed open, and the spring is here. I will be different, too. Feeling the sap rising, the same green flame.

But knowing in the dark tunnel that it will not matter. That pretense is part of the disease.

ABOUT THE AUTHOR

Ralph Dennis isn't a household name...but he should be. He is widely considered among crime writers as a master of the genre, denied the recognition he deserved because his twelve *Hardman* books, which are beloved and highly sought-after collectables now, were poorly packaged in the 1970s by Popular Library as a cheap men's action-adventure paperbacks with numbered titles.

Even so, some top critics saw past the cheesy covers and noticed that he was producing work as good as John D. MacDonald, Raymond Chandler, Chester Himes, Dashiell Hammett, and Ross MacDonald.

The *New York Times* praised the *Hardman* novels for "expert writing, plotting, and an unusual degree of sensitivity. Dennis has mastered the genre and supplied top entertainment." The *Philadelphia Daily News* proclaimed *Hardman* "the best series around, but they've got such terrible covers..."

Unfortunately, Popular Library didn't take the hint and continued to present the series like hack work, dooming the novels to a short shelf-life and obscurity...except among generations of crime writers, like novelist Joe R. Lansdale (the *Hap & Leonard* series) and screenwriter Shane Black (the *Lethal Weapon* movies), who've kept Dennis' legacy alive through word-of-mouth and by acknowledging his influence on their stellar work.

Ralph Dennis wrote three other novels that were published outside of the *Hardman* series but he wasn't able to reach the wide audience, or gain the critical acclaim, that he deserved during his lifetime.

He was born in 1931 in Sumter, South Carolina, and received a Master's degree from University of North Carolina, where he later taught film and television writing after serving a stint in the Navy.

At the time of his death in 1988, he was working at a bookstore in Atlanta and had a suitcase full of unpublished novels that he kept at George's Deli, where he was sleeping on a cot in the back room.